# HEART
### —of—
# LIES

**Also by Jill Marie Landis**
*Heart of Stone*

IRISH ANGEL SERIES

# HEART

## *of*

# LIES

*A Novel*

*Book Two*

# JILL MARIE LANDIS

***New York Times*** **Bestselling Author**

ZONDERVAN.com/
AUTHORTRACKER
*follow your favorite authors*

ZONDERVAN

*Heart of Lies*
Copyright © 2011 by Jill Marie Landis

This title is also available as a Zondervan ebook. Visit www.zondervan.com/ebooks.

This title is also available in a Zondervan audio edition. Visit www.zondervan.fm.

Requests for information should be addressed to:
Zondervan, *Grand Rapids, Michigan 49530*

Library of Congress Cataloging-in-Publication Data

Landis, Jill Marie.
     Heart of lies : a novel / Jill Marie Landis.
        p. cm. – (Irish angel series; bk. 2)
        ISBN 978-0-310-29370-5 (pbk.)
        1. Irish – United States – Fiction. 2. Street children – Fiction. 3. Bayous – Fiction.
    4. Kidnapping – Fiction. 5. Pinkerton's National Detective Agency – Fiction.
    6. Louisiana – Fiction I. Title.
    PS3562.A4769H424 2011
    813'.54 – dc22
                                       2010040115

Cover design: *Curt Diepenhorst*
Cover illustration: *Aleta Rafton*
Interior design: *Michelle Espinoza*

*Printed in the United States of America*

11  12  13  14  /DCI/  20  19  18  17  16  15  14  13  12  11  10  9  8  7  6  5  4  3  2  1

*To the people of Louisiana—past, present, and future.*

The LORD will guide you always;
      he will satisfy your needs in a sun-scorched land
      and will strengthen your frame.

Isaiah 58:11

# CHAPTER 1

**LOUISIANA 1875**

Beneath a crescent moon, a crudely built cabin rested on crooked cypress stilts planted in the chocolate-brown water of the bayou. A dock lined the front. The back of the cabin touched the edge of marshland that was illusive at best, a muddy bog at worst. A thousand eyes watched from the slowly moving water, tall reeds, and rises—alligators, muskrats, mink, rats, deer, an occasional bear. Silent denizens of the swamp, they existed here at the whim of the water and the storms that blew in without warning.

Fall had arrived. The muggy heat of summer was gone, gentled by cool air that drifted down from the north. Soon hundreds of thousands of birds would flock south to the marsh to escape winter's cold.

The bayou was a place of refuge for more than winged fowl. Humans, too, easily hid where back roads curled through dense overgrowth and miles of shallow, narrow waterways crisscrossed the swamp.

The cabin held one such human. Inside walls made of rough-hewn cypress planks lined with old newspapers, silence was broken by tormented sounds as Maddie Grande whimpered her way through a recurring nightmare. It was always the same, always terrifying. Maddie was a child again, running frantically. Her bare feet slapped the cobblestoned streets of New Orleans as she fought to keep up with the lanky man in the lead. A blonde girl, not much taller than Maddie, tugged her by the wrist.

All she could see of the man was his back. His greasy dark hair hung beneath his wide-brimmed black hat and over his hunched shoulders. His coat was well-worn, threadbare around cuffs that didn't reach his wrists. It swayed loosely from his shoulders, flapping as the three of them ran.

The other child, an inch taller, tightened her grip on Maddie's wrist and whispered a warning. "Keep up. You can do it."

Somehow Maddie knew that if she fell behind, a beating would be her swift reward. Like Mercury, fear fashioned wings on her feet.

The nightmare unfolded through a fog of forgotten memories, the edges of the vision blurred and tattered like the stained pages of a book left too long in the rain. The streets they traversed were cool and damp, the air close and warm. The sounds and smells around them familiar: New Orleans in early morning. Street lamps were extinguished as vendors at the French Market set up their wares and shouted to customers and each other in a patois of languages. Indians sold furs and herbs; farmers hawked fruits, vegetables, and spices. Hunters and butchers offered meats of every kind. Fishmongers promised a fresh catch and a bounty of seafood. People of every hue crowded the stalls.

Behind the scene, slaves hauled hogsheads loaded with tobacco, cotton, indigo, and cane to nearby warehouses. Refreshment stands lined the blocks near the market. The smell of gumbo and fresh-brewed coffee tainted the heavy, humid air.

No one noticed the ragtag trio fleeing past. Maddie, urged by the blonde, ran on.

Eventually they reached an area where homes stood alongside businesses. Now and again she glimpsed cool, shaded courtyards through gateway grilles. She longed to stop and dip her hand into one of the trickling fountains, to take a sip of water. But she was not allowed to tarry. Air burned her lungs as she fought to keep up the breakneck pace. She had no doubt that the blonde girl would drag her body down the street if she stumbled and fell.

When the man suddenly halted, Maddie clasped her free hand to her side where a stitch ached like fire. She stared up at the wooden planks in a huge door before them. It was anchored to a thick stucco wall.

The older girl turned, but the face of the blonde child who so protectively clung to her hand never fully materialized. In its place was nothing but a pale oval, a wavering, shadowy void where a face should be.

That faded, faceless image filled Maggie — not only with terror, but with feelings of intense sorrow and loss.

The faceless girl slicked down Maddie's hair and whispered, "I'll watch out for you. No matter what."

Maddie had suffered through the same nightmare countless times. Who was this child she mourned? Why did the nightmare haunt her, even in the best of times?

The skeletal man, just as unidentifiable, gave a phlegmy cough before he raised his hand and lifted the wrought-iron ring on the door knocker. It hit the wooden door with the hollow, ominous clang of a final heartbeat.

As the door swung open, the man faded from the nightmare. Maddie's hand tightened; she clung to the older girl's, and together they stepped over the threshold. The space around them narrowed to become a blood-red hallway. Flames licked the amber globes of flickering gas lamps along the walls. The girls' shadows wavered and danced over a decadently expensive textured wall covering.

Maddie's heart began to pound frantically. Scented perfume weighed heavily on the close air in the hall. She heard the sound of a door open and close. Now and again there came a throaty laugh, a moan, a cry.

Another man, different from the first but just as indistinguishable, suddenly appeared and came slowly toward the girls. Maddie's blood ran cold. He was as tall as the first but not as lanky. His crooked hat reminded her of a bent and broken stovepipe. The tails of his black coat flapped behind him as he strode forward.

Maddie was ever aware of the child beside her. She felt the other girl's panic, felt her stiffen, heard her cry out. Suddenly the older girl's hand was torn away, their hold broken.

The faceless child shouted, "No!" and tried to grab Maddie. Her cries were abruptly ended by the sound of a slap that cracked on the air between them.

Without warning, the man in the black coat hoisted Maddie to his shoulder. Handled with no more reverence than a bag of rice, she dangled head down, staring down at the whirling patterns of the red and gold carpeted floor. Her head began to swim. As the stranger scuttled along the crimson-lined hallway carrying her away, the other girl started screaming again and so did Maddie.

She kept on screaming as darkness closed around her. She screamed until shadows choked out the light. Everything faded away but the sound of her own voice.

Now her muffled cries broke the stillness on the bayou and filled the small cabin. Startled awake, no longer a child, Maddie Grande sat up drenched in perspiration and stared into the dark void around her. With the screams echoing in her head, she swung her legs over the edge of her moss-stuffed mattress and set her bare feet on the rough floorboards. She rose and stood for a moment beside her narrow cot listening to the creaks and groans of the cabin as the water lapped around the pilings. It was a comforting, familiar sound.

She padded across the room to where a tall pottery crock stood on a crooked shelf. Staring out a window above the shelf, she reached for a ladle, dipped fresh water from the crock, and brought the cool liquid to her lips.

Outside the window, a scant spoonful of moonlight filtered down through tall cypress trees, a wall of deep green that appeared jet-black in the darkness. Draped with gray Spanish moss, the ghost forest towered over the swamp. Maddie stared past her reflection in the wavering glass and out into the darkness, acutely aware that she was alone in the cabin, alone in the swamp. Yet she had no fear. She had survived the streets of New Orleans. Out here on the bayou, most of what she feared was of nature, not of men.

Besides, she was not frightened of death. She had already lost those she held most dear. She had nothing left to lose.

She sighed, listened to the barely audible sound of slow-moving water, then reached out to press her palm against the cool glass. Her own image stared back at her, elusive in the muted light. Thick, dark-brown hair with barely a hint of a wave tumbled past her shoulders. Eyes of nearly the same color but for a hint of green stared back. There was not enough moonlight to reveal the nearly faded scar near the end of her right brow. Of how it came to be there, she had no memory.

As she turned, intent on returning to her cot, she heard the scrape of a wooden pirogue against one of the piers. Relieved, she let go another sigh. The twins were back.

She fumbled with the temperamental oil lamp on the table. The golden glow illuminated the interior, revealing the side of the room where Maddie slept. It was neatly kept, in stark contrast to the jumbled lair where the twins piled their nests of clothing, old pieces of traps, and things they were "due to fix" heaped around.

She heard heavy footfalls against the dock outside and turned as the door opened. Red-headed Lawrence, burly and broad shouldered, walked in first. The freckles that spattered his face melded together in the lamplight. His eyes were blue, shadowed by heavy lids that gave him the appearance of perpetual drowsiness. Lawrence appeared slow-witted only because he was accustomed to letting his twin brother, Terrance, think for him. He was so adept at sleepwalking through life, Lawrence rarely needed to think at all.

He nodded to Maddie and headed straight for a brown-and-white jug full of white lightening. Hooking his forefinger through the ring on the neck, he lifted the cork and took a swig. Only then did he turn and smile at her.

But when he glanced back toward the open doorway, he wore a look of concern.

"What are you doing up, Maddie?" As if it were an after-thought, he took another swig and then set the jug in the middle of the table where Terrance would find it waiting.

She shrugged. She never talked about her nightmare, never showed any sign of weakness. Cowardice had always been ridiculed. Fears were not to be mentioned aloud, as if silence could wither them in their tracks.

She'd thought of the twins as her brothers for almost as long as she could remember. Impoverished urchins, they had grown up working the streets and back alleys of New Orleans. They knew how to pick pockets, to beg, to create a diversion while the others worked a crowd. They stole anything that wasn't nailed down. They'd been taught how to bite and scratch and escape the law, and they embraced their lives of thievery even as they matured.

When Terrance finally decided they should move to the bayou, Maddie welcomed the change. There was nothing left for her in the city. Nowhere she called home.

No one cared what she did or where she lived.

Lawrence shifted and turned for his cot. He brushed off a pile of clothes, ignoring them as they fell to the floor. The bed sagged as he sat.

"Where's Terrance?" She glanced toward the open door.

He shrugged. "Tying up the pirogue. He'll be along any minute."

She knew better than to ask where they'd been or what they'd been doing for the past three days. Even if they told her, the less she knew the better.

"Are you hungry?"

"I can hold till mornin'."

He was looking ready to bed down for the night when they heard Terrance's footsteps. Maddie turned and watched the second twin walk in. Equally tall and bulky, he moved stealthily for such a large man.

But he wasn't alone.

Shock hit her in a mighty wave when she saw the figure cradled in his arms. Two small feet shod in ankle-high black leather shoes dangled from beneath the frayed hem of a gray Confederate Army-issue blanket.

"What have you done?" she whispered, tearing her gaze away from the bundled child to meet Terrance's eyes.

His eyes, identical to his brothers except that they were cool and emotionless, narrowed in defiance. He silently dared her to criticize him. "I'm lookin' out for our future, that's what." He shot a glance at his brother seated on the edge of his sagging cot. "That's more than I can say for some around here."

He carried his burden over to Maddie's cot and gently laid it down near the wall. As he gave the blanket a slight tug downward, Maddie found herself staring at a beautiful little girl with a head full of coiled black ringlets. She was sound asleep, wearing a fur-lined red cape worth more than everything in the ramshackle cabin put together.

A twinge squeezed Maddie's heart. Unable to speak, she ached to reach out and touch the child's porcelain cheek so badly that she had to fist her hands in the folds of her skirt.

"Why?" She turned on Terrance, afraid there was only one explanation for the child's presence. "You're not thinking of starting a new tribe —"

Across the room, Lawrence laughed. Maddie and Terrance, locked in a battle of wills, ignored him.

"Those days are over, Terrance. They died with Dexter," she whispered.

Dexter Grande had been their leader, their father, keeper, mentor, and judge. He was the visionary, the glue who had held their tribe together, the one who "recruited" his band of children, the one who taught them to steal and to survive on the streets.

Two years ago, apoplexy had brought him down at the ripe old age of sixty-five, and without him, what was left of their tribe quickly scattered.

"It worked for Dexter; why not me?" Terrance speculated. "He's dead but that don't mean we can't start a new tribe — not just children, but men too. We can run the same games."

Maddie turned on him. "Look around. We don't live in New Orleans anymore."

She didn't want to think about moving back to the city. For the most part the twins were never here and she was alone, which suited her just fine. On the bayou there were no reminders of her own losses, only the gentle, healing sound of the water lapping against the dock and the hush of the wind through the lacy cypress.

He was at the table now, lifting the jug. He took a couple of deep draughts, set the jug down, and swiped the back of his hand across his mouth.

"All I need is the chance to make a few connections. For now, I'm thinking bigger than Dexter. I'm thinking we use her for a bankroll." He nodded at the sleeping child on the cot. "Why should we waste time havin' her dance for a dollar or two or picking pockets on the street when there's real money to be had?"

"You tell me," Lawrence said. It was one of his favorite sayings. Terrance always obliged.

Lit by greed, Terrance's eyes glittered. "One word: *reward*. Easy money, and lots of it, from the looks of her. We can get any orphan to run the scams, but this one . . ."

Maddie didn't know which would be worse: hiding the child until they could collect a reward or the idea that Terrance wanted to start a new tribe. One thing she knew for certain: the girl on the bed was no orphaned street urchin. This child belonged to someone wealthy. This child would be missed.

Her family would leave no stone unturned until she was found.

"What if there is no reward?" A pronounced belch followed

Lawrence's query. He rolled onto his side and folded his arm beneath his head.

Terrance shrugged and headed toward his own bed. "There will be. If not, we'll demand a ransom." He looked at Maddie. "If no one wants her, then I guess our new tribe will start sooner than we thought." His gaze pinned Maddie with an intensity that belied his twenty-two years. "You still know what to do in that case, don't you, Mad?"

A shiver ran down her spine. She knew exactly what to do. She'd done it often enough to know it would work and enough to know she never wanted to do it again.

"No." She raised her chin defiantly.

"What do you mean no?" Terrance took a step closer.

She didn't back down. "I won't do it. Not anymore."

He grabbed her arm and twisted. "You'll do as I say. I'm in charge now."

"In charge of what?" She pulled out of his grasp, marched across the cabin to put space between them while Lawrence watched from his cot. "You're not Dexter. Besides, you're never here. It's me that puts food on the table and me that keeps this place going while you two run off to New Orleans to drink and whore and gamble and steal. I'll not do your dirty work, Terrance. I'll not do anyone's dirty work anymore."

"You're a big talker, Maddie, but I know you'll do whatever I say because we're family. We're all that's left of the tribe." He softened his tone, held out his hand, almost pleading. "Come on, Mad. You took the same oath we did. You pledged your loyalty."

She knew he was just using the past to try to move her. He was loyal only to himself. She was just a means to an end.

"Those days are gone, Terrance. The tribe I pledged loyalty to has disbanded. All that's left is the three of us. I won't be part of that again."

"Think of how much easier your life would be with some money for a change."

"Not like this," she warned. "Not by kidnapping an innocent child."

"We could all move back to New Orleans, to the old place."

"I won't go back. I like it here."

His expression darkened instantly. He touched the handle of the knife sheathed on his hip, but she refused to back down and met his cold stare.

"You'd hate for anything to happen to her, wouldn't you, Mad?"

She stared at him in disbelief. Was it an idle threat, or could he possibly be serious? "Even you wouldn't stoop so low as to murder a child, would you?"

Silent seconds ticked by as they stared at one another across the shadows.

"Don't test me, Maddie. Just do as I say."

"Fine," she said grudgingly. "I'll look after her."

Across the room, Lawrence was already snoring like a bear.

"Then turn out the light and get some sleep," he ordered. "Mornin' will come sooner than you know. Me and Lawrence will be headin' back to the city to wait for word. Hopefully her folks will offer a reward soon. The longer we keep the girl hidden, the more likely the amount will go up."

Maddie glanced at the dark-haired child asleep on her cot. She didn't mind sharing the narrow bed with a little one. She'd done it often enough with her own, but this time both her heart and soul protested. She'd hoped she was done living on the wrong side of the law. She didn't want to survive this way anymore.

Especially not like this. Not by stealing a child.

# CHAPTER 2

Pinkerton agent Tom Abbott left his rented, sparsely furnished rooms in the French Quarter and made his way across the narrow cobblestone drive in the courtyard below. He passed through the open iron gates and walked along streets filled with noise and motion, the clatter of carriage wheels on cobblestone, ribald shouts, and high-pitched laughter. The occasional gunshot punctuated by strains of music drifted on the night air. New Orleans was a city that never slept, and because of his profession Tom was no stranger to long days and late nights.

He pulled his collar up and his hat down as he made his way toward Royal Street. He had dressed in worn clothing so nondescript as to render him nearly invisible as he moved through the dangerous streets of the city. He pushed back his brown wool jacket out of habit to expose the holstered Colt riding his hip. New Orleans boasted one of the highest murder rates in the country; a wise man took advantage of the law that made it legal to openly carry a gun or a knife.

When he neared Jackson Square, he slowed his pace and paused in the shadows of the imposing St. Louis Cathedral. Across the street from the huge church, a quartet of missionaries had set up an outdoor soup kitchen. There was a piece of pine tacked over the door of an empty storefront with the words *Jesus Is Your Savior* hand lettered in white paint. Outside the open door, two long planks of wood rested on sawhorses—a makeshift table for the small knot of the city's destitute who had gathered for a bowl of soup and a crust of bread.

Tom studied the missionaries carefully before he approached them. An elderly woman dressed entirely in somber gray with a matching poke bonnet kept time on a tambourine while the older man beside her read from an open Bible. Nearby, a woman in her early forties ladled soup from a deep pot at one end of the table. She smiled as she handed a full bowl to a prostitute.

Tom let his gaze scan the crowd. They were orderly, thinning out now. When the line finally dwindled, the younger woman began to walk around and collect the empty soup bowls. As Tom approached her, she paused to take in his faded coat and battered hat before her gaze shifted to his gun.

"We're a peaceable people," she told him.

He nodded and gave his hat brim a tug. "I understand, ma'am."

"If it's soup you're after, it's my husband's turn to serve." She smiled in the direction of a man who had paused at his task to watch them.

"I was wondering if I could have a moment of your time. I've a few questions. It won't take long."

"Pastor Bennett would be happy to counsel you." She turned her gaze toward the older man holding the Bible before continuing on to the table carrying a stack of thick ceramic bowls.

"It's not counseling I'm after. I'm a Pinkerton detective." He opened his jacket just far enough to reveal a badge pinned to the inside. He didn't want to advertise his identity to those lingering nearby.

"A detective?" He saw a flash of panic in her eyes. A second later she calmed. "What is this about?"

"I'm working on a missing person's case and I was hoping that since you work the streets you might have some information, anything that might help me find the woman I'm searching for."

"Oh. Well, then, yes. I'd be happy to answer a few questions."

"Is there somewhere we can sit and talk? Or, if you'd prefer, I can speak to your husband—"

"I don't mind." She set down the stack of bowls, walked over to her husband, and spoke to him in a barely audible voice. He looked across the table at Tom and nodded. The woman gestured. "Come inside with me. We've not much in the building yet, but there is a bench where we can sit and chat. I can't be long, though."

"I understand," he told her. "It will just take a few minutes."

Inside, she lit a lamp and carefully replaced the chimney. The room was cast in a warm yellow glow. "We've not the funds to set up our ministry office yet. Feeding the hungry takes most of our time and money."

She indicated a long bench standing against one wall. "My name is Elizabeth Henson. My husband is Pastor Bennett's nephew. We've just returned from five years in Singapore."

Tom was disappointed to hear they hadn't been in the city all that long. He doubted she could help, but since he had no solid leads, it was still worth a try.

"Will you sit?"

She sat down on the opposite end of the bench near the light and folded her hands in her lap. Even in the weak glow of candle-light, he saw that they were not the soft white hands of a woman unused to hard work.

She smiled and waited for him to begin.

"I've been hired by a woman in Texas to search for her sister," he began. "The last time she saw her was here in New Orleans, twenty-three years ago. The missing woman was nine then."

Mrs. Henson's brow knit. "Are you even certain she's still here? Or that she's even alive?"

"Not at all, but this is where she was last seen. I've found no records of her having been buried in any of the New Orleans cemeteries."

"She could be in a pauper's unmarked grave."

"She could, but I've not given up yet. The Lane girls lost their parents and shortly afterward were taken by their uncle and sold to a bordello somewhere in the French Quarter. They were separated within minutes of their arrival. The older of the two, the woman I represent, grew up there. She has no idea what happened to her sister, only that the girl was carried off by a man and never seen again."

Tom couldn't help but notice that Elizabeth Henson had gone very pale.

"Are you all right?" he asked. "I know it's not a pretty tale."

"Why are you questioning me, Mr. Abbott? Of all the people in New Orleans?"

"Like I said, because you are privy to things that happen on the streets. Because you have contact with women from the brothels. You do, don't you?"

She closed her eyes and gave a slight shake of her head. "Yes, of course, when they come to us."

He had the feeling there was something she was hiding.

"Would you rather I speak to your husband after all?"

"No." She shook her head. "I'm the one who can help you. I grew up in the city."

"Have you ever heard the name Megan Lane?"

Mrs. Henson's face was completely impassive. Staring across the room, she fingered a small wooden cross hanging from a thong around her neck. "I have no recollection of it."

"Have you ever heard the name Dexter Grande?" he asked.

Her eyes widened. Her hand gripped the cross. She said nothing.

"Mrs. Henson? Do you know him? Do you know where Grande is?"

Tom had searched through years of orphanage, school, and cemetery records in his search for Megan Lane. He'd gone through adoption decrees and whatever relevant paperwork had survived the war.

"Where did you hear that name? Dexter Grande?" Elizabeth Henson whispered.

"From a woman who works in the archives of the office of the mayor. She helped me comb through the Records of the Disposition of Destitute Children. She had no proof, but she has heard tales of a man named Dexter Grande who ran a gang of street thieves. He was supposed to be a Fagan of sorts, straight out of the pages of Dickens."

Tom noticed the woman's hand trembling as she lowered it to her lap. "Dexter Grande is dead," she said.

"You knew him?"

Her eyes had taken on a faraway look. "I knew him a long time ago. Before the war."

"Can you tell me anything? Anything at all?"

"Dexter Grande fancied himself a mastermind behind a band of street thieves, small children mostly. There were a few trusted older boys, but when they were around fourteen, he sometimes forced them out. Most of them, anyway. Younger children were more malleable and ate less."

"How did he come by these children?" Tom had a feeling he already knew but he wanted to hear it firsthand.

She shrugged. "Anywhere he could. There were so many orphans." She sighed. "There still are."

The records Tom had seen attested to as much. Yellow fever often struck the city with a vengeance. It had in the mid-fifties when Megan Lane disappeared. Relatives too poor to feed orphaned children often turned them over to institutions. From Elizabeth Henson's reaction, Tom was certain that she knew even more than she was willing to say. He glanced out the window and lowered his voice.

"Did you belong to Dexter Grande's street gang?"

She raised her eyes to meet his. Hers were wide, round, and very blue. Blonde curls showed beneath the brim of her hat. Laura Foster, his client, was a lovely woman too — fair-haired and blue-eyed. This woman could very well be her sister. Elizabeth Henson did not match the brief description Mrs. Foster had given him, but looks changed over time.

Was it possible that after meticulously combing through records and interviewing people all over New Orleans, he had inadvertently stumbled upon Megan Lane?

"Were you part of Grande's gang of thieves?" he asked again.

"His tribe." Her voice was barely above a whisper. "He called us his tribe."

*Us.*

"Did Grande find you in an orphanage?"

She started to stand, then sank back to the bench as if her legs wouldn't hold her. She stared through the open doorway to the dark street beyond.

"No, I know exactly where I came from and I know who my people were. I'm not proud of where I've been or what I've done, Mr. Abbott. It's not a story I will tell. Ever. Believe me when I say I'm not the one you are looking for."

"Is there anyone who might know for certain that Megan Lane was in the tribe?"

"No. If so, they're all gone now anyway. Disbanded. Besides, we all swore never to reveal anything about Dexter Grande or our lives. It was a blood oath."

"That explains why there is so little information on the streets. You took the oath as well?"

She reached up to wipe her brow. There was no breeze tonight. The air was close and humid.

"I took the oath, yes, but now I am beholden to a much higher Power than Dexter Grande." She smoothed her skirt, her calm smile back. She stood up and looked down at him. "I am reborn, Mr. Abbot. I don't like to look back on those times or talk about them. That's really all I can say."

He got to his feet, still not convinced that she wasn't the very woman he'd been searching for. But he was not willing to push her any further tonight.

"You're absolutely certain there is no one who might remember Megan Lane? It would mean so much to her sister in Texas to find her. Think of what it might mean to Megan herself."

Again she closed her eyes long enough to take a calming breath. When she opened them she admitted, "The only tribe members' names I've heard mentioned since I returned are Terrance and Lawrence, the Grande twins. If they are still in New Orleans, they may be able to tell you where to find a woman named Anita Russo, if she's still alive. She used to care for the children when they took ill. They may know where Anita is, if they're still here. She may lead you to others."

"Thank you, Mrs. Henson." Revitalized, Tom smiled as he waited for her to lead the way outside.

"Don't get your hopes up, Mr. Abbott," Elizabeth warned. "Tribe members lived in a shadow world, existing on the wrong side of the law. If you do find them, the Grande twins won't be willing to answer your questions, so take care. Be very wary. They're dangerous."

# CHAPTER 3

Maddie fell asleep sometime just before dawn and awoke with a start when the child beside her rolled over and kicked her in the shin. She lay there in silence as the sun's warm yellow light crept through the east window. Curled on her side, she surveyed the room.

The twins were already gone, no doubt headed back to New Orleans to celebrate their previous night's deed. She lingered in bed a while longer, thinking the child beside her was asleep.

"Who are you?"

Maddie nearly jumped out of her skin when she felt the whispered words against her ear. The girl was leaning over her, staring down into her face.

Still wrapped in her fine red cape, the child scooted over to make room. Her ink-black curls were a tumbled mess. Her eyes, an intriguing violet, were swollen from sleep and tears.

"Well?" the girl demanded. "Who are you?"

"I'm the one looking after you. Who are you?"

"I'm Penelope Charlotte Perkins. I'm eight and a half years old and I live at Langetree Plantation. At least I did until those two awful men stole me from my nanny. Where are they?"

The child certainly showed no fear. Maddie had expected her to start squalling for her mother.

"They're not here."

"Good. They kept telling me I was in danger. They told me to shut up too. Are they coming back?"

"Yes. Soon. But don't worry. You're safe." *For now.*

Penelope looked Maddie in the eye. "My papa is going to be furious with all of you. You had better let me go."

Maddie had no doubt about it.

The child had mentioned a nanny and her papa. What if there was no heartsick mother at home pining for her? Perhaps this lovely child's father, too busy to be concerned with her safety, had handed her over to a nanny. Perhaps the man didn't deserve her —

Maddie's mind began to dart in dangerous directions.

"What about your mother?" she asked.

"Mama cries a lot. Ever since the baby died." Penelope gave a heartfelt sigh. "She doesn't come out of her room much anymore, either, but Papa says that she'll get better. I was in the way so he was sending me off with Nanny for a while. Just till Mamma is feeling better." She shrugged. "Who knows how long that will be though. She's not been happy since the baby died. I don't think she cares where I go as long as I'm not around. I was headed to Paducah to visit my Aunt Gail for a spell when those two kidnappers stopped our carriage and grabbed me."

Maddie tried not to picture the already brokenhearted woman in mourning at Langetree Plantation. Surely she cared about this child too. Did she know her daughter was missing? Had word reached them yet?

"Do you have any other brothers or sisters?"

Penelope shook her head, and the ringlets that weren't in tangles managed to bounce prettily. She sighed and leaned against the wall. If she was at all frightened, it didn't show.

"Narry a one. We waited so long for the baby to get here, but then he was born dead. Papa said it was simply too much for Mama to bear. I couldn't do anything to cheer her either." She sighed. "It's better I'm not there, I suppose. I'm just in the way." She paused to look around. "I really don't want to stay here though."

Maddie tried to swallow around the lump in her throat and pictured her own little one, her firstborn. A daughter with blue eyes and ivory skin who'd lived no more than six hours.

The child would have been sixteen by now. *Near old enough to make me a grandmother.*

Penelope wrinkled her nose. "Why is this place such a mess?"

"I wasn't expecting visitors."

"Are you going to tell me your name?"

"Not yet."

"Are you going to take me home?"

"Not today."

"Then how about you take me to Paducah? That's where I was headed. It will be a lot more fun at my Auntie Gail's than at home, that's for certain."

Maddie had no idea when she would release Penelope, or how. She did not dare give Miss Penelope Charlotte Perkins false hope. The less said the better until she figured out exactly what she was going to do. She'd gone against Terrance a time or two in her life, with dark results.

"I'm starving," Penelope announced, looking toward the stove.

Maddie rolled off the cot and shook out her skirt. She, too, was surprisingly hungry.

"There's nowhere for you to run to and there are gators around," she warned, "so you stay put while I go see to my morning necessaries. Then you can help me check the crab trap and the fishing line out on the dock if you do as I say."

The girl gave her no trouble. Maddie helped her wash up and let her pull up the crab trap, then fixed a breakfast of fried catfish and grits.

"I need cream," Penelope said, staring down at the pile of grits.

Maddie laughed. "You'll have to settle for a cup of black coffee, missy. There's no cow around here."

"Why ever not?"

"We had one," Maddie said, feigning a serious expression, "but a gator ate it."

That, she thought, should keep Miss Perkins from wandering off anytime soon.

At Penelope's insistence, Maddie brushed out the child's hair and tried to restyle the crushed curls. She replaced a decorative silver comb in the shape of a bow tangled in the long strands.

"I had two of those," Penelope informed her. "Did you steal one? Those little sparkles are real diamonds."

Maddie looked at the finely wrought piece. "I did not steal the other one. You probably lost it on the road somewhere."

Penelope folded her arms, clearly angry. "That comb was worth a lot of money."

"I'm sure," Maddie agreed. "But I don't have it."

"One of those big brutes probably took it."

*Brutes?* Maddie thought. It was a perfect description of the twins. She bit back a smile. "Has anyone ever told you to mind your tongue or it will get you in trouble?" she asked.

"My papa likes me to speak my mind. He says standing up for myself will get me far in life."

Maddie pondered that as she continued fighting Penelope's hair.

"Nanny does my hair better," Penelope noted, "but I suppose this will have to do."

"Indeed," Maddie agreed. "I'm sure you're used to far better. You have a grand house, do you?" Maddie twisted up another lock of the child's thick hair.

"Oh, very grand. One day I heard Papa tell someone he stole it, but when I reminded him stealing is a sin, he explained he didn't actually *steal* it. He meant that he was able to buy Langetree Plantation by paying the back taxes. Before that he and Mama and I lived in New York. Did you know that saying you *stole* something can be a figure of speech?"

"I do now." Maddie wanted to add that there had been

carpetbaggers getting things for a steal all over the South since the war. Mr. Perkins was not the only one getting a whole lot for practically nothing.

"Sometimes Papa says he got it for a song. Can you imagine getting something for a song? How silly."

Silly? Dexter had always bragged that Maddie was his little golden songbird. She had earned them quite a bit of coin singing on street corners until he gave her other, more important duties. Her own childhood had been nothing like little Miss Perkins's; that much was certain.

"You'd be real pretty if you had a nice gown on and fixed up your hair some," Penelope decided.

Maddie looked down at her navy serge dress, one of the few articles of clothing she owned. There wasn't a hint of adornment on it. Nothing she owned was what Penelope Perkins would consider "nice."

Penelope looked over her shoulder at Maddie. Her violet eyes widened, sparkling with unshed tears, yet she raised her heart-shaped face in defiance and looked Maddie straight in the eyes. "*When* exactly did you say I would get to leave?"

"I didn't," Maddie reminded her. She took a deep breath and wondered how long she had before the twins returned.

# CHAPTER 4

Long before noon the next day, Tom was up and out of his apartment. He bought a newspaper from a young vendor on the nearest corner, then caught a hansom cab to the New Orleans Police French Quarter Precinct. Except for a growth of dark stubble, he appeared nothing more than a well-dressed man out for a stroll.

It wasn't long before he was seated in the office of Detective Frank Morgan of the metropolitan police. In America's most cosmopolitan city, where trouble simmered like a pot of gumbo, Frank Morgan was a man who spent day and night fighting a losing battle against crime. He wore the expression of a man overworked and underpaid.

Morgan sat back when Tom walked in and smiled. He studied Tom for a moment. "I was just going to have someone get me some coffee from the cart across the street. Would you like one? Had anything to eat yet this morning?"

"No food, please. Coffee sounds good."

Hot *café au lait* from a street vendor. Tom welcomed the thought but doubted it would soothe him. Closeted in the silence of Morgan's office, he hoped he wasn't wasting precious time chasing his tail.

Frank stepped out and spoke to one of his men. He was back in no time and sat down behind his desk again.

"Coffee will be here momentarily," he promised. "What can I do for you, Tom? Been a while since we've worked together."

"You ever hear of a Dexter Grande?"

"A little, but I've no idea how much is true. He was supposedly the mastermind behind a gang of child thieves for almost thirty years. He was elusive as smoke, which should have been impossible for a man who reportedly had up to twenty children of all ages working for him, but somehow he managed."

"So it's true."

"He called them his tribe. They were a well-trained band of pickpockets, hotel cat burglars, and sneak thieves. They considered Dexter their father and were completely loyal to him. They ran the streets like stray cats and were just as elusive. Impossible to catch and because of their ages, impossible to convict."

"They weren't all his, were they?"

"Some may have been. They all used the name Grande. "

"How is it no one really knows much about him?"

"This city has had more to deal with than petty thievery over the past twenty years. An informant we had claimed they were mostly orphans attracted by the promise of shelter, hot meals, and a place to call home."

"Is the tribe still operating?"

"Not that I know of. Grande died around two years ago."

The coffee arrived. The man who brought it needed to talk to Morgan. Once again the detective stepped out of his office, leaving Tom alone with his thoughts. He inhaled the scent of the café au lait before he took a sip.

Dexter Grande's tribe was just one more New Orleans legend in a long history of Kaintuck river men, pirates, cutthroats, and killers who mingled in a city perfumed by magnolias and the pungent musk of the swamps. The city's violent and colorful past was part of its mystique. The need for law and order was what kept him here.

Frank Morgan was back looking even more harried. "Why are you so interested in Grande?"

Tom quickly outlined his search for Megan Lane and said that more than one source had told him about Grande collecting children. "I thought you might have a lead for me," Tom admitted. "I have a feeling the missionary I spoke to, the former tribe member, knew more than she'd say about the Lane woman."

"You think a missionary would lie?"

"No, but I think she may have evaded the truth. She admitted there were so many children there over the years it would be hard to know."

"My hunch is you'll never find her." Frank finished his coffee and started shuffling through the paperwork on his desk. Tom knew the man needed to get back to work. "When you walked in here I thought maybe you'd been hired for the Perkins's case." Frank picked up a sheet of paper covered with his handwritten scrawl. "This is a report on a kidnapping that happened a few days ago. Figured the father would have hired private help by now, seeing as how we're notoriously overwhelmed around here."

"A kidnapping." Tom's gut spiraled.

During his training before the war, Tom had worked with a seasoned agent to solve the kidnapping of a wealthy congressman's son. The man was a Northerner who'd come South for the very purpose of being voted into office during the Reconstruction. A ransom was demanded, yet before Tom and his partner uncovered a single lead, the child had turned up dead. Though they eventually tracked down the murderers, he was still haunted by the case.

Allan Pinkerton himself had come down to New Orleans to convince Tom not to resign, but as far as assuaging Tom's guilt—no one but God could forgive him. Tom still hadn't forgiven himself.

"What have you got to go on? Anything?" Tom wanted to know.

"The child and her nanny were traveling together in a family coach when two armed and masked men rode up and demanded that the driver stop. They asked for money and ended up taking the child. The nanny said they looked a lot alike. She thought they might have been brothers."

Tom felt the hair on the back of his neck stand up.

"They looked alike?"

Morgan lowered the page and looked at Tom. "Yeah. Why?"

"You ever hear of the Grande twins?"

Frank's gaze was suddenly riveted on him. "Grande *twins*."

"Yeah. You heard of them?"

"No. Do you know where they are?" Frank's gaze shifted back to the paper and then to Tom.

"No. I was only interested because I hoped they might lead me to an older woman connected to the tribe. A woman named Anita Russo. The missionary told me the twins might know where to find her. She said if the Grandes are around, they're probably dangerous."

"How old are they?"

"No idea. You have anything solid on this kidnapping?"

"Nothing. Unfortunately, I've got far more to worry about than one missing child. Unless she turns up dead, I can't spare more than a couple of men to do the footwork. I'm trying to keep a lid on a lit powder keg here."

"If I find the Grande twins for you, you can haul them in for questioning on the kidnapping. All I want is a chance to get some information that might help me solve my own case."

"Always happy to let you make my job easier. There'll be a big reward posted for the girl in tomorrow's paper. If they turn out to be the kidnappers, you can collect the reward and we can close a case for a change."

"The minute I find the Grande twins, if I find them, I'll contact you for backup. Can I count on you to do the same?" Tom asked.

Frank stood and Tom got to his feet. "Of course." They shook hands to seal the bargain. "Just don't try to bring them in alone."

"Don't worry. I want them alive."

"So does the child's father."

"Take care of yourself, Frank."

"Heed some of that advice for yourself."

# CHAPTER 5

The pirogue slid across the top of the opaque water, the silence around its occupants broken only by an occasional splash from the long, forked pole Maddie used to propel the dugout craft. The sky above the bayou was cloudless and deep blue, the morning full of the promise of pleasant fall weather. Intent upon keeping the pirogue balanced and running true, she kept her gaze upon the water ahead of her.

When she was first learning, it had taken weeks before she felt confident maneuvering the craft. But she'd realized early on that if she was going to move freely about the swamp, she would have to become expert at poling.

She glanced down at the child seated cross-legged near the bow. When Penelope started trailing her fingertips in the water, Maddie nearly lost her balance.

"Penelope!"

The girl jerked her hand out of the water and crossed her arms in a silent pout. Maddie's gaze strayed to the water's edge where tall reeds met the lime-green duckweed floating on the surface. A huge alligator lazed in the sun watching them glide slowly by through slitted eyes.

The child had been in Maddie's care for two days. Long enough for her to come to a decision about both her future and the girl's. One that wasn't going to please Terrance in the least.

When she had nearly reached her destination, Maddie turned toward an opening to a second narrow channel cutting through the maze of waterways. She stopped poling to scout a cabin a few yards away.

"It's hot out here," Penelope groused. "I need a drink of water in the worst way. Water, water everywhere and not a drop to drink."

"Hush," Maddie whispered.

"Why?"

"Because I said so."

"But . . ."

"Hush, now. You'll get that water directly, but for now just enjoy the sights."

Penelope whispered back. "*Sights*? You call weeds and muddy water something to see? It's *very* boring out here. I'm sick of wearing the same clothes every day and sick to death of the bayou."

Maddie tried to ignore her. Across the water, the cabin door opened and a woman in her late sixties with thick salt-and-pepper hair walked out onto the dock and pulled up a crab trap. The woman dumped the contents into a bucket, then dropped the trap back into the water. She placed her hands on the small of her back and stretched, gazing around for a few seconds before she walked back inside.

Maddie righted the pole again, planted the fork deep into the swamp, and backed the pirogue out into the main channel. Not five minutes later they had reached the dock in front of the cabin.

"What are we doing here?" Penelope wanted to know.

"I'm going to visit a friend. She'll give you a drink of water."

Penelope eyed the place suspiciously. "Are those men here?"

"No."

They reached the pilings and Maddie called out, "Hooey! Anybody home?"

She called out twice more before the door opened and Anita Russo stepped out, wiping her hands on the stained apron over her mismatched skirt and blouse. She looked down at Maddie.

"Well, look who's here." Her smile faded when she saw the child. "What are you up to, Madeline?"

"Ha!" Penelope shouted, pointing at Maddie. "Your name is Madeline!"

For two days Maddie had refused to tell Penelope her name. The less the child could tell the authorities later, the better.

"What's going on?" Anita demanded.

"I'll explain later," Maddie said.

"May I have a drink of water?" Penelope asked. "I'm really thirsty."

The woman looked to Maddie, who nodded.

"'Course you can. Let me help you climb out of there, and you can come in and set a spell. If I'd known you were comin', I'd have done you up some flat cakes."

"Maybe you could do me some up right now. I'm thirsty *and* starving," Penelope assured her.

They went inside and as soon as she'd had a glass of water, Penelope turned her attention to a balding old coon dog lying in the corner. She asked permission to pet the dog and, once it was given, knelt down beside the old hound and began to chatter as if the dog understood every word.

Anita gathered up the makings for flat cakes, then walked back to the table and leaned toward Maddie.

"You want to tell me what's goin' on?" she whispered.

Maddie had known Anita Russo for as long as she could remember. The self-taught healer with a knowledge of herbs and potions had cared for the tribe's children as if they were her own. It was Anita who had delivered both of Maddie's children. It was Anita who had held her tight and rocked her as she mourned them. Anita was the closest thing to a mother Maddie could recall.

Maddie leaned an elbow against the table. She shook her head and rested it on her hand. "The twins brought that child home two nights ago," she said.

"Oh, no. I'm afraid to ask why."

"Terrance is hoping to collect a reward for her. Either that or he'll demand a ransom." She shrugged. "He may not give her back at all. He might even start a new tribe."

Anita made no comment as she poured herself a cup of coffee thick as oil and sat down across from Maddie. She watched Penelope pull the dog's ears up and attempt to tie them together. The dog's tongue lolled out of the side of its mouth.

"She's a beauty, that one," Anita observed.

Maddie nodded. "I can't let him do this, Anita. I'm through with that life for good."

She believed it was over, but the kidnapping had complicated things. She knew without a doubt that if she ever wanted a life free and clear of the past, she was going to have to walk away from the twins and start over. What she didn't know was how to accomplish that without a penny to her name.

"Changing your life would be like trying to shake your own shadow." Anita fell silent and watched Maddie, waiting for her to go on.

Maddie hadn't realized how age was catching up to her mentor. She had always imagined that Anita would be there to give aid and advice. But seeing her now with her stooped shoulders and face lined with the tracks of time, Maddie realized with sorrow that Anita would not be there for her forever.

Maddie forced her thoughts back to the little girl across the room. She lowered her voice to a hushed whisper.

"I can't do this, 'Nita. Look at that child. She's not like the others. She's from money. I hear it in every word she says. Her folks have the wealth and power to move heaven and earth to get her back. I have a bad feeling about this one. You always told me not to ignore what my heart says."

"If you came for advice—"

Penelope turned their way. The old woman paused and then rose stiffly, walked over to the dry sink against the wall, and dug into a pan to retrieve a stale biscuit. She held it out to Penelope. "That old hound loves these. Give her this."

The child ran across the room, grabbed the biscuit, and went back to sit on the filthy floor beside the dog. Anita returned to the table.

"What will you do with her?"

"I was hoping I could leave her here until I can take her back home. I'm afraid the twins will come back late today. At the latest, tomorrow. When they do, I'll convince them she ran off and lead them on a wild-goose chase. Once they leave, I'll take her back."

"I'm not up to keeping a child around here. I'm not as spry as I used to be."

"If I took off with her right now, they'd track me down. If you take her, I can stall them until they leave again."

"They could be back already. If they find you gone, they'll figure you're either here or at the trading post and come looking for you."

Maddie shrugged. "There's nothing wrong with me bringing her along on a social call, is there?"

"Terrance don't have your gentle heart, Maddie. He'll have my hide if he finds out I double-crossed him," Anita said. "He'll have yours, too, if you go against him. How you gonna keep him from killing you?"

"He'd never kill me."

"Mebbe, but he could hurt you pretty bad."

"She's constantly talking about going on to Kentucky. I'll say she ran off when I was out checking my traps and get them to head northeast."

"You're not a very good liar anymore."

Maddie shrugged. "I'm just out of practice."

Anita finished off her coffee and let the empty cup sit. "They'd know you'd never let her out of your sight."

Maddie leaned closer, lowered her voice. "You've got to help me get her home to her people. There is no tribe now, and I want no part of starting another one. I'm done thieving, but the twins are never going to change. It's high time I face it."

"You're right about the twins. They'll never make an honest living," Anita said.

"Orphans and abandoned street urchins are one thing, but stealing someone's child is unthinkable to me now. When I think of the suffering this little girl's mother must be going through—" Maddie took a deep breath, then let it out.

Seated on the floor across the room with one hand on Anita's hound, Penelope watched them intently. "Are you two whispering about me?"

"I'm leaving you here for a day or two," Maddie said.

"Where *is* here? Are we any closer to a town?" Penelope stood and tapped one foot and then the other. "I'm warning you; you better take me to Paducah to my Aunt Gail's—or you'll be in big trouble with my papa. B-i-g trouble."

"I'm going to take you back home, but I just need to pack up a few things first."

"What about those other two?"

Maddie took a deep breath and smoothed her skirt over her knees. "That's why you have to stay here. They'll be back any minute now."

Anita sighed and shook her head. "This is against my better judgment."

Penelope studied Anita for a moment and then crossed her arms. "I don't want to stay here."

"You'll be safer here."

"Are you coming back soon?" Penelope's voice cracked. Some of her bravado had diminished.

"Really soon."

"Then are you taking me to Kentucky?"

"I'm taking you back where you belong."

Maddie hardened her heart—at least she tried anyway. She turned away and headed for the door. It creaked on its hinges as she swung it open. Penelope and Anita followed her out onto the dock and watched as Maddie carefully climbed into the pirogue. Before

Penelope could attempt to follow her down the plank steps to the waterline, Anita placed a hand gently on her shoulder.

"Madeline, take me with you!" Penelope demanded. She stamped her foot hard against the dock. "I don't *want* to stay here. I *won't* stay here. I don't know this woman."

"It's just for a day or two."

Maddie heard Anita speaking softly to the child. She focused on the dark water, careful not to lose her balance. Once she was a few yards away, she glanced back over her shoulder.

Penelope and Anita stood side by side watching her.

"You had better hurry back!" Penelope called. "Or you'll be sorry. You hear?"

Maddie turned around. This time she didn't look back.

# CHAPTER 6

Two nights after he spoke to Frank Morgan, Tom was still sporting a growth of stubble on his jaw. Dressed in a battered hat and faded brown coat, he walked into the Yellow Moon Saloon on Gallatin Street and headed straight for a group of men crowded around the bar. The Yellow Moon's reputation as a den of sin was comparable to most of the haunts in the city's underworld district, yet Tom was as at home here as he was in fine cafe's like the Absinthe House.

Free lunches had recently become popular in the Crescent City. Not only could the wealthy partake of the saloon owners' generosity, but thousands of unemployed and impoverished men were assured one hot meal a day. For the price of a fifteen-cent drink, patrons could ladle up a bowlful of oyster soup accompanied by bread and butter and, depending on the menu, beef, *poulet*, mutton, stewed tomatoes, or macaroni *à la Française*.

He glanced around the room and knew for a fact that there were countless concealed weapons in the room. Not only was he wearing a pistol, but he had a knife strapped to his calf and a derringer tucked in his coat pocket.

He ordered a drink, dished up a meal, and headed for an open chair near a cold stove in the back corner of the room. That morning he'd bought a *Times Picayune* and read a full-page advertisement.

A hefty reward was being offered by the kidnapped child's father. There was also a sketch of Penelope Perkins accompanying a feature story.

Last night he'd haunted numerous saloons like the one he was in now, establishments that catered to the underbelly of New Orleans, but he hadn't discovered any leads. Now he sized up the room as he took a bite. The food was hot and decent enough, and thankfully the liquor was watered down. He finished his bowl of stew, then sat for as long as he could stomach the smoke-filled bar, scanning the crowd. Finally he shoved out of his chair.

"You leaving?" Nearby, a toothless man in a tattered jacket eyed his empty seat.

"Take it," Tom said, indicating the chair.

The man, along with a companion wearing a black patch over his left eye, sidled past. Tom was about to walk away until he heard what the toothless man asked his friend.

"You seen the Grandes lately?"

Tom paused, pretending to focus on straightening the brim of his battered hat. Sweat stains marred the band. He didn't recall where it had come from—a rubbish heap most likely. He was in the habit of picking up clothing for his various disguises from all manner of places.

"I just saw 'em at the Apple Tree." The one-eyed man was still waiting for a chair to open up. "Heard they was livin' somewhere in the bayou now."

"Wonder what they've been up to."

"No good, that's for sure."

A chair opened up, and as the one-eyed man sat down both men shared a laugh. Their banter turned to talk of gambling. When Tom finally stepped out onto the sidewalk, he felt more confident than he had in days. He had a lead that might help him find Megan Lane and even pay off for Frank Morgan. It was slim, but his intuition told him he was getting closer.

An hour later, after stopping by the precinct to confer with Morgan, Tom walked into the Apple Tree. Two undercover New Orleans policemen were not far behind. There were two more stationed outside the saloon. He spotted the Grande twins right away. They were hard to miss; both were big men, solid hulks of flesh and muscle. Along with a handful of boisterous braggadocios, the twins were seated at a poker table near the back of the room.

He silently signaled the officers that he would approach the Grandes alone. He hoped to leave with them and, after they were outside, let the officers approach to take them in for questioning. The last thing Tom wanted was to have the men turn on him in a room full of thieves and cutthroats.

At first he had a hard time telling the twins apart, but after a few minutes of observation he noticed one did all the talking while his brother either gazed into the bottom of his whiskey glass or stared at the barmaids.

Tom made his way across the room to the poker table. He turned around and faced the bar, keeping his back to the men engaged in card play as he listened to their exchange.

"So, then," said the more gregarious twin, "we thought we had it made."

"We *do* have it made," his brother said. He had the same voice, but in a slower drawl thanks to the alcohol he'd consumed.

"Shut up, Lawrence," the first said. Then he laughed and added, "He's drunk. We got nothing. We're livin' in a shack on the bayou with our sister — "

Tom imagined a big buxom woman with wild strawberry-colored hair and meaty arms until he remembered the woman they thought of as a sister was probably not blood relation at all. He pulled out his pocket watch, sprang the lid, and checked the time.

"But things is changin' — "

Tom heard what sounded like a *thunk*, and then the drunken twin whined, "What'cha wanna hit me for, Terrance?"

"Shut. Up."

Tom immediately picked up his drink and carried it over to an empty seat at the poker table.

"You gents mind if I sit in?"

Dark, suspicious glances sized him up from around the table. Across the room, the officers sidled up a bit closer. He didn't have to look to know they had his back. Tom held his breath for a second, let it out, and leaned back with as much nonchalance as he could muster. The twin called Lawrence paid him no mind. Terrance, on the other hand, appeared wary.

"Nice knife," Tom told him, eyeing the Bowie strapped to Terrance's thigh.

"Yeah. I took it off a dead Houma Injun."

"Didn't know there were any left," Tom said.

"What's left of them live along the banks of the Mississippi up north of here."

Tom wondered how much of an arsenal Terrance Grande carried concealed beneath his dirty buckskin coat and baggy wool trousers.

They finally dealt Tom a hand, and he let Terrance and the others win to keep things even. They talked and played for a good forty minutes. No one noticed Tom wasn't matching them drink for drink. But before he could suggest they move on to another establishment, the game broke up when someone at a nearby table threw a chair. It landed across Lawrence Grande's shoulders. He jumped up with a roar and the fight was on. Tom joined in the fray and made sure he wound up fighting alongside Terrance Grande, watching his back.

The fight pretty much broke up the card game for the night, and as the Grandes started for the door, Tom caught up with them.

"You gents calling it a night already? I'm still up for some carousing."

They agreed to accompany him to the Yellow Moon just down the street. Tom knew the police officers were on foot behind them. He slowed his pace, pretending to be on the near side of drunk. They matched his steps.

"I could sure use a couple of men like you." He focused on Terrance, who had rested his hand on the hilt of his knife.

Lawrence looked over and smiled. "We don't need to work no more."

Terrance scowled his brother into silence, then said, "We got a rich uncle about to die."

"Yeah. That's it. A rich uncle." Lawrence laughed so hard he started hiccupping.

Tom shook his head. "Then you probably aren't interested."

Terrance stopped walking. "All depends on what you're offering."

Tom lowered his voice and leaned closer to Terrance. The man's blue eyes were glassy, but lucid enough for a man who had downed as many rounds as he had.

Frank's men were in place, waiting for Tom to move. A sense of satisfaction came over him. He might not be any closer to finding Megan Lane, but he prayed that the kidnapped child's nanny was right about twin kidnappers. If so, then the Grande twins might be the ones responsible for taking the Perkins girl. Now Frank Morgan would have a chance to get a confession out of them, and Tom would not only help save the child, but might be able to track down the woman named Anita Russo in the bargain and find Megan Lane.

They stood in the shadowed doorway of a brick-and-mortar building that was over a hundred years old in a block of others just like it. A slow, steady drizzle began to fall. They ignored it. Nervous energy hummed through Tom as he glanced across the street. He didn't see the police but he knew they were there.

Terrance Grande shifted and cleared his throat. He scanned the seemingly deserted street. Tom had no doubt the man might rob him on the spot.

"So what about this job?" Lawrence asked.

Tom heard footsteps coming fast behind them. Frank Morgan's men were good at what they did. This tea party was starting right on time.

An undercover policeman dressed as a gent stepped out of a nearby alley and started walking toward them. Another stepped out from behind a parked hansom cab.

Suddenly Terrance was brandishing a gun, his sights centered on the two men coming in close behind Tom. Tom pulled his own gun and pointed it at Terrance.

"Don't move," Tom warned. "We just need you to answer a few questions."

That's when things went downhill. As an undercover policeman dressed as a waiter stepped up behind Lawrence, Terrance fired twice. Tom lunged for Terrance as the policeman went down, but the big man broke free and started pounding down the street.

Tom turned his gun on Lawrence, but shot by his brother, the second twin wasn't moving. His gun hand hung limp at his side, his eyes wide and wild as he stared back at Tom. He opened his mouth to speak, but nothing came out. A blood stain spread fast and high across the left side of his buckskin shirt.

Down the street, Terrance was wrestling with three officers. The fourth officer was on the sidewalk holding his thigh. From the way he was cursing, Tom figured the man would live.

Suddenly Lawrence's gun clattered on the street. He looked down at his shirt front and covered the blood with his meaty hand just before his legs folded and he sank to the ground.

"Did you kidnap the Perkins girl?" Tom asked him.

"What girl?"

"Did you kidnap Penelope Perkins?"

"Where's Terrance? Is he dead?"

Ignoring Lawrence's gasp, Tom grabbed his shoulders and tried to force him to focus. "Where is she?"

Three officers were dragging Terrance closer. One of the policemen was bleeding from a knife wound on his forearm.

"Don't you say nothin', Lawrence," Terrance yelled. "Keep your trap shut, you hear me?"

Lawrence was battling to stay conscious. Blood continued to

bubble from the wound near his heart. Tom doubted the man would make it.

"Where is she?" Tom leaned close to be heard over Terrance's shouting. "Where's the girl?"

Lawrence grabbed Tom's shirtfront with his bloody hand. In a voice barely above a whisper he said, "Tell my sister," he wheezed. "Tell Maddie ..."

"How do I find her? Where is your sister?"

"Bayou," Lawrence whispered. "A cabin ... near Clearwater. Ask ... asssk around. Ask for Maddie Grande."

# CHAPTER 7

Something was wrong. Maddie could feel it as sure as she sensed a storm brewing. The sky matched the color of the spidery gray moss that hung limply from the trees. The air was close and still, so hot and heavy she could almost taste it.

Worry unraveled her thoughts and kept them jumping like fleas on a wet dog as she scuttled around the dock, pulling up the nets and tossing her crab catch into a bucket.

She'd spent three days waiting for the twins to return, anxious to get back to Anita's, collect Penelope, and take her home. Anita had been on her own with the child far too long. In payment, Maddie intended to give the woman her crab catch. She owed Anita much more.

She lowered the bucket into the pirogue, straightened, and then stared off in the direction of New Orleans and wondered what was keeping the twins.

She was headed back inside when she heard someone shout hello. Maddie walked through the house, picked up her shotgun, and made sure it was loaded before she went out the back door. She wouldn't hesitate to use it.

A stranger stood on the small trail behind the house that led through the marsh and out to the road to Clearwater. He was leading a fine chestnut horse that was worth a pretty penny. His eyes were hidden beneath the shadow cast by the wide brim of his low-crowned hat. Dark stubble covered the lower half of his face. All she could tell from a distance was that he had a straight nose, even features, full lips, and the slightest cleft in his chin. His looks gave her pause, and she studied him carefully. He was handsome, she'd give him that. She'd married a man with similar dark hair and eyes — but the last thing she needed or wanted right now was a man.

"Hold it right there, mister." She aimed the gun at his chest and held it steady.

He slowly raised his free hand to his hat and pulled it off in a move that gave her a better look at his face. His hair was black; so were his brows. They had a slight cynical arch to them. His eyes were dark, and even though he was a few yards away, his gaze held hers longer than she liked. Long enough to make her uncomfortable. His eyes kept his secrets well hidden.

His smile was slow in coming and fleeting when it finally appeared. He took her measure as sure as she took his. His expression was unreadable.

"Are you the Grande twins' sister?" He put his hat back on, his gaze returning to the shotgun in her hands.

"Who wants to know?"

He sure didn't have the look of any lawman she'd ever seen, but a body couldn't be too careful. His jacket was raggedy, his trousers worn and stained at the hems. His brown, watermarked boots had seen better days, and there was a rusty spot on the front of his shirt that very well could have been blood. She made note of his sidearm. Even without a weapon, he posed a threat.

"My name is Tom Abbott," he said. "Lawrence told me where to find you."

"He's not here."

"I know. That's why I'm here."

Maddie's heart stumbled. "What about?"

"Terrance is in jail."

Terrance in *jail*?

"What about Lawrence? Where is he?"

Still clutching the reins in one hand, he took a step toward her.

She leveled the shotgun. "Hold it right there and start at the beginning. I'd just as soon plug you as not, sir. The gators around here are not particular about what they eat," she warned.

He stopped moving.

"Mind if I at least tether my horse?" He studied the cabin behind her and then met her gaze again. She shifted the weapon, using it to point out a hitching post to his left.

"Throw down your gun first," she ordered.

He nodded to show he understood. Her hands tightened on the shotgun as he slowly reached for the handle of the Colt and slipped it out of its leather holster. Bending his knees, he sank low, stretched out his arm, and carefully set the weapon on the ground.

"Go on, then." She indicated the hitching post again with a tilt of her head. "Tie up your horse."

He led the animal to the post, looped the reins, and then glanced again at the cabin. She ignored his curiosity.

"Now start talking," she ordered.

"Your brothers were suspected of kidnapping. They were wanted for questioning by the New Orleans police."

She tried to hide her shock. The twins had always gotten away with their crimes. What he told her hardly rang true.

"You keep saying 'were.' Did they confess?" Careful, Maddie warned herself. Be very careful. "Where are they now?"

"Well, as I said, Terrance has been jailed."

"For kidnapping?" She hoped she looked disbelieving. She could see Abbott was hedging.

Finally he said, "For resisting arrest, shooting a police officer, and murder. He hasn't confessed to the kidnapping yet."

"What about Lawrence? Is he in jail."

"Maybe you should sit down."

Maddie took a deep breath. "Say it, mister."

"Lawrence is dead."

Her mind raced as she tried to grasp it all. Terrance hadn't confessed to anything and Lawrence was *dead*.

"How? How did he die?"

"He was shot. By your brother."

Terrance *killed* Lawrence? Was it an accident? Or had Terrance made certain his twin held his silence? It was nearly unthinkable, but she wouldn't put it past him.

"Do you know anything about a kidnapping, Miss Grande?"

She nearly blurted everything out until the intensity in his stare stopped her cold.

"I . . . they didn't much tell me what they were up to." Not a lie. Not the truth. "You're a policeman?"

"No. I'm a Pinkerton." He held up one hand. "If I may . . ." He carefully opened his jacket to reveal the Pinkerton Agency badge pinned inside.

"A Pinkerton." She was still trying to wrap her mind around Lawrence being dead, and now this.

"A private detective."

"I know what a Pinkerton is." Just as she knew good and well that if she told him about hiding the child for the twins, if she led him to Anita, both of them would be implicated in the crime as accomplices.

"If you do know anything about a missing child, you could make it easier on yourself by confessing. Your cooperation might help lessen your time in prison."

Her ears were ringing, but not so loud that she didn't hear him mention prison.

"I don't know what you're talking about, Mr. Abbott."

Abbott was still watching her closely. She pictured Lawrence, dying of a bullet wound. Had he known Terrance shot him? Lawrence couldn't abide having as much as a hangnail. If he'd been arrested, the police would have gotten the truth out of him without hardly trying. Terrance hadn't talked or the law would be here, not just one Pinkerton.

The minute Abbott found out Penelope Perkins was being held against her will, then she'd be as guilty as her brothers.

Sweat dampened her hairline and trickled down her temple. The heavy gray sky hung so low it looked close enough to touch the tips of the cypress trees. It was too sultry to think. She wished there was at least a lick of breeze.

Aware of the detective, she knew she had to pull herself together. If she could just get rid of him, demand a ransom for the child, and then turn her over to her parents, she would have a stake for the future. It wouldn't have to be much. Just enough to help her start over on her own.

She nearly jumped out of her skin when Tom Abbott touched her shoulder. She took a step back and wondered how he'd managed to sidle up so close.

"Miss Grande? Are you all right?"

"I'm fine. I'm trying to wrap my mind around what you just told me."

"I'm sorry about your brother. Mind if I have a drink of water?"

He didn't look sorry. She doubted he was really thirsty.

"You said your piece," she told him, "and I thank you for bringing word. Help yourself to some water out of that rain barrel at the corner of the cabin and then be on your way."

He shrugged and looked around the unkempt yard.

She wanted him gone. She wanted to go inside and collect herself. To come to grips with Lawrence's death and the notion that Terrance was in jail. If it wasn't for Penelope, she'd be free to do whatever she wanted. Her stomach was in knots.

She turned, forgetting that he was so close, and nearly ran into him. His dark eyes gave away nothing. His stare was completely disarming. She found herself inexplicably drawn to him and took a step back.

"I'm real sorry I had to bring you bad news," he told her.

"I thank you," she said, "for your trouble." He had come a long way to deliver it. It was a far piece back to the city too.

"It's obvious you're innocent." His conclusion surprised her but she tried to relax, to appear as if he was right. She needed to keep him believing she had no knowledge of the kidnapping. No part in it. With Penelope safely out of sight at Anita's, there was no harm in putting his mind at ease.

"I guess you may as well come in and have some coffee. I fixed up some biscuits earlier. You're welcome to have some."

"What about my gun?"

She'd forgotten all about it. He could have grabbed it but hadn't.

She walked over to where it lay on the ground, bent, and picked it up.

"I'd prefer to hang on to it for a while," she told him and then added, "if you don't mind."

"You're one suspicious lady." He lifted his hat and wiped his brow with the stained cuff of his sleeve.

"It's a dangerous world, Mr. Abbott. A body can't be too careful."

She was beside him again. Together they turned to walk toward the cabin.

"This is a far cry from New Orleans," he said.

"I feel safe here." As they continued to dance politely around each other, she was forced to keep her stewing emotions hidden. She pointed to the rain barrel. "There's the water."

Abbott walked over to the barrel, took the ladle down off the nail on the side of the cabin, and dipped himself a drink. She watched his Adam's apple bob as he swallowed it in three long gulps.

Just then thunder ripped through the air and the sky opened up, shaking the ground beneath them. Across the yard, his horse reared and strained against the reins. Its eyes rolled wildly.

"Put him in the shed," she hollered over the pelting rain. "Looks like a bad one."

Together they dashed across the yard. Abbott untied the chestnut gelding and followed Maddie into the small shed that smelled of muck and old leather. She watched him move with purpose in the shadows. She wasn't exactly a petite woman, but Tom Abbott was still a good head taller. His wide shoulders filled out his jacket, straining the seams. Unlike the twins, this man was fit and firm. He had no gut hanging over his waistband.

She glanced outside to where rain fell in sheets. She thought of the pirogue tied at the dock and the crabs in the bucket. She couldn't afford to lose the craft.

"We'll have to make a run for it," she told him. "You go first."

She nodded toward the door on the back wall of the cabin. Abbott didn't hesitate as he took off running with his hand on his hat.

By the time they reached the building they were completely drenched. Maddie stepped inside the back door, aware of the way the worn fabric of her sopping dress clung to her. She ignored her discomfort, afraid to call unwanted attention. Her long hair was heavy, dripping down her back.

She turned away from Abbott, propping her gun against the wall near the sink. When she glanced over her shoulder she caught him looking around the shack. With his attention elsewhere, she quickly slipped his Colt behind a large tin of flour on a shelf. He took off his weather-beaten hat, brushed off the water droplets, and continued to gaze around. He gave the impression he wasn't really interested in what he saw, but she had no doubt everything he did was with purpose.

"You can put your saddlebags on one of the twins' beds." She pointed across the room.

He turned, his expression one of surprise.

Color rushed to her cheeks. "It's just temporary, Mr. Abbott. You won't be sleeping here."

"I never assumed so, ma'am."

"It's Madeline. Folks call me Maddie."

His stare never wavered. "You're welcome to call me Tom."

She went over to the stove, stirred the coals to life, and put a

Dutch oven over the front burner. While she was still soaked, she figured she might as well go back out and check the lines to make sure the pirogue was tightly lashed to the dock. She left the door open as she hurried out, glancing back now and again to keep an eye on Abbott. He'd walked to the door to watch her through the rain as she grabbed the crab bucket. He stepped aside to let her back in.

"Now you're really drenched." Abbott looked around until he noticed a towel on a peg near her bed. He grabbed it as she stood just inside the threshold, her rain-soaked skirt dripping on the floor.

The rain pelting against the tin roof sounded as if it would bring the cabin down. Thunder cracked again, closer this time.

"Thank you." She raised her voice over the din. His gesture hadn't gone unnoticed. Neither of the twins would have lifted a finger to get her a dry towel, or anything else for that matter. She warned herself not to let her guard down, not even a fraction. "A body might take you for a gentleman, Mr. Abbott."

"Tom. And I'm hardly a gentleman." He rubbed the stubble on his chin.

"I hope you're enough of one to have a seat and turn your back while I put on some dry clothes," she told him.

He pulled out a chair and sat with his back to her. "I never argue with a lady when she's got a shotgun within reach."

# CHAPTER 8

Tom listened to Maddie's footsteps as she moved around the room. She'd been a surprise since the moment he'd laid eyes on her. He hadn't really known what to expect of a woman raised the way she had been, a woman who had grown up on the wrong side of the law. He certainly hadn't expected Madeline Grande. She appeared to be in her mid- to late twenties, long limbed, lean and elegant, despite her faded dress. Her rich, dark hair was nearly black. Thick and wavy, it hung loose past her shoulders. Her eyes were huge, deep brown with a hint of hazel. They were full of intelligence and speculation. Pale copper freckles, prominent across her cheeks and the bridge of her nose, dusted her skin all over.

Miss Maddie Grande was actually a pleasant surprise. The minute he laid eyes on her, he realized she fit the description of Megan Lane, except she appeared younger than thirty-two. Finding Penelope Perkins was more important right now. He'd question Maddie about Megan Lane later. The fact that Penelope Perkins was nowhere to be seen was a heavy disappointment. As far as he could tell, there was no place to have hidden her in the cabin, no side rooms, no closets or armoires. There had been no cupboards, no hidey-holes in the shed. If Madeline knew about the kidnapping, she wasn't about to let on. If her brothers were involved and she knew nothing of it, she had nothing to tell, but if she did know where Penelope was, *if* she was hiding the girl for them, then sooner or later he'd find out. For now he couldn't afford to have her panic and do anything rash.

Except for the twins' bunks, the cabin was neat and tidy. A few pieces of Maddie's clothing hung from pegs. Household items and cooking supplies were carefully arranged on sagging wooden shelves lined along one wall.

He was aware of her every move. He heard the squish of her sodden dress when it hit the floor. Then the rustle of dry fabric. He shifted on the hard wooden chair, trying not to imagine what was going on behind him, and studied her neatly made bed. The blanket hung over the edge but didn't quite reach the floor. Something beneath the bed sparkled and caught his eye. He didn't know much about women's geegaws, but it looked to be a small hair comb.

Too small for a grown woman.

He didn't turn until he heard Maddie's soft footsteps as she padded barefoot across the wood-plank floor. Now dressed in a brown skirt and yellowed blouse, she paused before the stove and lifted the lid off a cast-iron pan. A rich, delicious smell began to fill the room. His stomach grumbled and she must have heard it because she said, "Guess you were telling the truth about being hungry."

"That's not something I'd lie about," he told her.

She glanced over her shoulder. "What *would* you lie about, Mr. Abbott?"

She didn't appear to be teasing or making idle conversation. He tried to laugh off the question, but her eyes were deep, dark, and serious.

"Well, if that grub turns out to be a disappointment, I might tell you otherwise so as not to offend."

"It's stew." She reached for a bowl and started ladling out a goodly portion.

"Where'd you learn to cook?" he asked, changing the subject.

She shrugged, noncommittal. "Here and there."

He respected her silence. He liked folks who didn't need to hear themselves talk. She surreptitiously watched him, thoughtful all the while. Her quiet confidence was evident in every move she made. He wondered if she enjoyed living in such isolation.

He finished off the stew in record time. Though she didn't have any herself, she made certain he ate his fill and gave him a second helping. When he was all done, he leaned back in his chair and sighed.

"That was delicious."

"You would have said so anyway, remember?"

He laughed, surprising himself. "If it was bad, would I have had a second helping?"

She shrugged but a slight smile teased her lips. He found himself wishing it had lasted longer.

Tom glanced toward the window where rain streamed down the glass. Leaks had sprouted in the ceiling, and Maddie had carefully placed bowls and buckets on the floor to collect the drips. Now the room was full of a chorus of plinks and plops.

"I brought along a paper. You mind if I sit and read a bit?"

"Read?"

He nodded, noting there were no books, no papers around other than a few yellowed sheets of newspaper pasted up on the wall to cover the cracks.

"Go right ahead."

As he stood, he purposely knocked his spoon to the floor, causing it to slide off in the direction of Maddie's bed. As he had hoped, it fell where he could both reach for it and scoop up the trinket. His hand closed over both. After he placed the spoon back on the table, he slipped the comb into his vest pocket. Then he stretched and walked over to the bed against the far wall where he had tossed his saddle bags. Pulling out a copy of the *Times*, he shook it out, shoved aside a pile of dirty clothes, and sat down.

After pretending to read for a while, he let the newspaper fall and feigned dozing. Through half-shuttered lids, he watched Maddie quietly straighten her kitchen and putter. She picked up a broom and swept the floor, then washed the dishes stacked in the dishpan, dried them, and put them on the shelf. After that, she walked over to the table and struggled to light the oil lamp. The wheel that turned the wick gave her trouble, and she mumbled beneath her breath. Finally the flame caught, and she carefully slipped the glass chimney back on. The scent of burning lamp oil filled the cabin.

He waited until she returned to the sink and worked a while before he sat up. Rubbing his jaw and then his eyes, he yawned.

"Guess I dozed off," he said.

"Not for long."

"Hope I'm not a bother."

She glanced out the window, not really answering. "It's sure dark early with the storm."

He got up slowly and walked over to the window. Hands on hips, he stared out into the pouring rain. Behind him Maddie remained silent.

"It hasn't let up much yet." The storm appeared content to hang over the bayou. "I can be on my way—" He paused, wondered whether she'd make him leave in this weather.

They exchanged a long, silent stare, and then he heard her sigh.

"Might as well bunk down out in the shed with your horse," she suggested. "Leave in the morning."

Her offer surprised him. Innocent or not, she probably didn't want a stranger or a Pinkerton around.

"I don't want to put you out, Madeline."

He turned and found her standing closer than he'd expected. So close he could have touched her. He was shocked to realized how much he wanted to. Maddie Grande radiated an inner strength, yet there was nothing hard about her. Now dry, her hair gently curled around her shoulders. Except for tinges of hazel, her eyes were liquid brown, the color of the bayou waters. Her lips were rosy.

How many men had kissed her, he wondered. Surely a woman this lovely had been kissed. Something in the way she stared back assured him she wasn't innocent in the ways of men. She was no child.

"It's nothing to me if you sleep out in the shed with your horse," she said softly.

"If you're certain you don't mind?" He'd slept in worse places. The twins' beds weren't any better than the shed.

"No. I don't mind." She took his place at the window as he moved away.

Worry creased her brow, and he found himself wondering if she was thinking of the twins. She tended the place, cooked for them, might even worry about them, though to his way of thinking they didn't deserve it. Unlike her crude, lawless brothers, she appeared to be a woman with a kind heart — at least enough of one to give a stranger shelter from the storm.

But she knew he was a Pinkerton and if the Grande twins had kidnapped the Perkins girl, then Maddie was most likely involved too. If the child was hidden somewhere nearby, it wouldn't do to alarm Maddie.

While she had her back to him, Tom folded the newspaper and left it next to the pile of bedding so it appeared he had forgotten to take it with him. He shouldered his saddle bags, picked up his hat, and walked to the back door.

He didn't ask for his gun. She'd hidden it someplace, and if it made her feel better to think she'd disarmed him, so be it. He had other weapons on him.

Maddie turned away. She walked to the shelf over the dry sink and moved a tin. Retrieving his Colt, she brought it over and handed it to him.

"Thank you for the delicious meal." He lowered his hat onto his head.

"No trouble, Mr. Abbott."

"It's Tom."

"Thank you for letting me know about ... Lawrence." She looked as if she were about to say more but didn't.

"I wish it wasn't such dark news for you." In truth, he wished this had all been simpler, that he had found the Perkins girl in the cabin and hadn't had to spend the last few hours alone in Maddie Grande's company.

Most of all he wished he hadn't found her so attractive.

"I'll see you in the morning." He stepped out into the rain and sensed her watching from the doorway. He turned and raised a hand to the brim of his hat in farewell. She leaned against the door frame, arms folded, staring at him through rain pouring in streams of silver rivulets off the tin roof.

Water had collected in low spots in the yard and formed puddles as big as small ponds. He sidestepped what he could and finally reached the shed. The door creaked in protest when he opened it. He stepped into the pungent, shadowed interior. His horse nuzzled his shoulder.

"Looks like it's you and me tonight." He spoke softly to the animal as he pulled the small piece of metal out of his pocket and looked at it.

There, lying in his palm, was a small comb. It was ornamented with an intricate silver bow encrusted with tiny diamond chips. A much finer piece than anyone the likes of Maddie Grande might own.

As twilight faded into dusk, darkness gathered in the corners of the cabin. With Tom Abbott tucked in the stable, Maddie could concentrate on his shattering news.

She walked to an empty chair and sat down, feeling slow and heavy as she tried to come to grips with the idea that Lawrence was dead. How could it be? She'd known him since he was four. Watched him grow up. With all his faults, she considered him family. That was one of the only things that had kept her here for so long.

Dexter's words were ingrained on her heart. *"We're not like anyone else. We're a family with a strong will and that strength helps us survive and thrive. We protect each other from those on the outside who would do us harm."*

"*We protect each other.*"

Now Terrance was in jail, Lawrence was dead, and she was alone.

If she told Abbott about the Perkins girl, she'd seal Terrance's fate and surely go to jail herself. So would Anita.

The wind rammed the rain against the cabin so hard that it was beginning to seep through the paper covering the cracks in the wall. Storms in New Orleans always slowed life to a standstill. Dexter had hated rain for that very reason. There had been no working the streets when it rained, which was perhaps why she found storms somewhat comforting. She'd loved hearing it beat down on the roof and watching it fall in thick ropey strands from the eaves of the tall buildings. The rain washed away the dust and grime on the buildings and put a shine on the leaves and windowpanes. After a passing storm, droplets glittered like diamonds around the city.

Despite the pounding rain, the cabin seemed hollow with emptiness. It was a blunt reminder of just how lonely her life had become.

She sat idle in the gathering darkness with her hands limply folded in her lap. At times like this she desperately missed Louie, the young husband she'd lost long ago. She missed Dexter too. She had always been his favorite. He called her his shining star. And he'd been hers. Dexter Grande was the force behind them all. He was a genius. He'd told them so himself.

Hunger nagged as she thought about the Pinkerton in the shed. Tom Abbott had eaten more than a fair share of her stew, but she'd had no appetite at the time. She was beginning to feel a bit lightheaded, though, so she got up and ladled a small portion of stew into a bowl and carried it over to the table. As she passed by the cot where Abbott had slept, she noticed he'd forgotten to take his newspaper.

She thought about how content he'd looked with the newspaper spread out across his chest. And then she looked closer.

The paper was folded so that only half of a child's smiling face showed, but that was enough to set her heart pounding. Maddie set down her bowl, picked up the newspaper, and opened it.

She found herself staring down at a very good likeness of Penelope Perkins.

Maddie hurried back to the table and spread the paper out near the lamp. She strained to make sense of the marks on the page, but it was fruitless.

"Girls don't need to read," Dexter had always said. "They probably aren't even capable of it. It's a great waste of time to try to teach them."

She ran her fingertips over Penelope's likeness and shook her head. She had no idea how long ago the story had been printed. Newspapers were sold all over the city, which meant that Penelope Perkins's image had been seen by countless New Orleanians. The papers were no doubt being spread all over Louisiana. This couldn't be the only copy to have reached this corner of the bayou.

She pictured the Pinkerton out in the shed. Imagined his dark, shrewd eyes.

One thing was clear: she had to get to Penelope and get the girl away from Anita. But she couldn't leave until Tom Abbott was gone.

# CHAPTER 9

The next morning, the storm moved on, leaving a brilliant blue sky overhead. Tom was lured to the cabin by the aroma of bacon. He paused outside the back door, pulled off his hat, and ran his hand over his hair before he knocked.

He heard Maddie Grande's footsteps as she crossed the cabin. A jolt of expectation coursed through him at the thought of seeing her again. He tried to shake it off, irritated by his undeniable attraction to her. As she opened the door, he reminded himself that she was no better than her lowlife brothers, no matter how innocent she seemed. Now that he'd found the diamond comb, he had to tread very carefully. Even so, before he left, he hoped he had an opportunity to ask her about Megan Lane.

"Mornin'," she said, stepping back to invite him inside.

He couldn't help but notice there were dark smudges beneath her eyes, shadows that attested to a sleepless night. She indicated with a wave of her hand that he should sit at the table. As he crossed the room, he saw the paper there. It was folded and waiting for him.

She dished up a plate piled high with bacon and bits of crab sautéed and scrambled with eggs and onions, served beside a mound of grits, and then went back to pour his coffee. It was as opaque as the muddy bayou water and strong enough to kill a weaker man. He took a few sips and smiled.

"I forgot to ask if you'd like some sugar with that," she said.

"Don't mind if I do."

She brought over a cracked sugar bowl along with a plate of hot biscuits. He loaded the coffee with sugar, looked up, and found her watching. When he caught her staring, a hint of a smile graced her lips and her face lit up. His blood warmed to the sight despite his best efforts to ignore it. He wouldn't let himself be taken in.

"The twins are of the opinion my coffee could be used for tar and featherin'."

He couldn't help but chuckle. "Maybe they're just weak of heart." Staring at all the food he said, "You must have been up long before dawn."

"I didn't sleep much." Her smiled faded. "You know how long Terrance will be in jail?"

"That depends on whether or not he confesses to the kidnapping."

She nodded that she understood.

"But when he doesn't?"

"Confess, you mean?"

"That's right. When he doesn't confess?" She knew they'd have to light Terrance on fire to get him to talk. She doubted that would happen, so sooner or later they'd have to let him go.

"Do you think he did it?"

"I can't say."

"Then he could have? Is that what you're saying?"

"He's not the confessing kind. That's what I'm saying."

He let her lead the discussion. If Maddie did know something, he wanted the information to come from her voluntarily. He wasn't about to spook her and make her bolt—or worse, panic her into getting rid of the child to escape prosecution.

"Which is why we need to find the girl. Terrance wounded a policeman. He won't be getting out of prison anytime soon." Tom looked at Maddie. "I wouldn't fret too much unless you know more than you're telling." He picked up his fork and dug into the meal.

It was some of the best food he'd ever eaten. Simple, flavored just right.

"Never had bacon and crab together before. You concoct this recipe yourself?"

She shrugged. "Crab is easy to come by. Bacon came from ..." She paused and studied her hands. "The bacon came from a friend up the bayou near Clearwater."

"Must not be easy to make friends out here. It's pretty isolated."

She didn't respond. Her gaze fell to the paper and then darted away. He noticed but pretended to ignore it, with the niggling feeling she knew a lot more than she would admit.

He polished off half the meal and took a long swig of coffee. Maddie shook her head and ran her fingernail over an indentation in the tabletop. There were a few burn marks here and there, as well as oil stains. She was quiet, lost in contemplation as he finished his breakfast.

She tucked her long hair behind her ear. "Would you like more?"

He leaned back and sighed. "That was delicious, but no thanks. I couldn't swallow another bite."

She surprised him by reaching for the *Times Picayune.* Opening it, she set it on the table and tapped the drawing of Penelope Perkins. "What does this say?"

He leaned over the paper. His heartbeat accelerated. "It's a story about the kidnapped child. Why?"

"I can't read. I was just wondering what it says."

Her expression gave nothing away. If the twins were guilty and if she *did* know something about the child, then Maddie Grande was a consummate actress.

He picked up the paper and read the article to her word for word.

" 'Penelope Perkins, eight years old, was kidnapped by two men on the river road as she and her nanny occupied a carriage headed for Kentucky where she was to visit her maternal aunt. Her parents, Peter and Mary Perkins, are offering a reward of two thousand dollars for her safe return, no questions asked.' "

"A mother's heart can't bear losing a child."

He had to strain to hear her. There was something so bleak in Maddie's voice, such heartfelt understanding in her whisper, that he couldn't help but wonder if she was speaking from experience.

"You almost sound as if you know—"

Pushing out of her chair she picked up his plate and crossed the room.

"Two thousand dollars is a king's ransom," she said.

"The Perkinses are desperate." He added, "It says here they lost a baby boy a month ago."

He watched her shoulders sag. Her hands stilled. She recovered quickly and slid his plate into a tub of soapy water before she dried her hands on a rag draped over the dry sink.

"You sure you don't know anything about this?" He tried to sound as if he didn't care. As if this wasn't the very heart of the reason he was here.

She kept her back to him, stared down into the dishpan. "How could I?"

But when she finally faced him again, her eyes were haunted. A frown marred her brow. "You'd best be going, Mr. Abbott. I've got to see to my traps today." She sounded distracted as she headed for a rack of antlers with hats and an oilcloth slicker hanging on it.

If the Perkins child was on the premises, he'd have seen or heard her by now. Last night it had struck him that the Grandes could have hidden her somewhere nearby. There were hundreds of waterways threading through the swamp. She could be hidden in a shed on a spit of land somewhere, in a hidey-hole where they stashed stolen goods.

"Mind if I go along?" He figured he'd worn out his welcome, but why not press his luck?

"Would it do any good to tell you no?"

He shrugged. "I'm not the law, Maddie. You don't have to have me along."

He could almost see her mind working.

She wasn't happy about his request but she said, "It's up to you. Come along if you want."

She didn't seem overly concerned. Perhaps because she wanted him to think she knew nothing of the kidnapping.

Or maybe he was just hoping that she was innocent.

The longer Tom Abbott hung around, the more desperately Maddie wanted him gone. She had a feeling he was just waiting for her to accidentally reveal Penelope's whereabouts. That he was just waiting to pounce. She'd seen him weigh every word, watch her every move, while they discussed the newspaper story.

She reached for an oilskin coat on the antler rack and pulled it over her brown serge skirt and stained blouse. She'd trimmed the deep hem off the coat and cut the sleeves down but it was still four sizes too big across the shoulders. She sat on the edge of her bed to unfasten and slip off her shoes, then shrugged into a pair of tall leather boots. Once she had the shotgun in hand and her skinning knife sheathed and dangling from her waist, she was ready to leave. Because of the storm, her trap line had gone unchecked yesterday. With the swamp full of predators, if she didn't get to them soon, there'd be nothing worth saving of the muskrat catch.

Tom Abbott finished off his coffee. She watched with curiosity as he carried his mug and the rest of his dishes and cutlery to the dry sink before he followed her out onto the dock. As she went about preparing the pirogue, her thoughts were consumed with the Perkins girl.

She could not shake the sound of Abbott's voice as he read the story to her. The reward money offered was more than she could fathom.

*"No questions asked."*

No questions. If she could just deliver the girl, collect the reward, and escape, she'd be free. But even if she *did* take the child home, there was no way to keep Penelope from telling her parents she had been in league with the twins all along.

Maybe instead of handing Penelope over, she should have a lock of the child's hair delivered as proof she had possession of her. Or better yet, the red cape. Maddie could then demand a meeting and exchange Penelope for the reward.

If she could shake Abbott.

*"Trust no stranger."*

It was a cardinal rule of Dexter's.

Maddie lowered the gun into the pirogue and climbed down from the dock, careful to keep the craft balanced. She held firm to the iron ring where she'd lashed the craft for the night. Catching a glimpse of movement out of the corner of her eye, she glanced up. Abbott was waiting to join her.

"Take care climbing down. Don't make any sudden moves or you'll upset the balance and we'll go over." She waited until he was aboard before she took up the forked push pole. She loosed the rope and they floated free.

Abbott sat in silence in the bow of the boat, watching the banks intently. The bayou had had the same seductive affect on her the very first time she'd taken to the water. The twins were unmoved by the haunting, natural beauty of the swamp. The silence did not speak to them the way it did her. Unfortunately, the notion that Tom Abbott was in awe of it too brought her defenses down another notch.

She studied the way he sat there so casually, one arm propped across his knee, his broad shoulders thrust forward as he studied one side of the bank and then the other. They passed a blue heron poised on one leg near the reeds along the bank and then floated silently past a black snake on the surface of the water.

"Where are we headed?"

She jumped at the intrusion of his voice and nearly dropped the pole. She took a deep breath.

"To the heart of the marsh. Muskrats make tunnels in the soft ground away from the water. When we get there, I'm going to tie up and get out, but you stay put. Walking around on damp ground with tunnels beneath takes some practice." She feared he might be too heavy-footed to make his way safely across the marsh.

"I'll stay put. Guard the pirogue," he said.

"Most likely you won't see anyone out here. If you do, just wave and don't look threatening."

She slowly edged to the left and poled along between an ever-narrowing thread of water until the boat refused to go any further.

"How do you know where to set the line?" Abbott had his hand to his brow, shading his eyes as he scanned the landscape. "It all looks the same to me."

"A friend told me I'd begin to feel where the rats might be. I choose spots where I've found them before and set traps in tunnels and holes. If you look close you'll get better at recognizing paw prints. Sometimes there are gnawed roots and droppings around the entrances to tunnels."

"Your brothers make a lot selling pelts?"

"My brothers wouldn't do this on a bet. I do all the trapping and skinning myself, sell the pelts in Clearwater. First town up the road."

Abbott turned slowly and carefully, his hands steady on the sides of the pirogue, and stared up at her. "You aren't joshing, are you? You catch and skin muskrats yourself?"

"I don't make jokes, Mr. Abbott." There wasn't much in her life to tease about and never had been.

Carefully, she set down the pole and picked up an axe handle she used to club muskrats that hadn't died in the traps.

"Hand me the rope," she instructed.

He grabbed the end and stretching toward her, held out his hand. Their fingers touched as he passed the rope over. At the slow brush of his warm skin against hers, Maddie's gaze involuntarily flew to his eyes. They were dark, unreadable, and held her gaze far longer than she would have liked.

Did he know what she was thinking? Did her reaction give away just how long it had been since she had been close to someone?

She was the first to look away. Shaking off her surprise at her reaction, she picked up the shotgun and stepped out. She tried to concentrate on the soft ground beside the boat. This was no time to let her mind wander. If she wasn't careful, she'd end up halfway to her waist in muck.

"You leaving me here alone?" His voice shattered her concentration.

"You've got your gun. I won't be that long."

"What about alligators?" He looked around.

"Keep your hands in the boat. I'll be back shortly." She'd try to hurry, but haste fueled accidents.

"Maybe I should go with you."

"Maybe you should stay put and let me get on with it. You're safer here, believe me."

"Just don't dawdle."

She almost smiled. The unaccustomed lightness fluttering deep inside her was more than a little disturbing. She thought of Lawrence and reminded herself she had nothing to smile about.

The ground was soggy from yesterday's downpour. Her boots were mud-caked after the first two steps and her hem was quickly soaked, but she kept her footing.

The first trap held the mutilated remains of an otter. The pelt was unsalvageable. She carefully opened the trap, pulled out what was left of the creature, and flung it as far off into the marsh as she could. It sailed out over the high grass and landed without sound.

When Anita first suggested she learn to trap and skin to provide for herself, Maddie had found the blood and guts disgusting. Her life had always been far from glamorous, but she was a city girl at heart. She knew the streets and warrens of New Orleans like the back of her hand. On her first few trips into the swamp, she would have been impossibly lost if she'd been alone, but Anita was wise and patient, and that, coupled with the lure of the bayou, helped Maddie quickly learn to read the signs. Nature always pointed the way.

Torn-up and half-eaten critters no longer disgusted her. A

ruined carcass represented no more than a lost pelt. She moved on, checked six more traps. Five of the six held round-eyed muskrats. They were compact little animals with wide heads, round ears, and dark, brown-black pelts. Many had red-gold tints running through their dark coats. Their underbellies were silver.

There was good money to be made selling the thick pelts — she not only used her earnings for food and supplies, but for rent on the cabin — yet there was never any left over. Nothing to save for a new start.

She kept her promise to Abbott and soon made her way back to the pirogue with the heavy line of muskrats dragging from her hand. He was stretched out with his arms folded over his chest, his hat brim pulled down to shade his eyes. She tossed her catch into the bottom of the pirogue, where they hit the wood with loud, wet slaps.

Abbott quickly sat up. Even without looking at him, she felt his gaze. As before, he was a master at masking his thoughts.

They passed the journey back to the cabin in silence. She grabbed the shotgun and climbed up onto the dock, and Abbott handed her the string of muskrats. She turned away to let him climb out of the pirogue on his own and was about to head around the house to wash the muskrats with fresh water when the cabin door opened and Anita Russo stepped out.

Maddie stared in shock but quickly covered her dismay.

"Hey, Anita." She was certain Abbott could hear her heart pounding. Maddie glanced back and saw him climb onto the dock. He made certain the pirogue was secure. She held her breath, expecting Penelope to bound out of the cabin behind Anita, but thankfully, the child failed to appear.

Maddie knew it was too much to hope that Anita had taken the girl home.

"You been here long?" Maddie spoke to Anita, fully aware that Abbott was making his way toward them.

"No." Anita eyed Abbott with suspicion. "Just got here."

"I caught five rats." Maddie held up her catch with two hands. The muskrats dangled by tails as long as their stiff bodies.

Anita's brow creased. She opened her mouth and then closed it since Tom Abbott was now within hearing distance.

Maddie stared into the shadowed interior of the cabin, but there was no movement, no sign of Penelope. Anita remained silent. Obviously she'd realized something was going on.

"This is Mr. Abbott." Maddie quickly added, "He's a Pinkerton."

"Tom," he said with a nod to Anita. He opened his coat so she could see his badge. "Tom Abbott."

"Howdy, Mr. Abbott." Anita stared at the silver badge a moment and fell silent, but her expression spoke volumes. She looked to Maddie for a cue.

"This is Anita," she told Abbott. "The one who taught me to trap. She lives up the bayou a ways."

Abbott gave the brim of his hat a tug. "Pleased," he said.

"I need to talk to you," Anita told Maddie.

"I'll go see to my horse," Abbott suggested and started to walk toward the stable shed.

Maddie set the muskrats on a skinning table near the back of the house, wiped her hands on her filthy skirt, and indicated that Anita should follow her. Once they were inside, Maddie glanced around the room. Still no sign of Penelope. She closed the back door.

Anita started. "I came as soon as—"

Maddie shushed her with a shake of her head. She led Anita through the cabin and out the front door, where they stood close together on the ramshackle porch over the water. Maddie glanced over her shoulder and then turned to Anita.

"Where's the girl?" she whispered. "Did you take her home?"

"What's going on?" Anita's thick salt-and-pepper brows beetled. "A Pinkerton? Why's he here? Does he know about the girl?"

"Where *is* she?"

Anita massaged the spot between her brows and then shrugged. "I don't know. She ran off. I awoke after the storm and she was gone. I tried to get into Clearwater, but I couldn't leave till early this morning. I asked around but no one's seen her."

"You *asked* about her?" Maddie thought of the newspaper article.

"I told them she was my niece and that she was a bit teched in the head." Anita rolled her eyes. "Told folks she might spout nonsense and not to pay her any mind; just bring her back to me if they found her."

For a split second, Maddie didn't believe her. Saying that the child had run off was too close to the tale she was going to tell the twins.

"Did you collect the reward, Anita?" She didn't want to believe the woman would double cross her, but two thousand dollars would turn anyone's head.

"What reward? She ran off, I'm telling you. Till then I kept her hid, just like you asked me to."

Maddie bit her lips and stared out over the bayou. There wasn't a hint that the sky had opened up and a deluge had fallen just yesterday. A snowy white egret landed atop a cypress knee. Fluffy white clouds scudded across an azure sky.

*She ran off. She ran off.*

"She could have drowned. Or been eaten by a gator. How could a little child survive out there alone?" Maddie pictured the mauled otter. She couldn't think past anything else.

"She's got spunk. Maybe with luck—" Anita rubbed her hand across her mouth, thinking.

"Her likeness is in the New Orleans paper," Maddie said. "There's a two-thousand-dollar reward for her return. Everybody and his brother will be looking for her soon as they see or hear about it."

"The boys back yet?"

Maddie shook her head no. "That's what *he's* doing here."

She nodded toward the back of the house. "Came to tell me what happened."

"What? What happened?"

"Terrance is in jail. Lawrence ..." She hesitated. Took a deep breath. "Lawrence is dead."

"How is that possible?" Anita stared in disbelief. Her shoulders sagged. "Those two were more slippery than a basket full of eels. How did they ever get caught?"

Maddie walked to the edge of the porch, watched the muddy water slide by.

"They were wanted for questioning. Tried to run. Lawrence was shot."

"Did he confess before he died? Did Terrance?"

"No."

"How did he find you?"

"Lawrence sent him to tell me what happened."

"Well, then, that's that. No need worrying about the girl anymore."

"That reward money could have been the key to all my tomorrows." Maddie shook her head. "Now she's gone."

She threaded and unthreaded her fingers, staring at the bayou, trying to imagine a new life, a new beginning. She had no notion what it would be like to live without fear of the law. Without nightmares. But she would sure have liked to give it a try.

When Maddie turned around, she saw that Anita had sunk into an old, overstuffed purple chair that was losing its innards. She had her elbows propped on her knees, her hands dangling between them.

"When did you say she ran off?" Maddie tried to run her fingers through her hair, but it was hopelessly tangled.

"Sometime after the storm." Anita reconsidered. "I got up to use the necessary and it seemed daylight was just about to break. She was there. Then I went back to bed, and when I woke up, she was gone. Can't say as I wasn't glad to see the last of her. Never heard a body who could talk a blue streak like that. She's a handful."

"I was ready to go back to your place yesterday until Abbott showed and the storm hit."

"What are you going to do now?"

Maddie rubbed her upper arms and shook her head. "I don't know. I just don't know, Anita."

"How'd you hear about the newspaper?" Anita was watching her intently.

"He brought one with him. I saw Penelope's likeness on the front page. He read me the story."

"You get the feeling he knows for sure we had her?"

"Terrance hasn't confessed."

"You think it would be better to tell him? Maybe they'd let you go."

"I don't know if I can trust him to help me if I do."

Maddie could see Anita was still shaken by the news of Lawrence's death. Her bottom lip trembled. "I've been taking care of those boys, taking care of all of you, since you were little. Maybe I could have saved him."

Maddie felt her heart stumble but ignored it. She couldn't let herself fall apart now. She had to think clearly and come up with a plan. The key to her own freedom just might be Penelope Perkins.

Anita pushed herself to her feet. It was a minute before she started walking across the wooden deck toward the front door. Her steps were heavy and slow.

"Don't get old," she warned when she paused to look back over her shoulder. She reached for the doorknob. "Everything aches."

Maddie nodded. She didn't know about the physical aches that came with old age, but she figured if she'd been schooled, she could write a book on heartache. There was only one way to save herself from any more of it, and that was to do whatever it took to walk away from her life.

# CHAPTER 10

When the cabin door opened and the old woman walked back out with Maddie, Tom was staking his horse in the shade in high grass near the shed. Both women were silent but the glance they exchanged spoke volumes. Something was definitely wrong. Maddie had looked jumpy as a frog on a hot griddle from the minute she'd laid eyes on her friend Anita.

Tom studied the woman, certain she was the one the missionary suggested he find. She was a good head shorter than Maddie, with dark eyes and graying hair slipping beneath the edges of a paisley scarf wrapped turban style. Her complexion was creased with deep wrinkles, her cheekbones high. He figured there might be some Indian blood in her family tree. Though her walk was slow and steady, there was strength and determination in her short strides.

Maddie bid the woman farewell. Anita nodded to Tom and began to walk past him.

"You knew Dexter Grande?" he asked.

His question stopped her dead in her tracks. She eyed his expensive horse. "I did." She grew even more wary.

"I was told that you might be able to help me solve a missing person's case."

"Maddie told me you were looking for a kidnapped child. I ain't seen her."

He looked for the truth in her eyes. "I wasn't talking about the recent kidnapping. I was talking about child who would be a woman full-grown now. Thirty-two or so. Her parents were Irish. From Irish Channel. Her name was Megan Lane. You ever heard of her?"

She shook her head no. "I don't recall anybody by that name."

"She disappeared around 1853. Brown hair. Fair skin. Brownish eyes." The description Laura Foster had given him fit thousands of women. It even fit Maddie Grande.

"Nope, sorry, mister. Sometimes I don't hardly remember what I et for breakfast."

He opened his jacket, pulled a calling card out of his vest pocket, and handed it to her. "If anything comes to mind, you can reach me here."

"What's it to you?" she asked.

"Her sister is searching for her. I'm authorized to offer a reward for information leading to her whereabouts."

She tucked the card into the folds of her skirt and walked past him without another word. Her diminutive figure was soon swallowed up by high, dense growth along both sides of the path.

He looked up. Madeline was standing nearby.

"I heard part of what you said. Who told you about Anita? I know it wasn't Lawrence or Terrance."

"It was a missionary in New Orleans. A woman named Henson." When she showed no recognition of the name, he asked, "What was your name before it was Grande?"

Her chin went up a notch. She looked him straight in the eye and said, "My name was *always* Maddie Grande."

Maddie frowned. "I 'spect you'll be leaving now," she said.

"I guess I will."

She seemed more impatient than ever. He was hesitant to leave before flushing out Penelope, but there was no obvious sign that she was still around anywhere. He hated to leave suspecting she was nearby, but until he had someone identify the comb, he might be wrong.

Maddie was headed toward the skinning table with a long, lethal-looking knife in her hand. He followed her at a decent distance and leaned a shoulder into the side of the house where he could watch from the vantage of the shade.

"You'll be on your own without your brothers."

"They weren't around much."

"You ever get lonely?"

"Folks are only as lonely as they let themselves be."

She sorted through the muskrats, picked the fattest one first. Filling a bucket with clear water from one of the rain barrels beneath the eaves, Maddie doused one muskrat at a time and then ran her hands down the stiff bodies. With a firm grip, she stroked and squeezed the water out of the thick pelts. Her expertise showed. Taking up a razor-sharp knife, she commenced removing the pelts one after another.

"The meat makes for good eating. Too bad these are so far gone," she said offhandedly.

"They're edible?" They looked too close to fat gutter rats for his liking.

"When they're fresh."

When she smiled over her shoulder, he found he had to force himself to look away.

"That was muskrat stew you lapped up yesterday."

"You don't say." As he met her gaze again he tried not to think about the two heaping bowls he'd polished off.

"A body will eat anything if it's starving," she added. "They're pretty good if you bake them all day smothered in onions."

He reached for an empty bucket, turned it upside down, and sat to watch her work, glad skinning wasn't a task he had to undertake. More than once he saw Maddie heave a heavy sigh and give a slight shake of her head. He finally stood and walked over to the skinning table. Ignoring the blood and guts on the table and her hands, he stepped up close behind her.

"What's wrong?" he said softly. "Maybe I can help you."

She jumped at the sound of his voice, apparently unaware he'd even moved. She gasped on a swift intake of breath. They both glanced down at once. There was a thick slice across her forefinger, not deep, but enough to draw blood. She dropped the knife.

Without thinking, he reached for her hand, held it between them as he inspected the cut. When she stiffened, he looked up. He caught himself falling into her eyes, and after another heartbeat, he let go.

A drop of blood slid down her finger. She wiped it off on her skirt. "I could have lost a finger."

"I'm sorry. I didn't mean to startle you."

She turned slightly toward him, stared deep into his eyes. Hers were dark, troubled. There was more to her worry than just a shallow cut.

"That girl," she said. "The one in the paper—"

He nodded. "What about her?"

Maddie looked so grave, so hesitant, that Tom held his breath. *Don't let her say the child is dead.*

"I hope they find her, is all," she whispered. "I surely hope they do."

Maddie was more than relieved when Tom Abbott finally rode off, leaving her alone. She worked quickly and efficiently as she hung the pelts to dry, freshened up, and then gathered her shotgun and wrapped up a few supplies. She boarded the pirogue and headed to Anita's.

"Did he follow you?" Anita glanced over Maddie's shoulder as she ushered her inside the cabin. Maddie watched her pace over to the window overlooking the dock. The old woman planted her hands on her hips as she stared out at the duckweed floating on the water.

"Not unless he swam after me. I've got to find that girl and get her home, Anita. Will you lend me your horse?"

Anita stared out the window, ignoring her request. "If he finds you here—"

"He won't."

"So you think. Pinkerton's known as The Eye That Never Sleeps."

Anita's hair hung limp around her face. She raised the hem of her apron to wipe a bead of sweat from her temple. The air was oddly close and humid. Maddie could feel it thickening around her and wondered if there was another storm coming in close on the heels of the last. She hoped not. She needed clear weather to search for Penelope.

She hated to think the child was wandering around alone in the swamp—although by now she might have been picked up by a rescuer ... or someone worse.

"Where are you going?" Anita wanted to know.

"To Clearwater to ask after her again. If nobody's seen her, I'll head up the road. Then I guess I'll have to head back toward New Orleans. I have no idea where Langetree Plantation might be, but I'll have to find out somehow if she's made it back. I'd hate for somebody else to collect the reward."

Maddie was anxious to leave. She started for the door, paused. "So can I use your horse?"

"'Course. The old nag's not very fast but she's steady." Anita chuckled and added, "Kinda like me."

Maddie saddled up the swaybacked old mare and almost felt sorry for her as she mounted up. Anita handed up her shotgun and then told Maddie to wait while she ran back into the house and brought out a felt hat that had seen better days. The brim was so tired it flopped up and down.

"At least it'll keep the sun off your face," Anita said.

"Thank you again. And I'll bring the mare back as soon as I can," Maddie promised.

"No hurry," Anita assured her. "You just watch out for yourself."

# CHAPTER 11

The wide canopy of oaks draped with hanging moss formed an emerald tree tunnel that awed as much as welcomed. At the end of the lane, a two-story home with ground-to-roof columns gave the illusion of a Greek temple. Built during the 1830 boom years, Langetree's grand structure was a testament to all the South had been before the war.

Tom put his heels to his horse and headed up the oak-lined drive toward the sumptuous forty-year-old mansion resurrected by Yankee money. As he drew nearer, he saw the outbuildings beyond the house—offices, kitchen, servants' quarters. A traditional *garçonnière* and a *pigeonnier*, twin round structures, flanked the main house.

The front door was draped in black crepe, and black curtains were drawn over the windows. A drapery across the glass sidelight beside the front door shifted when Tom dismounted. A moment later, a servant stepped outside onto the portico. Dressed in black livery, the man nodded and came forward to take the reins of Tom's horse.

"Mister Perkins is expectin' you," the man said in a deep drawl. "Go right on in."

Tom thanked him, took off his wide-brimmed black hat, and walked through the open door. Inside, the house was quiet as a tomb. The wide central hall bisected the structure from front to back. Fifteen-foot doors opened into rooms with impossibly high ceilings on each side of the hall. Tom took in the long, winding staircase that ascended from the center of the hall and wished he was anywhere but here facing a grieving family.

As he waited in the foyer of the mansion at Langetree trying to shake off his melancholy, a door to his right opened. A man well over six feet with dark hair and a handlebar moustache that met his wide muttonchop sideburns stepped out. He smoothed the front of an amethyst brocade vest and offered his hand in greeting.

"Mr. Perkins? I'm Tom Abbott, a Pinkerton Agency detective."

"I'm happy to make your acquaintance. Frank Morgan sent word that you'd be coming. I took the liberty of wiring Allan Pinkerton in Chicago. He recommends you highly."

The two men, both of equal stature, shook hands.

"I'm sorry for your loss, sir."

"Our son was stillborn not quite a month ago. My wife has yet to recover from that blow, so you can imagine what she's suffering knowing Penelope is out there somewhere in the hands of criminals. Or worse." The big man, brought low, choked on his words and fought to collect himself.

"I've gone through all the information the police have, but perhaps you have some details that might help," Tom told him. "The sooner the better."

"Of course." Peter Perkins indicated the opulently appointed sitting room behind him and ushered Tom in. "Come. Have a seat."

The servant who had taken Tom's horse slipped silently into the room. Perkins turned to him. "Armand, have Sally bring in a tray of coffee and refreshments for Mr. Abbott."

The man nodded and left without a moment's hesitation.

"Thank you, sir." Tom took a seat on a settee upholstered in a rich blue silk.

"Have you been a detective long?" Perkins asked.

"I was hired on as a Pinkerton operative during the war," he said.

"It was brilliant of General McClellan to appoint Pinkerton as his personal spy. I assume you carried out similar duties?"

Tom nodded. "I played many roles in order to infiltrate Southern society to gather vital information for the Union. After the surrender, I opted to stay on in New Orleans."

There was something about the Crescent City that haunted and seduced him, something that kept him here despite the fact that all of his family resided in Michigan.

"The local sheriff is useless. For that matter, so are the New Orleans Metropolitan Police. I haven't had much help from that quarter."

"Morgan is sparing what manpower he can. He has a suspect in custody."

"So I heard. But the man in custody still hasn't confessed. He would if I could have five minutes alone with him." Perkins poured a whiskey from a crystal decanter on a side table and offered it to Tom.

"No, thank you." Tom shook his head. "Hard liquor and I parted ways years ago." He only drank on occasion, or pretended to when his cover depended on it.

He watched as a maid entered bearing a silver tray covered with a tea service, a plate of sweet bread slices, and cookies. She set them down, poured Tom a cup of tea, and silently slipped out of the room.

Tom drew a small notebook and pencil out of his pocket. He opened the notebook, licked the lead tip, and watched Peter Perkins sink into a wide armchair opposite the settee.

Tom nodded toward a large portrait in an oval gilt frame above the fireplace mantel on the wall opposite him. "Is that Penelope?"

He studied the portrait of the beautiful child with black hair, violet eyes, and a mouth that formed a perfect bow. Her hair was drawn away from her heart-shaped face. He wondered if the impishness in her smile was a facet of Penelope's personality or simply a charming addition by the artist.

Perkins nodded. "Yes. That's our Penelope Charlotte. She's only eight, nearly nine now, and very precocious. Very well-spoken for her age. She's a lovely child when she wants to be." Perkins's hand holding the brandy snifter began to shake. He finished off what was left of the liquor in one swallow. Tom watched him closely.

"When was the last time you saw her?"

"When I put her in our private coach and told her good-bye. I was sending her off to my wife's sister, Gail, in Kentucky." He gazed around the room, indicated the crepe-covered mirror over the fireplace and the heavy curtains at the windows. "I thought it would be better for the child to get away for a while. My wife rarely comes out of her room, and Penelope has been extremely upset. She blames herself for her mother's sadness. Nothing she did could cheer Mary."

He paused and a deep sigh shook his heavy frame. "If I hadn't sent her away, she'd be here safe and sound."

Tom knew words of consolation would do little to salve the man's guilt.

"Could your driver or the child's nanny have been in cahoots with the kidnappers? Given them the route or schedule?"

Perkins set the brandy snifter down on a table beside him. "Absolutely not."

"How do you know for certain?"

"I've made it my business to handpick my staff. I pay them generous wages and provide housing. My wife has even set up a school on the property where all who wish may attend and learn to read, write, and cipher. I know my driver, Jeb, to be a good, honest man. And as far as Nanny is concerned, she treats Penelope as one of her own."

"From what the girl's nanny told the police, the kidnapping sounds like a robbery gone sour," Tom said. Then he asked Perkins a few questions about his business dealings and if there was anyone who might be seeking revenge.

"That's always possible, Mr. Abbott. I'm a wealthy man and I didn't get this way by mincing words. I've stepped on a lot of Southern toes, but there's no one in particular I can think of offhand who would do anything this dastardly."

Tom gave him details about finding the twins, the shooting, and Terrance's arrest. He added that he was sorry there'd been no confession.

Perkins asked if he cared for more tea. Tom had just declined when there came the soft rustle of silk, and a young woman walked through the drawing-room door. She was draped in black from her neck to the tips of her shoes. An oval mourning broach of gold and glass with a wisp of dark hair encased inside was pinned to the fabric at her throat. Her hair was braided and swept up into two coils pinned on either side of her head. She was petite, not much taller than five feet and a few inches. Violet shadows stained the skin beneath her eyes. She was pale as a wraith, thin to the point of emaciation—a grown-up, sadder version of the lovely child in the portrait.

Tom quickly stood the moment she entered. He nearly went to her aid, doubting that she could make it across the room, but her husband moved quickly, rushing to her side, helping her to the nearest chair.

She never took her eyes off of Tom.

"Are you the detective?"

Her voice was so very soft he had to strain to hear her. He moved to the edge of the settee and leaned forward. She looked so in need of comfort that he was tempted to take her hand, but she held them clenched in her lap.

"Yes, ma'am."

"This is Tom Abbott, Mary. He comes recommended by Allan Pinkerton himself," her husband assured her. "Mr. Abbott, my wife, Mary."

If Mary Perkins had one tear left in her, it was impossible for her to shed it now. She mirrored Tom by leaning toward him. Her voice was barely a whisper, almost as if she were unaccustomed to speaking anymore. She didn't ask the usual questions clients wanted answered: Did he think he could find their daughter? When did he think the kidnappers would contact them for a ransom? Should they offer a reward and how much?

She merely stared deep into his eyes with all the anxiety, fear, and daring it took for her to hope and said, "Bring my daughter home, Mr. Abbott. Whatever you do, please find Penelope and bring her home. She's all we have."

Tom reached into his pocket, held out his hand, and opened his palm. "Is this your daughter's, Mrs. Perkins?"

The silver comb sparkled on his palm. Mary Perkins leapt to her feet. Her hand flew to her throat and lay there limp as a pale, fallen dove. Her eyes met Tom's.

"Where did you find that?" she whispered.

"Is it hers?" he asked.

"Yes. She was wearing two of them when she left."

Shaken, Mary slowly listed to her right. Her husband's arm went around her waist, and he lowered her back into her chair. She sank onto the brocade upholstery.

"Where did you get that, Abbott?" Perkins's expression was a study of a man grappling with anger tempered by fear.

"In a cabin on the bayou not far from New Orleans." Tom was dealing with his own reaction to the verification, forced to accept that Maddie was an accomplice. She was part of the scheme causing these two good people so much pain.

"Penelope wasn't there," Tom told them. "But this is proof that she had been. I'm going back to find her. I wanted to make sure I was on the right track first."

Perkins's pent-up frustration exploded. "I want my daughter found. If you know where she is, where the perpetrators are, spread the word. I want everyone in Louisiana looking for her."

"If we panic the kidnappers, Penelope could end up—" He glanced at Mary and stopped. "We could place Penelope in very grave danger. Not only that, but you would open yourself up to a host of extortionists demanding money for false leads."

Tom knew it was up to him to convince the man to let him see this through on his own. He didn't want Maddie panicked. He didn't want everyone in the state breathing down on her.

"These are desperate times." Tom hoped the man was listening. "People will do anything for money. If I knew exactly where she is right now, that would be one thing. But I don't. I only know where she *was,* but now I have a solid lead to follow."

"Listen to me, Abbott. If I have to, I'll contact Pinkerton himself and—"

"Stop it. Both of you." Mary Perkins's voice might have been weak, but there was underlying strength in it. "Please."

Tom and Peter both turned to her. Her gaze drifted to Penelope's portrait before she eyed both men with a preoccupied detachment.

"Peter, Mr. Abbott knows what he is doing. Let him do his job. I want my daughter back, and the sooner you let the man be on his way, the sooner he can find her."

Perkins's anger still radiated but he held his silence.

Tom bowed to Mary and then offered his hand to Perkins. The man was slow to take it, but after a strained moment they shook hands.

"Thank you for understanding." Tom turned to Mary. "Thank you, Mrs. Perkins, for your confidence."

"Thank you, Mr. Abbott. Only faith has gotten us this far. I pray God will guide you to our Penelope."

"I do too, ma'am." Tom bowed again and made his way out of the house.

It wasn't until he mounted up and was halfway down the drive that he realized instead of handing over the silver comb, he had slipped the proof of Maddie's guilt back into the watch pocket of his vest.

Penelope's fate might still be unknown, but one thing was now certain: Maddie Grande was involved. There was no way he could let her walk away now.

The handful of buildings that made up the hamlet of Clearwater lined the road that ran along the banks of the bayou. The homes were modest, some fashioned in the old Spanish style of moss and mud, others weathered, gray shanties or more substantial raised cottages surrounded by shady galleries.

Palmettos and willows lined the banks as well. Beyond, silent cypress stood surrounded by jutting knees poking up through the water. Water hyacinths bloomed in floating lavender blankets.

A small sugar mill, abandoned since before the war, showed signs of neglect. Weeds grew around the doors. Boards that had once barricaded the windows now hung broken and rotting, showing the holes that gaped in the windowpanes. Maddie slowed the mare and glanced up and down the road. There was no one in sight, so she rode around to the back of the building and tied the mare's reins to a broken-down wagon.

She walked to the nearest window and looked inside. Shafts of sunlight sifted through holes in the roof. The place was empty, but Maddie knew plenty about hiding and hoisted herself in through the window. She carefully listened for any odd sound, searched every possible hiding place before she gave up. There was no sign of Penelope anywhere.

A few minutes later she was back on the road, headed for Smythe and Co., Inc., the one and only store in Clearwater. It was the place folks gathered to buy, to barter, and to chew on gossip. Three old trappers, permanent fixtures, lounged on the front porch. They fell silent when Maddie rode up.

Under their watchful eyes, she tied Anita's horse to the hitching post and paused to wipe her muddy shoes on the iron scraper beside the step. She didn't know the men by name, but she'd seen them most every time she'd come to the village. Nodding in greeting, she lifted the wide brim of her borrowed hat and smiled.

"Don't suppose you gentlemen have seen a little girl around anywhere? About so high." She held out her hand. "Eight years old."

All three of them shook their heads in unison. One spat a stream of tobacco juice off the side of the porch. Finally the one in the middle volunteered, "'Nita was asking around. Already told her no."

"Thank you kindly," Maddie said.

She forced a smile and walked into the dim interior of the store where Gilbert Smythe was in the process of lining up tins of peaches on a high shelf. He turned when he heard Maddie's footsteps against the plank floor and smiled down at her from his perch on a tall ladder.

"Hey, Miss Grande. How you doing today? What brings you to Clearwater? You bring any pelts with you?"

"None today. I have a few that will be ready soon, though." She paused, pretended to be interested in a bowl of buttons. She sorted through them, shuffling them around with her fingertip, trying to appear casual, hoping her nervous impatience didn't show. "I'm helping Anita look for her niece."

Gilbert set the last can in line, turned it left, then right. Finally satisfied, he climbed down the ladder.

"No one's seen her far as I know. I've been asking folks when they come in. Told them Anita's nigh onto frantic. It's a shame. I hate to think——"

With his unfinished thought hanging in the air between them, Maddie silently cursed Terrance. Because of him, Lawrence was dead and a child was lost somewhere in the bayou.

"She couldn't have gotten very far on foot," Maddie said, thinking aloud.

"'Bout all you can do is follow the road to Stonewood. Ask at places along the way."

She thanked him and left the store, walked past the men on the porch, and stepped out onto the deserted road wishing she had an inkling of where to look next. She tried to keep her jumbled thoughts focused on finding Penelope and collecting the reward, but the image of the child's heartsick mother kept coming to mind. She knew the ache of Mrs. Perkins's empty arms, knew the suffering of a woman's longing for a child she had nurtured, cradled, and lost. She knew it all too well and wished she didn't.

*Don't*, Maddie warned herself. *Do not remember.*

She tried to shake off her dark thoughts as she unhitched Anita's nag. Heading north, she followed the road toward Stonewood, an abandoned sugar plantation a few miles away. It was as good a place to search as any, though she'd never been that far herself.

She rode past the village blacksmith's barn. Clement Stanton, bent over a sorrel's hoof, smiled at her around a mouthful of nails, and waved. She rode closer but didn't dismount as she asked if he'd seen Anita's niece. She described Penelope. He shook his head no and shrugged.

"I'll sure keep an eye out," he mumbled around the nails.

Maddie turned the mare onto the road again, leaving behind the sounds of Clement tapping a nail into a horseshoe.

As she passed the last of the homes along the road, her gaze scanned the bayou along both sides. Her tension slowly eased. The swamp, even with its innate danger at so many turns, offered silent comfort. The varied shades and depths of greens, the songs of the birds, the hum of insects, the rustle of the palmetto fronds and cypress lace calmed her jangled nerves. She took a deep breath and rode on.

*Please. Let me find her.*

She had no idea how to pray. Dexter hadn't been beholden to any god and had raised his tribe to answer to no one but him. Yet in her darkest moments, Maddie always found herself seeking solace, asking for mercy, asking for help from somewhere, someone, although she had no notion of whom that might be.

Lost in her thoughts, she let the mare plod along at her own pace, unwilling to push the old nag and have it drop dead under her. Suddenly, not far from the outskirts of Clearwater, she saw a flash of color in the foliage along the road. Something unnatural to the surroundings. Something that gave her pause.

She reined in but remained in the saddle, scanning the undergrowth just beyond the road.

*Nothing.*

Thinking she'd been wrong, she was about to ride on when she saw it again.

*There.* A flash of bright red against the green winding its way through the forest.

Silently she slipped off the mare and led her over to a willow with a broken branch. She found it strong enough to hold the reins, wrapped them quickly. Grabbing her shotgun, she began to carefully pick her way through the marsh. She brushed aside curtains of leaves, pausing now and again to scan her surroundings, to listen for the crack of a twig or the rustle of debris.

Nothing. Nothing ... until she heard someone humming. Afraid of making a single sound, she crept toward the music. Within a few feet she saw it again — scarlet against the green.

She reached out, gently pushed aside an overhanging willow branch.

In a small clearing, Penelope sat on a log with her back to Maddie. She was humming "Rock-a-Bye Baby," then softly chatting and pretending to pour tea for a rag doll seated across from her.

Maddie's heart pounded. She took a step closer ... and snapped a twig beneath her shoe. The sound was overly loud in the silence.

Without even glancing back, the child jumped to her feet and started to run. The rag doll fell face down into the decaying leaves. Maddie stepped over it as she burst into the small clearing. Holding her shotgun tight in one hand, she took off after Penelope.

The way the girl evaded her astounded Maddie. She zigged and zagged through the trees and undergrowth as if she'd been born in the swamp. But Maddie's longer stride gave her advantage, and before they went hopelessly deep into the forest, Maddie reached out and made a grab for the child. Not only did she catch hold of the cape, but she managed to get a firm grip on the little girl's arm.

She whipped the girl around ... and stared in shock at the face of a child she didn't recognize. Surprise loosened her grip long enough for the girl to bolt and run again. This time Maddie was close enough to grab her. She whirled the girl around and stared down into the upturned, dirt-streaked face. The hood on the cape fell back, revealing strawberry-blonde braids.

"Who are you and where did you get that cape?" Maddie demanded. It was definitely Penelope's. There was no one in Clearwater who could afford such a well-tailored garment lined with such fine fur.

"I never stole it." The girl stuck out her lower lip and tried to pull out of Maddie's grasp.

"I never said you did. Where did you get it? I know it's not yours."

"It *is* mine." The girl nudged the toe of her worn shoe in the decaying leaves on the forest floor.

Maddie gave her arm a shake but softened her tone. "You may as well tell me. I'm not letting you go until you do."

"My pa will kill you if you harm one hair on my head."

"Your pa isn't here."

"She *gave* it to me."

"Who?"

"That girl. Penelope. She said I could have it if I—"

"If you what?"

"If I helped her get away." Tears began to trace muddy tracks down the child's face as she eyed the shotgun.

Maddie was afraid the child would start bawling, so she calmed herself down and led the girl back to where she'd been having her tea party. Maddie set down her gun, picked up the rag doll, and handed it over. The girl clutched it close.

"What's your name?"

"Betty."

"Betty what?"

"Betty Stanton."

"Clement your daddy?" Maddie pictured the blacksmith.

Betty was wise to look frightened. "Yes," she whispered.

"Well, Betty, I know your daddy real well, so you don't need to be scared of me. Let's sit a spell, and you tell me all about Penelope. Start at the beginning."

Betty's breath hitched. She sat down on a log and rested her chin on her cupped hands.

"Go on," Maddie prompted. "Tell me about how you got the cape."

"I found her in the old shed behind the house."

"Penelope."

"Yep. I found her after the storm. I was looking for my cat. She just had a whole passel of kittens and —"

"I want to know about Penelope, not the cat."

Betty wiped her nose on the back of her arm. "She told me she was headed to Kentuck', to her mama's kin, and asked if I could help her get there. I said we should ask my pa for help. She begged me not to tell nobody, that her mamma and daddy had enough troubles lately and that she wanted to surprise them by gettin' there on her own. Said I should help her, seein' as how we're the same age and all. Said I could have her cape if I helped and didn't tell nobody." Betty shrugged. "So I found her a way to Kentuck'."

Maddie lowered herself to the log across from Betty and sat down heavily.

Penelope was headed to Kentucky on her own as if it was the next town down the road. Maddie was astounded by Penelope's pluck.

"Where is she now?"

"On the way to Kentuck', of course."

"On foot?" If she kept to the road, Maddie was certain she could track down the child in no time at all — if someone else hadn't already picked her up.

But Betty shook her head. "Nope. My grandpa was going to Parkville, up north of here."

"He agreed to take her?" She couldn't imagine a grown man with any sense letting an eight-year-old talk him into taking her anywhere alone. Then again, there were some men—unscrupulous, dangerous men—who wouldn't have thought twice.

Betty shook her head no. "He didn't know nuthin' about it. I put her in the back of his buckboard and covered her up with a tarp. He was haulin' cane to Parkville."

"How far away is that?"

Betty shrugged.

"When did they leave?"

"Hours ago. Just after first light."

"Headed north?"

"Yep." Betty rubbed the ermine cape lining against her cheek and sighed. Then she unfastened the silk frog at the neck of the cape, slowly slipped it off, and handed it over to Maddie.

"I 'spect you'll want to give this back when you find her."

Maddie took the cape and folded it over and over. It felt a bit damp but was no worse for wear.

"Didn't your folks ask where you got this?"

"I never showed it to them. Kept it out here at my secret spot." She picked up her doll and held it close again. "I surely do love that cape." Betty sighed.

"It's lovely, that's certain." Maddie forced herself to be patient. Having dealt with Penelope, Maddie knew it wasn't Betty's fault that she'd been badgered into helping. Given enough time, Miss Penelope Perkins could probably talk a muskrat out of its pelt.

Maddie smiled down at Betty. "Now, why don't you tell me what your grandpa looks like and where he usually stops along the way to Parkville?"

# CHAPTER 12

It took Tom hours to return to the bayou and Maddie's cabin. He tried to imagine what she would say when he confronted her with Penelope's silver comb. Obviously an accomplished liar, would she continue to feign ignorance?

It was almost dark when he reached the shanty on the water. The interior of the place was shadowed. He called out and knocked on the door, finding it unlocked. And the place empty.

Frustrated by imminent nightfall, he stabled his horse in the shed and made himself at home. But Maddie never returned. After a restless night trying to sleep with one eye open, he rummaged through her larder until he found soda crackers and cold biscuits and helped himself. Then he mounted up and headed for Clearwater.

Along the way he noticed a white poster nailed to a tree up ahead. He nudged his horse into a canter, thinking it might be one of Perkins's reward posters. What he discovered was not a reward poster but a playbill announcing performances by a troupe of actors. The poster touted them as being "well versed in the works of Shakespeare and various original plays." They were touring the back roads of Louisiana hoping "to ease the woes brought on by the chaos and upheaval that once descended over the land."

Tom rode on. The closer he came to the small settlement, the more dwellings he saw lining the road. When he finally reached Clearwater and began to nose around, he realized the local inhabitants were highly suspicious of outsiders. Inside the town's trading post, he asked the owner for directions to Anita Russo's cabin.

"I doubt she's there," the man replied. "She been out searching for her runaway niece. The poor child went missing a few days back."

"Her niece." Tom rested his elbow against the counter.

"She was through here asking if anyone had seen the girl, about eight years old."

Hiding a rush of anger, Tom studied scuff marks in the oak countertop. He recalled how Russo's sudden appearance had had Maddie acting as nervous as a sparrow in a nest of crows.

For a moment he pictured Maddie's sure hands, her confidence in the swamp, her fleeting, wistful smiles. If she had let him go along with her in order to soften his heart, it had worked. His attraction to her had tainted his objectivity. She'd been part of the blackhearted scheme all along, and she'd managed to keep him from getting to the truth.

The twins had left the girl with Maddie and the Russo woman, and somehow Penelope had escaped. He wondered if Maddie was worried about the child wandering around the bayou alone or if she even had a conscience.

Then, out of nowhere, he recalled her words: *"A mother's heart can't bear losing a child like that—"*

He forced himself to concentrate on the facts at hand. He'd found the comb. Maddie had had the child at some point in time. Now Penelope had somehow given Maddie and the Russo woman the slip and they were both searching for her.

He had to find Penelope before they did, and would make certain Maddie was held accountable for her part in the kidnapping. Russo too.

"Can you tell me how to find Anita's place? I've a message for Maddie Grande."

The other man eyed him suspiciously. "How do you know Maddie Grande?"

"I've got a message for her from Terrance."

The storekeep frowned at the mention of Terrance's name. He though it over a minute and then said, "Maddie took the road north yesterday and hasn't been back."

"You sure?"

"Did you see those codgers settin' on the front porch? Nothing gets past them. If she'd have come through, I'd know about it."

It was nightfall once more. Maddie hadn't relished sleeping in an abandoned shack on the swamp last night, nor did she feel any easier about camping out tonight, but she had survived the streets of New Orleans thanks to Dexter and now, thanks to Anita, she knew how to survive in the bayou.

She found a small clearing surrounded by oaks and cypress with enough dry wood and sticks to use for kindling. She gathered a few stones for a fire ring and started a fire, kept it low enough to hold critters at bay and yet not be seen from afar.

Unrolling a saddle blanket, she spread it in front of Anita's saddle and sat down with her shotgun across her lap. She dined on cold, dry biscuits and some slices of ham she'd wrapped in a dish towel and then stared at the glowing embers, fighting sleep.

A slight breeze moved through the treetops. In her mind she heard them whisper her name. Shadows thrown by the flames danced on the forest floor. She tightened her hands on the shotgun and cursed Terrance for putting her in this situation.

Tomorrow she would not push herself as long. She'd leave the road, find a secluded spot, and sleep while the sun was still high. That way if she was forced to camp another night, she would be able to stay awake, to scan the darkness for danger.

Exhaustion claimed her and the dream came with the stealth of most nightmares. She saw the faces of her children, heard their laughter, then suddenly she was a child being tugged through the streets of New Orleans. The faceless girl had a death grip on her hand. The tall scarecrow in black was leading them both.

The long crimson hallway appeared. The faceless girl started screaming ...

Maddie let out a cry and awakened. Heart pounding, she straightened against the saddle and stared into the dying embers of the fire ... and suddenly remembered where she was. Too late, she started to close her hands around her shotgun, but it no longer rested across her thighs.

Her gaze darted around the clearing. She let out a gasp when she saw the man seated on the ground to her left, watching her from beneath the wide brim of his low-crowned hat. She couldn't see his dark eyes, but she felt their intensity and his simmering anger.

"That must have been some nightmare," Tom Abbott said.

She made no comment.

"You cried out before you woke up."

"What are you doing here?" She was shaking but kept her tone calm and even.

"Same thing you are," he said.

"I have no idea what you're talking about."

"I'm fairly sure that there's only one thing that would inspire a lovely lady such as yourself to sleep out here alone in the middle of the night."

His words dripped with cool sarcasm. She didn't bother to tell him she hadn't intended to fall asleep. "And what's that?"

"Money."

Her mind raced around in circles until she hit upon a lie.

"You're right. I came out here to hunt. Thought to get a few extra hides, add the earnings from their sale to my savings. Someone mentioned seeing a panther out here recently. I figured a pelt that fine would earn me a heap of money."

"A panther."

"Yes." It sounded ridiculous and she knew it.

"Seems knowing a panther was around would keep you awake. I figure you're out here hunting something else."

Her heart tripped. "And what would that be?"

He brushed aside his coat, reached into the pocket of his vest. When he held out his hand, something caught the red glow of the embers and sparkled in his palm.

She stared at the piece of silver and diamond fragments twisted into a bow and tried to hide her shock.

*"That comb was worth a lot of money . . . One of those big brutes probably took it."*

Maddie ran her tongue over her bottom lip and looked away. "That's a mighty pretty bobble. Where did you get it?" she asked.

"On the floor of your cabin. Under your bed."

She had nothing to say, nothing she could say. She stared back in defiance.

"What now?" he asked.

"What do you mean?"

"There's no sense in pussyfooting around it anymore. I know you're involved in the kidnapping of Penelope Perkins, Miss Grande. You have been all along. Those no-account brothers of yours kidnapped her and somehow you or that Russo woman managed to lose her. Now you're desperate to find her. Why else would you be out here in the middle of the night?"

"You're crazy."

"How do you explain this?" He held out the comb again.

"It's mine."

"Funny, but it matches the description of some the kidnapped girl was wearing."

"The story you read me didn't mention any combs."

"Maybe I didn't read it all to you."

"Maybe you're a liar."

"Something we have in common, then?"

She eyed him carefully, certain that there was no escape, not with him so close. She might be able to bolt, but he'd be on her in an instant.

"You should be glad I found you." He tucked the comb back into his pocket. "I can keep the panther away while you sleep."

"I'm safer alone than with you."

"Miss Grande, I'm offended. Have I ever been anything but polite?"

She was furious. She hated the sarcasm in his tone and, truth be told, she was more than a little disturbed at the way he was looking her. Gone was the admiration she'd seen in his eyes when he'd arrived at her cabin. He was staring at her as if she were no better than the thief and liar she was. Though it shouldn't have, the notion hurt.

She stared at his coat where it hid his vest pocket. The comb proved her guilt. There was no use arguing.

He shoved his hat back a notch. "How about you go back to sleep? I'll keep watch, seeing as how I've got your shotgun," he offered.

She didn't bother answering. For now she had no choice and they both knew it.

Tom had to give her credit for playing her cards close. When he showed her the hair comb, her only reaction had been a slight widening of her eyes, but she knew she'd been caught. He added a few pieces of dry wood to the fire and sat back, watching the way the flickering glow of firelight played across her skin.

In the semidarkness, the details of her mud-brown skirt and oft-mended blouse were muted. Yet even in her ragamuffin clothing, she was lovely. It was easy to picture her turned out in fine clothing, silk and lace and crinolines, her hair styled in a manner befitting a lady. Polished and fluffed and dressed in a gown of high fashion and expense, she would be stunning.

On his journey along the backwoods road searching for her, he'd kept reminding himself that he was bringing a kidnapper to justice even as he pondered over what her hair would feel like in his hands or pictured her delicate features.

*She's a liar and an accomplice in a kidnapping.*

All the more reason to keep his distance.

They sat staring into the fire, avoiding each others' eyes. He realized she wasn't going to go back to sleep, not sitting there ramrod straight against her saddle, her arms folded over a small red blanket on her lap.

"Tell me about that nightmare," he prodded.

"No."

"It'll help pass the time."

"Telling won't make it stop."

"You've had it before?"

She nodded. "For years."

"So tell me."

"I don't want to."

He sighed, raised one knee, propped his elbow on it. "Something's been bothering me," he said.

"Good."

That made him smile. She didn't.

"Back at your cabin you said, 'A mother's heart can't bear losing a child.'" He still couldn't shake the raw heartache and pain he'd heard in her voice. "How do you know?"

She was quiet for so long he was certain she was bent on ignoring him. He was about to change the subject until he heard her softly say, "I just do."

"You've had a child, then?" It wasn't something he had considered.

"Two."

*Two?* That one word made it perfectly clear that he'd barely scratched the surface of her past. Had she had a husband? Or merely a lover or two? All he knew for certain was that she was an accomplished liar and might very well be lying to him again. Trying to play on his sympathies.

"So where are they now?"

When she tightened her arms about her midriff as if he'd gut punched her, he wished he hadn't asked.

"My children are dead," she whispered. "Both of them."

# CHAPTER 13

Afraid she would cry, Maddie bit her lips together and turned away from the man beside her. If he'd pulled hot coals from the fire and laid them on her skin, he couldn't have caused her greater pain.

Her children's faces danced before her eyes. Selena, had she lived, would be sixteen now. Maddie wasn't certain, but she herself might have been around that same age when Dexter married her to Louie Seuzeneau.

She had fallen in love with Louie the moment she first laid eyes on him.

Before he came into the tribe, she'd imagined living another life, an honest life. It was a dream that sparkled like a newly minted coin. But then came Louie. Despite his youth, Louie Seuzeneau was already worldly wise, young and handsome in a dashing, roguish way. With his dark, flashing eyes and broad teasing smile, he stole her heart as deftly as he could steal a man's pocket watch or a purse of coins. From the moment she saw him standing beside Dexter in the center of the upheaval in the warehouse, she was in love.

"I found him for you," Dexter had said. "This one we'll keep."

Dexter knew her well. As he predicted, she lost her heart to the handsome young rogue. Dexter found their young love amusing and started to plan their wedding. It would be the first marriage within the tribe and he would officiate.

"How fitting," Dexter had said, "that my dearest treasure will be the first of our tribe to wed, and I will perform the ceremony."

Anita was not at all happy, but after a whispered argument with Dexter in the dark of the night, the woman had held her silence and deferred to him as always.

Louie became Maddie's sun, moon, and stars. Selena was born nine months later. She lived but a few hours. The year the war began, she gave birth to a son. They named him Rene. Her son thrived, but two years later, Louie was stabbed and left to die in an alley.

"God gives and He takes away," Anita told Maddie as she mourned Louie.

Dexter overheard and laughed. "There is no god. Only me."

There was no leaving the tribe, no fulfillment of the dream of a real home with her little family. Louie was gone and her life began to revolve around Rene. Beautiful Rene, the image of his father. For ten years he was the light of Maddie's life, until yellow fever took him and left her alone with a heart full of broken dreams and fading memories. Alone with the twins and Dexter and the few who were left of their slowly dwindling tribe.

She had loved her children with all her heart and soul, but they were gone. Dead and buried in paupers' graves in St. Patrick's Cemetery.

"I'm sorry," Abbott said, reminding her he was there. He didn't sound sorry at all. He sounded as if he doubted her story.

Why should he believe her now? He'd caught her in a lie. A very big lie. She didn't want his sympathy anyway — real or false. She turned her anger, her bitterness, on him.

"I don't expect you to care. You didn't know them. You don't know me. Keep your sympathy to yourself. You may need it."

She could tell that gave him pause.

"Should I worry about your husband showing up tonight?"

"If he found us together like this he would kill you, but ..."

"But?"

"Like my children, Louie is dead too."

Speaking his name aloud should have brought his image to mind, but when she tried to picture them, his dark eyes looked too much like Tom Abbott's. She silently cursed herself and the man beside her for tainting her memory.

She stared at Abbott now, daring him to say something more, but there was a new, deeper pity in his eyes.

"Do not pity me, Abbott. Save it for someone who needs it."

"Why did you agree to keep the girl?" he asked. "If you are aware of the suffering this has caused, how could you?"

She ignored his question and asked her own. "Can you arrest me? Can Pinkertons do that?"

"I can hold you until I turn you over to the police, yes. Which is just what I intend to do after we find Penelope."

She had no doubt he'd see her behind bars. Would it make a difference if she forgot about the reward and told him that she only agreed to hide Penelope because she knew as long as the child was in her keeping, she would be safe?

"Do you know where she's headed?" he asked.

"No."

"Then why *this* road? Why go north and not south?"

"It's as good a guess as any."

"I don't believe you, Madeline."

She was exhausted after the fright of the nightmare and finding him here. He was smart enough to know she wouldn't wander around aimlessly. She had to throw him a bone.

"There is an old plantation not far north of here. Stonewood. I wanted to be there before nightfall but I didn't make it. It's as good as anywhere to look. Enough talking. I'm tired."

So what if he had her shotgun? Her skinning knife was tucked in her saddlebag behind her. Let him think that he had the upper hand. As soon as he was asleep, she would be on her way.

"I'm tired." She pulled Penelope's cape tight against her midriff. So far he hadn't noticed that the red wool was actually a garment, one much too small for her to wear. "Leave me alone and let me sleep."

"My pleasure."

The way the word lingered between them made her all too aware that they were alone in the dark. She relied on the fact that his manners at the cabin had been without fault. He was a man of honor, which was why she had to escape. He stirred too many conflicting feelings in her, made her feel less than human. Made her feel guilty as Terrance. And he was determined to take her to jail.

She scanned the perimeter of the campsite where the fire's glow failed to illuminate the darkness. For now escape was impossible. Weighing her options, she decided to trust in what honor Abbott possessed rather than to be stupid enough to try to hide in the swamp unarmed.

Determined not to let down her guard, she was certain it would be a very simple matter to feign sleep while she planned her escape.

Tom awoke at dawn's first light. He hadn't intended to drop his guard, but he had dozed off more than once. Thankfully, Maddie had slept through the night. He got to his feet slowly, set the shotgun on the other side of the camp, and then rubbed the back of his neck. He was stiff and sore from a night on the ground but determined to ignore the discomfort.

Maddie slept on as he checked their horses. Hers was an old swaybacked mare which explained why Maddie hadn't gotten any farther.

As he walked around the camp collecting firewood, he continually glanced back at Maddie. On his way back to the fire he noticed she was finally awake. She shifted on the hard ground and winced as she rubbed her backside.

He almost smiled.

"I need some privacy," she said, shoving a wayward lock of hair away from her eyes.

He looked away to hide his embarrassment and nodded toward the deeper growth just beyond them.

"You've got three minutes. If you're not fast enough, I'm coming after you."

It was her turn to color with embarrassment but she didn't argue. She rolled up the red wool blanket on her lap and was gone and back in no time.

She watched him walk over to his saddle, open a saddlebag, and take out some biscuits. He had two left. He offered her one. Maddie accepted and took a bite.

"This isn't half bad," she said.

"I expect not. You made 'em."

"You *stole* my biscuits? When?"

"I went back to your cabin looking for you. If you'd have been there, you'd have probably offered me some anyway. That's how I saw it."

"You saw wrong. I wouldn't have offered you anything."

He stared at her long enough to bring the high color to her cheeks before he turned away. "We're heading to Stonewood."

She nodded. He found her compliance far too easily won and knew she was only humoring him until she could escape. No matter, he thought. He'd be vigilant.

"It's just up the road a piece," she volunteered.

"We'll stop there, ask around."

They arrived at Stonewood Plantation a couple of hours after breaking camp. Once thriving, the former owners' mansion was abandoned, the slave quarters out back taken over by squatters.

One look around and Tom figured that the former slaves now living on the property would be too frightened to hide a white child in their midst. He described Penelope anyway, asked if anyone had seen her, and was told no. He and Maddie were offered a midday meal, which they gratefully accepted before they rode off.

Maddie traveled beside him in stoic silence, staring down the road ahead. If she was at all concerned about Penelope's safety or what the child was going through, she didn't let on.

"You sure you have no notion where Penelope is headed?"

Maddie ignored him as the mare plodded along, never faster, never slower, but at a constant, irritating pace. Finally she faced him.

"I have no idea where she is right now and even if I did, I wouldn't tell you."

He wasn't surprised. Despite what Maddie had done, he couldn't help but admire her spunk. During bouts of sleeplessness last night, he had thought about her revelation, of how she'd lost two children and a husband. If that was all true, then it might explain why she was still living with the no-account twins, why she'd agreed to become their accomplice. She had nothing to lose.

He glanced over at her, and his glance became a leisurely perusal. She was awkward on the horse but too stubborn to show her discomfort. As she kept her back ramrod straight and her hands clenched around the reins, her vulnerability tugged at his heartstrings. Her long dark hair had escaped its pins to tumble about her shoulders. The floppy hat she wore kept the dappled sun from beating down on her freckled nose.

They left the swamp behind and crossed fertile farmland, stopping at each property they passed to inquire if anyone had seen or heard of a lost child in the area. They continued north all day, passing creeks lined with dogwood and wild honeysuckle. It was a bucolic pastoral setting that would have made for an enjoyable outing had she not been a kidnapper and he a Pinkerton.

In the late afternoon they stopped at a farmhouse they'd seen from the road. As they approached the wide-covered porch of the well-tended home, he made her promise to let him do all the talking.

"Are you going to tell them I'm a kidnapper? That you're taking me in?"

"These look like nice people. I don't want to spook them. We need food and we need a place to stay. Just go along with whatever I say."

When he dismounted, she remained in the saddle. Before he reached the porch steps, the front door opened, and they were greeted by the mistress of the house, a woman in her forties with lines carved by care around her eyes and lips. Her name was Susan Cole.

He introduced himself as a Pinkerton, showed them his badge, then introduced Maddie as his sister. Two girls who appeared to be around twelve and fourteen followed their mother out onto the porch. A little boy no older than five clung to Mrs. Cole's skirt.

The Cole woman looked out at Maddie, who lifted a hand in greeting.

Tom indicated Maddie with a nod. "We're searching for a runaway. She took off a couple of days ago. Have you seen or heard of a lost child around here, Mrs. Cole?"

She showed immediate concern by glancing worriedly at her own girls and absently stroked her son's sandy-red locks.

"How terrible," she declared. "We haven't seen or heard anything at all." Her gaze drifted from Tom back to Maddie. "My husband's in back scrubbing up. We're just about to have supper. Why don't y'all come sit a spell and take the evening meal with us. We've enough to go around and would be delighted to have you."

Tom wished he was alone. It would make things a lot easier. As it was, Maddie had started to wilt a few miles back, but that didn't mean she wasn't capable of slipping away. He thanked Mrs. Cole and accepted her invitation.

The woman told him where to hitch their horses and wash up before they came inside. Tom walked over to Maddie's horse, prepared to hold the reins while she dismounted. Despite what he thought of her, when their eyes met, his heart involuntarily quickened.

Before he thought about what he was doing, he reached up to help her down. She surprised him by leaning toward him. His hands slipped around her waist. It was slim and firm, yet womanly. The instant he felt her warmth through the thin fabric of her worn blouse, his hands tightened at her waist. He heard her gasp. Her eyes widened, as if she, too, was startled by the connection.

She slid off of the mare, trapped between him and her mount. Lost in the moment, neither of them moved. For a heartbeat the world stopped as he stared down into her upturned face, inexplicably drawn to her. He slowly leaned nearer. Captivated, he heard no sound, saw nothing but Maddie.

"Mama? Should I set two more places at the table?" The Coles's oldest daughter's voice drifted to them, breaking the spell.

Tom quickly stepped away from Maddie and grabbed the mare's reins. Shaken by his reaction to her nearness, he refused to look at her again. Nor did he look at the woman on the porch waiting for them to wash up and go inside. He stared at his boots as he walked both horses to the hitching post outside a barn with a sagging roofline, cursing his loss of discipline. Spontaneous magnetic attraction had to be the only explanation for what had just happened. He'd been alone with her for too long, that was all. Despite who and what she was, there was no denying that she was a beautiful woman. He'd be a fool to let her work her wiles on him. Better to acknowledge the power of her beauty so that he could guard against it.

There was no way he would ever let himself nourish deep feelings for a woman like Maddie Grande, no matter how beautiful or how much she played on his sympathies. No way on earth.

He hitched the horses, stalling when he saw Maddie poised near the rain barrel in the shadows beside the barn. He watched her cup her hands, close her eyes, and lift the water to her face. She washed in the clear rainwater, eyes still closed, a slight smile of relief on her lips as droplets slipped down her throat, dampened the collar and bodice of her blouse. She paid no heed, cupped more of the clear water, dipped her face and opened her mouth to take a drink. He watched her bare throat move as she swallowed.

When she straightened, she slowly turned his way as if she had felt his stare. When she caught him watching, her face colored and her hands flew to her damp bodice. She turned on her heel and headed for the house, bending down to wipe her face on the hem of her skirt.

Tom realized he had been holding his breath. Before he went to wash up, he waited until she disappeared inside, reminding himself over and over that not only was she an accomplice in a kidnapping, but a liar and thief like her brothers.

He was not just a Pinkerton. First and foremost, he was a man who believed in honor, in doing his job and seeing things through. He wasn't about to let a thief like Maddie Grande steal his heart.

# CHAPTER 14

Mr. Cole ushered Maddie to the long wooden table in the middle of the kitchen where his family gathered for dinner. He seated her beside Tom Abbott. Still embarrassed about what had happened outside, Maddie refused to look at Tom. Unfortunately, she was therefore forced to watch the Cole children seated across from her. Her heart soon ached for what might have been.

The two girls flanked their little brother and filled his plate for him. They seemed adept at caring for him, as if it were second nature. Not only was Maddie reminded of life with the tribe and her duty to care for the younger ones, but of Rene. As the first surviving child born into the tribe, he'd been coddled by one and all.

Seated at the well-laden table filled with serving bowls heaped with mashed potatoes, home-grown vegetables, and a platter full of sliced ham, Maddie couldn't help but notice and admire not only the abundance, but the way the Coles behaved toward each other.

There had been no organized meals in the tribe. They never sat down to break bread together. They worked the streets in twos and threes, and when they were hungry and couldn't steal food, they made their way back to the warehouse where Anita would have a pot of gumbo or beans and rice simmering on the stove. They ate whenever and wherever they desired.

Dexter was usually seated in his overstuffed chair holding

court, collecting earnings and treasures the children brought to him and tossing them into a communal pot. It was the same with their food. Whatever they "earned" they shared.

On national holidays when other Louisianans went out in celebration, the tribe worked the streets. On solemn holidays when families gathered together in churches and homes and the streets were nearly deserted, the tribe complained about the fact that they were not plying their trade.

The food on the table smelled wonderful. Maddie's mouth watered as she started to reach for a bowl filled with a mountain of creamy mashed potatoes beside her plate.

"Let's join our hands in thanksgiving," Mr. Cole said.

She jumped as if caught stealing, but none of the Coles noticed. They had already bowed their heads and were holding hands with one another. Mrs. Cole, seated at the opposite end of the table from her husband, was holding Tom Abbott's left hand.

Maddie slipped her hand into Mr. Cole's, who was on her own left, but hesitated before she reached for Abbott's right hand. He must have sensed her reluctance. He turned to meet her gaze for the first time since they had entered the house.

Heat seared her cheeks. She quickly ducked her head and stared at the table.

His hand was on the table palm up, waiting for her to take it. Without meeting his eyes again she took a deep breath and slipped her palm into his. When his fingers closed around her hand, dwarfing it, her pulse jumped erratically. She felt herself flush even deeper. Instinctively she tried to pull her hand away and sever the connection, hoping to end the unwelcome emotions sweeping through her.

His touch was cool, firm, and inescapable.

She forced herself to breathe slow and evenly.

Mr. Cole gave thanks for the food. While Maddie sat in silence, everyone, including Abbott, said amen. He finally let go and Maddie pulled her hand away. She folded her hands together in her lap until her heart stopped hammering.

She was tempted to see if Tom showed any sign of having felt anything when they touched. Fear that he had kept her from looking his way.

"You may pass the mashed potatoes around, Miss Grande," Mrs. Cole said. The woman's voice lacked its earlier warmth, and Maddie wondered if that was because she hadn't said amen like the rest of them.

As the meal progressed, she caught Mrs. Cole studying her a number of times. Halfway through, the sound of rain started hitting the roof. The smell of damp, newly tilled earth filled the air.

Mr. Cole kept up a steady stream of conversation.

"Where did you say you lived?" Mr. Cole asked.

"Bayou Sauvage," Maddie said.

"New Orleans," Tom said at the same time.

Mrs. Cole put down her fork.

Tom spoke up, "I live in the city. Maddie prefers a quieter life."

"Did you ever see a gator?" the youngest girl asked.

Maddie nodded. "Lots of them."

"Did you ever shoot one?" The other girl's eyes were wide as saucers.

"Once, but I didn't hit it between the eyes and it ran back into the water." Maddie took a sip of water and noticed everyone was listening. "Why don't you tell them how you became a Pinkerton, *Thomas*," she suggested.

She was pleased when his right brow rose ever so slightly, but he accepted the challenge and soon the Coles were hanging on his every word.

"Is gambling still prevalent in the city?" Mr. Cole wanted to know.

Tom nodded. "The statute passed six years ago legalizing gambling hurt more than it's helped. Sure-thing men are coming in from all over the North and Midwest to open all manner of gambling halls. Some consider this a prime time to be a confidence man." He looked at Maddie. "But it's never really a good time to be on the wrong side of the law." He smiled. "Is it, Madeline?"

Cole leaned back in his chair and patted his full stomach. "That, Mrs. Cole, was a fine, fine meal," he told his wife.

"Thank you, Mr. Cole."

Maddie wondered what it would be like to live like these law-abiding folks. To live an upstanding life in a house where the family gathered together to share each meal. How would it feel to tend to her home, to prepare every meal for her family, to wash and clean and polish and set a fine table full of a bounty of food?

She knew nothing of manners nor how to teach them. She wasn't adept at polite conversation. She knew nothing of God or prayer.

*I never gave my child this. I never even knew how.*

She knew how to survive on the wrong side of the law, and for most of her life she'd been content because she knew of no other way. She had been part of the tribe, but it was made up of a group of individuals. All that bound them together was Dexter and the need to survive. Her life had been worlds away from the kind the Coles lived, and yet there was something hauntingly familiar about seeing them gathered together at the table. Some misty memory that she couldn't grasp and wouldn't know what to make of even if it did pulse at the ragged edges of her mind. All she knew for certain was that being here made her feel melancholy and empty and she had no idea why.

She watched Mrs. Cole in the act of reminding her son to sit up straight and found herself wondering if this placid life was enough for her. Did the woman ever long for more than her children, her house, and her farm? Was Susan Cole content with such a settled life?

Maddie looked at the children. *If only I could have my children back for an hour, for even a minute, I would be happy no matter what the circumstances. I would hold them close, treasure each and every precious heartbeat and beg for more.*

When tears threatened, she forced herself to think of the bayou.

She pictured herself in her pirogue, poling across the still water, wading through the marsh. She saw the banks lined with trees. She would miss her children always. She would miss Louie and Dexter and, yes, even life in the tribe, for it was often as exciting as it was terrible. But she would survive. She wasn't completely happy, but she was content. She had been at peace listening to the hoot of a night owl, staring at the full moon reflected on the surface of the still waters. She had learned there were treasures that came with solitude if one was open to accepting them. There were small jewels of happiness in every life if one had the ability to see them.

"The rain doesn't appear to want to let up tonight, does it?" Mr. Cole said. "You two might just as well bed down here and start off fresh in the morning."

Maddie could see that Mr. Cole was far more enthusiastic about having them stay the night than his wife. The woman grudgingly suggested, "I can put a cot in the girls' room for Miss Grande."

"I'll sleep out in the barn," Tom volunteered.

"You'll do no such thing," Mr. Cole insisted. "We'll put a pallet on the sitting-room floor. You'll be comfortable enough for one night."

Though Maddie told Mrs. Cole she didn't want them to go to any trouble, she was thrilled at the prospect. She didn't dare look at Tom Abbott, afraid that if she did, he would see her renewed energy and determination.

If there was any way to slip out of the Cole house during the night, she would find it.

Tom stretched out on the pallet Mrs. Cole and her elder daughter had made up for him on the far side of the sitting-room floor. His body may have been exhausted from a restless sleep at Maddie's camp the night before, but his mind was churning. Even more frustrating, he knew he should be focused on finding the Perkins girl, but his mind kept coming back to Maddie.

After dinner she'd jumped up to clear the table and help with the dishes. Shortly thereafter, she excused herself to go up the narrow stairs to the children's rooms on the second floor. Before she went up, she paused and with a defiant lift of her chin said, "Sleep well, brother."

Sleep well, indeed. He was worn out from watching over her last night. Tonight things were no different. He'd laid her shotgun on the floor beside him and was perfectly situated with a view of the front door and the kitchen. There was no way that she could get out without him seeing her.

He propped his head on his stacked hands as the occupants of the house quieted down and took to their beds. He heard one of the girls giggle upstairs and wondered if Maddie was thinking of her children. She'd been silent all through dinner, watching the Coles closely. Her wishful expression told him more than words could say.

He knew now that her loss accounted for her air of loneliness. But he was certain she was not seeking his pity.

The Coles's room was on the other side of the sitting-room wall. As Tom lay there wide awake, the couple's voices drifted to him, first on a whisper or two until Mrs. Cole spoke loud enough to hear clearly.

"I'm telling you, Jed, he wasn't looking at her the way a brother should look at his sister. There's something very wrong here and I want them gone in the morning."

"Calm down, Addy. I think your imagination is working too hard."

"That man's interest in her isn't brotherly. And she wasn't any better. Did you see the way she pinked up every time he looked at her?"

"No, I didn't."

"Well, that's because you're a man and men don't notice things like that." Her words were followed by what sounded like one of them giving a pillow a good punching.

"Now, now, dear," Jed Cole murmured.

"Don't *dear* me. I want them gone after breakfast."

They fell silent and within a minute or two, Cole's snores filled the air.

Tom found himself wide awake, staring at the ceiling.

Rationalize as he might, his attraction to Maddie was obviously impossible to hide if Mrs. Cole had noticed. Surely Maddie had noticed as well, which would account for her "pinking up" whenever he looked at her.

Staring up at the ceiling, he wondered if Maddie was awake. Every time he closed his eyes, he saw her face. Her hazel eyes, the freckles across her nose, her high, smooth brow. Her full lips.

He groaned in frustration and opened his eyes.

Staring at the ceiling was far safer.

Sometime during the night, he fell sound asleep and awoke the next morning to the sounds of a house stirring—the clatter of dishes and flatware against one another as plates were laid out for breakfast, the sound of a cast-iron skillet against the stove.

Tom threw back the quilt, rolled off the pallet, and got to his feet. He was just tucking his shirt into the waistband of his trousers when the younger Cole daughter came running downstairs barefoot.

She glanced his way and then walked into the kitchen, where the aroma of frying bacon had set Tom's stomach to rumbling.

He heard the girl ask, "Where's Miss Maddie?"

"Isn't she upstairs?" Mrs. Cole asked.

There was a pause, the sound of a chair scraping across the floor. Tom reached for his boots and hurried toward the kitchen.

"Maybe she's in the outhouse," the girl said.

Tom paused at the kitchen door, saw Mrs. Cole glance out the back window.

"No. The outhouse is open," she said.

His heart picked up double time.

"Maddie's not upstairs?" He tried to hide his alarm.

The Cole girl shrugged. "Her cot's empty."

Mrs. Cole ignored the bacon she'd been moving around the skillet and pinned Tom with a look that spoke volumes. "Is there any reason she'd take off by herself?"

He ran his fingers through his hair and then rubbed two days' worth of stubble on his jaw. "She hasn't run off," he said.

Mrs. Cole looked out the window again. She sounded smug when she said, "Well, then, someone else must have ridden off with your horse and left that old swaybacked mare behind."

# CHAPTER 15

Tom Abbott's horse was a far better mount than Anita's mare, but being an inexperienced rider, Maddie was afraid to push the gelding as fast as she might have. Clutching the reins, she carefully glanced over her shoulder, convinced she would see Tom Abbott closing in on her any minute now. She was amazed that in two days he still hadn't found her.

She'd slept in her clothes at the Coles's, so all she had to do was put on her shoes once the house was quiet and the girls had fallen asleep. She had slipped out of her cot and tiptoed to the window at the end of the hall that divided the two rooms beneath the gabled roof. Not about to risk Tom catching her, she avoided the sitting room. Inch by inch she opened the upstairs window until she could fit through.

She gauged the distance to the ground. It was too far to jump without breaking anything, but she had options. She hadn't learned to escape from second- and third-story windows and dash across the rooftops of New Orleans for naught.

Surveying the back of the house, she quickly spotted what she was looking for and lowered the window. Silently she crept into the little boy's room. He was sound asleep with one arm thrown above his head, his fingers curled inward, making a soft fist. She had the urge to stop and brush his tousled hair off his forehead, to lean close and inhale his little-boy scent. She resisted and moved on.

His window slid up easily. On the corner of the house within reach of the window was a sturdy drain spout. Unlike so many places since the war, this house had been kept up. Maddie had no doubt the drain would hold her weight.

She climbed out the window and shinnied down the drain spout without a sound.

Both horses were corralled close to the barn. She moved quickly and quietly as she grabbed Anita's saddle blanket and saddle and toted them over to the corral. Tom had her shotgun. She knew she could make do with the skinning knife in her saddlebag.

She had just slipped the bit into the mare's mouth when it dawned on her that Tom's horse was much younger and faster. If she truly wanted to put distance between them, then she should leave him the nag.

Now, after two days alone on the road and looking back once more, she was glad she had traded. Tom Abbott was still nowhere in sight.

She kept to the road that meandered through pinelands and wooded swamps. Before the war the idea of a white woman traveling alone was unheard of, but since the surrender there were countless displaced and homeless of every race and gender still on the move even now, nearly ten years later.

She stopped at plantation homes and modest farmhouses alike to ask for whatever folks could spare in the way of food. No one turned her away. She told the same story over and over—that she and her niece had been on the road, bound for Kentucky.

"We were separated," she said mournfully. "There was confusion at a ferry crossing. I've been searching for her ever since."

Describing Penelope, she would go on to say that her niece would be bound and determined to get to Kentucky on her own in the hopes that they would be reunited. It was no surprise that the child wasn't afraid to hitch a ride with just about anyone.

If folks doubted that she had a young adventurous niece wandering the countryside on her own, they never admitted it. Dexter used to say, *"Most people are gullible enough to want to believe a well-told tale that tugs at the heartstrings. It gives them the chance to help someone worse off than they are. Makes them feel superior."*

Maddie found it was true. Not only had she received sympathy, but generous packets of leftovers to tide her over.

She finally reached Parkville before nightfall. She stopped at a sawmill just as the manager was locking up for the day. He directed her to the trading post where the owner claimed to know old man Stanton, but Stanton had already come and gone. As far as the trader knew, there had been no child with him. Nor had Stanton seen or heard of any matching Penelope's description.

If Penelope had managed to hop out of Mr. Stanton's wagon undiscovered, then she was still on the run. Maddie asked for directions to Kentucky.

At first the trader laughed, but he sobered when he realized she was dead serious. He pointed northeast.

"What's the next sizable town directly up the road?"

He scratched his head and smiled. "Follow the road and you'll come to Baton Rouge eventually. When you get that far you'll have to cross the river to get to Kentucky. Ask somebody the way from there."

He watched her mount up. She was about to bid him good-bye when he said, "What's a gal like you really doing out travelin' on her own?"

*"A gal like you."*

*What kind of a gal am I, exactly?*

*Kidnapper. Thief. Liar.*

If she gave up the search for Penelope, she could take off in any direction, hide out, and start over. But right now, she was the only one who knew where Penelope was headed. If she did find her and made an attempt to turn the child over to her parents, things might go easier for her. At least she hoped so.

Maddie sat a little taller in the saddle and told herself she was doing the right thing. "I'm heading to Kentucky. Looking for my niece, like I said."

"You wouldn't want to change your mind, maybe stay here and settle down, would you? My wife up and died and left me with eight young'uns and—"

"Thank you kindly, but I'm not looking to get married, mister."

"Never hurts to ask, does it?"

"I expect not."

Disappointed but not surprised that no one had seen Penelope, Maddie left Parkville behind and rode on until twilight stained the sky a dusky violet. She veered off onto a side road and came to a deserted cabin with a crumbling barn behind it. Abbott had found her easily camped beside the road last time. Tonight she would sleep in the barn.

There was as much sky showing through the roof as there was cover. Pulling out her oilcloth slicker, she slipped it on. She rolled up Penelope's cape and used it for a pillow. Despite a slight mist that fell off and on through the night she slept well. Thankfully, she was too tired to dream.

By the time Maddie reached Baton Rouge, it was hard to imagine Penelope could have come all this way alone, but with the Pinkerton on her trail, she refused to give up. She'd reached the banks of the Mississippi again, and this time she would have to cross the river to Kentucky. But she had no fare money, no matter how small the fee. She was out of food, filthy, and so saddle sore she could barely walk. She couldn't keep going without supplies.

Although larger than any of the country towns she'd been through, Baton Rouge was smaller than New Orleans. Nothing she had learned about surviving on the streets of New Orleans would serve her here. There were far fewer people crowded together, far fewer pockets to pick. Even the city market was nowhere near crowded enough for her to get away with stealing food.

Weighing her options, she walked Tom's horse down St. Philip

Street, passing a burned-out ruin that she was told was the Louisiana state capitol building. It had been lying in a heap since the war. She rode on until she came to the Louisian Hotel at the corner of Lafayette and Main. The ferry landing was across the street from the hotel's back entrance. She hitched her horse and carried her saddlebag as she went to talk to the ferryman. If Penelope had boarded, perhaps he had noticed her.

Before the near toothless gent answered her query, he squinted into the afternoon sun on the western side of the Mississippi and hiked up his pants.

"A child, you say?"

"An eight-year-old. About this high." Maddie held out her hand. "Black hair, talkative. Pretty."

"By herself, you say?"

"I'm not sure."

He looked Maddie up and down so thoroughly she wanted to squirm. She tried not to let his stare unnerve her.

"Runaway, you say?"

"Yes," she nodded. "I'm her aunt."

"There's always people through here with children. Two days ago some folks had a passel of young'ins with 'em. Couldn't tell one from another."

If Penelope had gotten this far, she must have had help. She was certainly cagey enough to talk her way into traveling with a family headed in the right direction.

"How much to carry me and my horse to the other side?" It wasn't a small thing, crossing to the other side of the Mississippi. She'd lived on its banks all of her life yet never crossed. It appeared as wide as the ocean.

He named a price that was next to nothing but far more than she had.

"Could you make it half?" She knew how she must look by now. She didn't have to pretend to be pitiful.

"Sorry." He spat again. "It ain't all that much and this ain't no charity. Come back when you got the money. I don't expect it will take your type long to earn it."

Insulted, she trudged over to the Louisian where she'd left her horse, ignoring passersby long enough to splash water from the horse trough on her face, wash her hands, and tidy up as best she could.

She sighed and wished she'd never heard of Penelope Perkins or Tom Abbott. All she knew how to do was steal. She had no idea how to go about finding honest work, but trying was better than risking time in jail in the middle of nowhere. She smoothed her hair and walked up to the back door of the hotel.

Tom rode the Russo woman's old nag for a day and a half before the horse went lame and he was forced to walk through the middle of nowhere until it grew dark. He camped out and the next morning came upon a house where a planter offered to sell him a horse at twice its value. There was nothing he could do but dig into his stash of money tucked inside a hidden pocket in his coat. The expense would go on the Perkins's account when he found the girl—and find her he would.

He ran into enough people in small towns along the road to know Maddie hadn't turned back yet. Then he met a trader in Parkville who told him she had asked for directions to Kentucky.

*"I was sending her off with her nanny to Paducah to stay with my wife's sister, Gail."*

So Maddie thought the child was headed for Kentucky. Tom was forced to make a choice; return to New Orleans or keep trailing her. If by chance Penelope had somehow found her way home to Langetree already, then she was safe. But if Penelope was still on the run and Maddie was tracking her, then there was every chance he could find them together.

# CHAPTER 16

After two days of washing bedding and scrubbing and polishing everything from silver to woodwork, Maddie was convinced picking pockets was a whole lot easier than earning an honest wage. Her hands were raw and every muscle ached. Her legs were tired and her feet swollen. When she wasn't working, she was walking the streets of Baton Rouge hoping to catch a glimpse of Penelope somewhere. She checked with the ferryman morning and night, and at the end of the day she fell into bed exhausted enough to keep her nightmare at bay.

She had a small room with a cot tucked under the stairs and had been given a starched white blouse, plain black skirt, and a mop cap by the hotel manager. By the end of the week, she would have enough money put by to purchase supplies and outfit herself for the journey.

As she hurried through the back rooms of the first floor with an armload of freshly ironed sheets, she paused near the back stairs unnoticed. She shifted the load and waited patiently while a heavy-bosomed woman argued with a mustachioed man.

A traveling troupe of actors had recently arrived and were camped a few blocks away, living in their brightly painted caravans near the cemetery. The owner of the Louisian had agreed to let them perform in the main dining room for a percentage of the door and the actors were constantly underfoot. Whenever Maddie tried to negotiate the huge kitchen, laundry room, or pantry in the back of the hotel, one of the actors or stagehands was in her way. Tonight was opening night and tensions were high.

Arabella the Magnificent, billed as "The Star of the Show and the Queen of the Boards," was arguing with Hammond Cutter, proprietor, director, and lead actor of the Phoenix Rising Theatre Troupe.

"I'm telling you, Hammond," Arabella shrilled. "She is *constantly* upstaging me at every turn." Arabella's voice rose an octave at the end of every sentence.

Cutter, whose only claim to fame was that he had been an understudy at the Ford Theatre the night Lincoln was assassinated, heaved a melodramatic sigh. "Darling, she only has a few lines. I don't know how she could possibly upstage you."

"Well, I want her gone before the curtain opens tonight."

"Our take has risen tenfold since we added her to the production."

"Some things just aren't worth it. You put her in her place or I will."

"How about we run through the first act again. Shall we?"

As soon as they walked into the dining room and launched back into rehearsal, Maddie scooted out of the shadows and went upstairs.

The scene reminded her of Dexter, who'd thought himself an accomplished thespian and coached the children in singing and dancing. Those blessed with a little talent performed on street corners, and as soon as a crowd gathered, the other children stationed on the outskirts started relieving the unsuspecting audience members of diamond bracelets, gold watches, coins, and jewelry tucked on their persons.

She shook off a bout of melancholy, completed cleaning two rooms, and was headed down the hall when Steven Williams, the young hotel manager who'd hired her, appeared at the top of the landing.

"Maddie. Just the one I'm looking for."

Steven was in his mid-twenties with light hair and blue eyes. His hands were soft, his fingers long and thin. As he walked toward her, he nervously adjusted his cravat.

"Is there something you'd like me to do?" She sensed he might be sweet on her and had done her best not to encourage him.

"Are you going to attend the production tonight?"

"You mean the show?"

"Yes. In the hall."

She shook her head. "I'm afraid not."

She wasn't about to waste even a penny of her hard-earned money, no matter how much she'd like to see what the fuss was all about. Though New Orleans had claimed some of the finest opera houses in the country before the war, the closest she'd ever come to the theatre was working the crowds as they exited.

"I'd be happy to escort you." He hooked his thumbs in his waistband and rolled onto the balls of his feet before settling back on his heels. "As management, I was given two complementary tickets."

She started to decline, then paused. Williams hadn't disguised the fact that he was smitten, but she knew how to handle herself should he make any unwanted advances. What harm could there be in accepting his invitation? It would be a far cry better than sitting alone in her small cubicle.

"Why, thank you, kindly, Mr. Williams. I'd be happy to be your guest."

His smile was as wide as the Mississippi as he hurried back downstairs. Maddie watched him go. For the first time in a long while she found herself with something to look forward to.

There was standing room only in the crowded dining room of the Louisian Hotel. Dinner guests remained seated at their tables. Extra chairs were peppered around the room in every available space. The lights were low except for a semicircle of lamps on the floor surrounding a makeshift stage area. Plush velvet curtains were suspended on a wide, thick pole across the back of the room.

Tom walked in and kept to the shadows as he slowly scanned the room.

He had arrived in town a couple of hours before dark and described Maddie in a few of the establishments along Main Street. It wasn't until he inquired at the river crossing that the ferryman said a woman fitting her description was working at the Louisian.

The lobby was deserted when he walked in. He followed the sound of the crowd to the dining room where a show was about to begin. He scanned the room but didn't see Maddie anywhere. The theatre production would be enough of a diversion for him to slip into the back of the hotel and search the kitchen and workrooms. Biding his time, he folded his arms and leaned against the wall near the door, ready to walk out as soon as the makeshift curtain opened.

Then he spotted Madeline seated beside a young man with wavy blond hair. The gent was unable to take his eyes off Maddie.

Though she didn't appear to be paying him any mind, a wave of unbridled jealousy hit Tom with the force of a runaway wagon. As he watched Maddie with his pulse pounding erratically, all he could think was that it should be *him* sitting beside her. He should be the one smiling down at her. Most of all, she shouldn't be a thief and a kidnapper.

The gas lights were lowered, which made the lamps surrounding the stage seem to glow brighter. He watched Maddie, ignoring the players as they entered. He paid no attention to what they were saying. He didn't care. When he finally looked at the stage, he saw a very tall, dark-haired man in a Georgian costume complete with white stockings, satin knee-length pants, and high-heeled shoes competing with a tall, lushly built woman dressed like Marie Antoinette. They were hopelessly melodramatic as they wrestled with the lines of an obviously amateur piece.

During the second act a child actress stepped out from the wings. She had a commanding presence despite a lack of lines, a ridiculously frilly milkmaid's costume, and an overly large red wig that made her appear as if her head was on fire. Sporting two spots of rouge on her cheeks, the little girl pranced over to an upended barrel on the left side of the stage and made a dramatic pause beside it. She rolled her eyes, leaned an elbow on the barrel, then rested her chin on her hand. As the lead actress continued to shout out her lines, the child tapped her toe impatiently and winked at the audience.

Giggles and muffled laughter rippled through the crowd. Tom couldn't help but smile until he realized the ridiculous wig and makeup did not hide the child's identity. He glanced over at Maddie but she wasn't laughing like everyone else. She had scooted to the edge of her seat and leaned forward, her gaze locked on the stage. Even in the shadows of the large room, he could tell her face had lost all color.

His gaze cut to where the girl was skipping slowly across the stage, still holding everyone's attention. She stopped in front of the lead actress, planted her hands on her waist, looked up, and shouted her lines.

"Alas! You dare speak ill of me? I'll tell my father, you shrew. He will no doubt see you in chains!"

Tom looked back at Maddie. She sat spellbound.

The act ended, and the audience broke into thunderous applause. Someone was fumbling behind the curtain, trying to close it, but the fabric was caught. The actors all held their places, waiting.

Maddie jumped to her feet and tried to move toward the stage, but she was hemmed in by those seated around her. Suddenly the child actress let out a high-pitched squeal. "Help! Somebody save me!"

The girl darted past the red velvet curtain and through a side door.

The audience, assuming it was all part of the performance,

watched as Maddie pushed through and ran after her. Tom also tried to shove his way through the crowd, but by now everyone was on their feet, rushing out of the room to watch the unfolding drama.

Breathless, Maddie tried to shake off the shock of seeing Penelope walk out on stage. As she ran through the hotel pantry, she caught sight of the girl's bright-red wig and chased her through the kitchen. Penelope zigged. Maddie zagged and nearly knocked over one of the two cooks who stopped what they were doing as she barreled past.

If Penelope made it through the back door, Maddie feared she'd never catch her. Penelope banged through the door with Maddie on her heels. As she gained on the girl, she lunged ... and was left holding nothing but a handful of wig. She tossed it aside, cleared the steps, and this time when she reached Penelope, she grabbed the girl's upper arm.

Penelope started screaming at the top of her lungs. "Let go of me! She's trying to kill me! Let me go!"

Hammond Cutter was the first to reach them, oblivious of the crowd behind him. Not only the cooks, but the rest of the staff, followed by the cast and half of the audience, streamed through the back door.

"Unhand her, woman! She's the star of my show," Hammond yelled at Maddie.

"She's my niece. I've been looking all over for her."

Penelope tried to twist out of her grip. "Let go of me! I am *not* your niece, you *kidnapper*, you."

"Don't be silly, Penelope, honey." Maddie turned to Hammond. "She's just scared. She's in a heap of trouble for running away."

Maddie leaned close until she was nose to nose with Penelope. "Just settle down and come with Auntie like a good girl. I'm going to take you home to your mama."

Hammond grabbed hold of Penelope's other arm and a tug-of-war commenced.

Penelope dug in her heels as Maddie tried to pull her away. "She's not going to take me home. She's going to kill me!" Penelope glared at Maddie. "You're gonna skin me and hang me on a clothes-line like you do those nasty rat-tailed varmints of yours."

Hammond suddenly let go. Momentum propelled Penelope toward Maddie.

"So you *do* know this woman?"

"No!"

"Like I said, she's my niece," Maddie said, calmer now that she had a tight grip on the girl. She smiled up at Hammond Cutter, whose face was coated with an inch of grease paint. Kohl encircled his eyes. Seeing him up close made it hard to concentrate.

"She ran away and I've been searching for her," she said.

"I am *not* her niece. She's a liar, Mr. Cutter. She kidnapped me. Her and her *evil* twin brothers."

Maddie's hand tightened on Penelope's arm, and she forced a high laughing trill. "Evil twin brothers. Such an imagination. She's quite the actress, as you know, Mr. Cutter." She looked down at Penelope and shook her head. "How many times have I told you not to lie, honey?"

*"You're* lying!" Penelope raised her foot, and Maddie moved her own in time to keep from being stomped on.

"Someone should get the sheriff." Steven Williams stepped out from the crowd. "This woman is Maddie Grande. She's been working here for the last three days." He leaned closer. "You never mentioned a missing niece, Maddie."

She whispered back, "I needed money to continue my search—"

Maddie could see Williams wanted to believe her; that much was crystal clear. She batted her eyes. He cleared his throat and tugged his collar away from his Adam's apple.

Another man was pushing his way through the crowd. Maddie recognized his hat first, and then he parted the two cooks who had been flanking Maddie like bookends. He stepped between them, tall, dark, and furious.

Maddie groaned. Tom Abbott had finally found her. *And* Penelope.

I'm a Pinkerton from New Orleans." Tom flashed his badge at Williams and Cutter. "I'm taking Miss Grande into custody and returning this child to her parents."

"You are *not!*" Penelope kicked and twisted.

Maddie said, "He's not a Pinkerton. He means to kidnap my niece."

Tom watched in amazement as Maddie reached for the hem of her skirt and used it to dab at her eyes. She was as consummate an actress as the Perkins girl. When she looked up, tears actually sparkled on the tips of her lashes.

Hammond Cutter stepped forward. "Hold on, mister. How do I know you're who you say you are? Anybody can sport a tin badge."

Maddie looked so bereft, Tom almost believed her himself.

"Is there somewhere we can all go and straighten this out in private?" Tom asked Hammond.

"You *cannot* do this to me!" Penelope was at it again. With Maddie still clinging to one arm, the child grabbed Hammond's pant leg.

"Please, please, *please* don't let them take me. Please! I was *born* to act. You said so!"

Behind Tom someone whispered, "This is a lot better than the two acts we saw inside."

By that time Arabella the Magnificent, trailing a flotilla of perfume and male admirers, had made her way into the center of the crowd encircling the unfolding drama. "Let them have her, Hammond. We don't need her." Arabella looked down her nose at Penelope. The child started wailing in earnest.

Hammond gave Tom a look that spoke volumes. "Let's go over to our encampment and we'll talk this out in private, Abbott."

"I'll stay here and comfort Penelope," Maddie volunteered.

Since Maddie had a death grip on Penelope, Tom reached for Maddie's arm and held on tight. "Come on. You're both going with me."

# CHAPTER 17

The actors' camp was comprised of four caravans drawn into a circle on open ground near the cemetery. A low fire burned in a central fire pit, casting light on gold-leafed advertisements painted on the wagon.

Hammond Cutter's hand shook as the actor reached up to slick back his hair. "Would you like a drink, Abbott? I'm in dire need."

"No, thanks." What Tom wanted was to get Maddie and Penelope somewhere secure before they could give him the slip again. But he said he'd wait while Cutter went to get himself a drink.

Tom watched the man enter his caravan. He didn't trust Cutter not to take it upon himself to steal his star actress back.

Across from him, the child pouted, glaring at Maddie, refusing to talk—a blessing to be sure. She looked none the worse for wear and had obviously been adequately treated or she wouldn't be begging to stay on with the troupe.

Tom tried to keep his gaze from straying to Maddie, but it wandered of its own accord. Now that they'd found Penelope, it wouldn't be long before they were back in New Orleans, and he'd have to turn Maddie over to the police. He tried to forget about his reaction to seeing her in the shadowed light of the hotel dining room but found it impossible.

Maddie hadn't loosened her grip on the child and didn't look like she was about to.

Hammond Cutter reappeared as promised, carrying a tumbler full of whiskey.

"So, Mr. Abbott, why should I believe you over Penny? It would be irresponsible of me to hand over a child to just anyone. Especially since she so vehemently protests. Have you proof to back up your claims?"

Tom looked the man over. He was tall himself but Hammond was a good two inches taller, a commanding figure on stage.

"You can wire Allan Pinkerton himself or you can telegraph Detective Frank Morgan of the New Orleans Metropolitan Police. But when you do, you should probably consider that it was highly irresponsible of you to put a child in your show without her family's permission," Tom warned. "I'd hazard a guess that you found her wandering around alone after she ran off near Clearwater?"

"It's none of your business where I found her."

"I found *him*," Penelope hollered. "I asked him to help me get to Paducah and he said he would."

"I'm sure her father will make it his business to find out exactly where you found her and how long she was in your care," Tom said.

"I was planning an entire production around her." Cutter nursed his drink.

Hovering behind them, listening to the exchange, Arabella fumed. "You *what*?"

Hammond Cutter held up his hand to silence her.

"Sorry to ruin your plans," Tom said. "I'll be taking Penelope home where she belongs."

"I *don't belong* with them. Her brothers stole me from my real family." Penelope reached out, appealing to Cutter. Huge croco- dile tears ran down her face. "My mama doesn't want me anymore because I'm too much of a bother. Please, Mr. Cutter," she sobbed, falling to her knees. "They *stole* me."

Cutter finished the whiskey before he turned back to Tom. "She's really very convincing."

"Your audience thought so too," Tom said. "We've wasted enough time here. I can be fairly convincing myself." He reached for his waistband and drew out a bag of gold coins. "How about I reimburse you for your trouble, Cutter? Would that make it easier to part with her?"

Cutter accepted twenty dollars to cover Penelope's board and care. The child refused to go quietly until she was allowed to collect her clothes and shoes. Cutter let her keep her costume, and as Tom and Maddie led her away from the caravan campsite, there was much sniffling and foot dragging from the little milkmaid walking between them.

"Where are we going?" Maddie wanted to know.

Tom hadn't thought past getting Penelope away from Cutter.

"We're leaving Baton Rouge," he said.

"Tonight? It's too late. And what about my things?"

He sighed. She was stalling.

He nudged Penelope until she started walking again.

"I don't recall you bringing much." He was far more concerned about where they were all going to spend the night.

"The hotel gave me new clothes. And I'm owed money for the work I did over the past few days."

It was Tom's turn to stop walking. He pictured Williams. "Exactly *what* did you do?"

She squared her shoulders and kept walking. Penelope trudged along beside her. Tom caught up.

"Do you still have my shotgun?"

"I do," he said.

"Well, don't forget it's mine."

"Don't worry. You'll get what's coming to you."

"Where are we going?"

"Yes," Penelope piped up. "Who are you? And where are you taking us?"

Tom sighed. It was going to be a long, long night. "Somewhere I can keep an eye on you both."

"I'm *not* staying with you," Maddie said.

He lowered his voice and leaned over Penelope. "Of course not. You're only a kidnapper, not a loose woman."

With no idea where to go, he headed for the hotel so Maddie could collect her things. The cooks had long since finished for the night. A lone maid was mopping the floor. Steven Williams was waiting for them in the kitchen, seated on a barstool drawn up to the cooking table with his head propped on his hand. When they came through the back door, he tugged down the shirt cuffs beneath his jacket.

"So you'll be leaving, then?" Williams asked Tom.

"I'll be taking them back to New Orleans."

"You owe me my pay," Maddie told the manager.

Williams glanced at Tom and then focused on Maddie again. "You lied about who you were."

"I did no such thing. I told you my name."

"You didn't tell me you were a kidnapper." He sounded more disappointed than angry.

Tom planted his hands on his hips and turned a hard gaze on Williams. "She did the work; now pay her what she's owed. We've got to leave."

Williams excused himself to go to the office and collect Maddie's pay. Tom shifted his attention to the open back door. Across the street on the river, not only was there a ferry, but a riverboat that had just docked. The floating palace was lit up like a sky full of Chinese fireworks. Music and gambling would go on all night long.

Tom figured it was the only place he could ensure there was no escape until the boat docked in New Orleans. It was the safest place to keep Maddie and Penelope for the night.

Williams hurried in, started to hand Maddie her money. Tom held out his hand. "She's in my custody. I'll be holding that for her."

Maddie started to protest, but Tom silenced her with a glance.

"How'd you like the show?" Penelope asked Steven Williams.

"The guests thought it was the best they've ever seen."

"All because of me," the girl sniffed. "But now my illustrious career as a thespian has come to a close."

Tom waited outside Maddie's door as she gathered her freshly laundered clothing, her saddlebag, and Penelope's cape. Penelope had stopped arguing. *No doubt*, Maddie thought, *the child was busy hatching another plan*. Once they were settled, she would start thinking up one of her own. For now she'd have to content herself with irritating Tom Abbott as much as humanly possible.

Tom followed her and Penelope out the back door. As soon as they cleared the hotel, he reached without warning for her saddlebag.

"How dare you?"

He flipped it open, pulled out her skinning knife, and cocked an eyebrow.

"I guess I was lucky on the trail," he said. "You could have filleted me in my sleep."

"I guess you were. How did you know it was there?"

"Thank Miss Perkins here. She mentioned your affinity for muskrats, and I remembered the knife. Figured you'd have it with you."

He held up the lethal piece. Light from the riverboat danced along the blade.

"I'm surprised you didn't try to run when you had the chance," he told her.

She returned his stare. "I think you know why I didn't. I've as big a stake in Miss Perkins as you do."

"Nanny says it's rude to talk about people as if they aren't around," Penelope informed them.

"We've one more stop." Tom laid his hand on the child's shoulder and led them two doors down to the hotel stable for guests. Money exchanged hands as he arranged for their horses to be delivered by barge to New Orleans.

Then he headed for the river.

"Where are we going?" Maddie demanded.

"We're not going to stay on the riverboat, are we?" Penelope slowed down, forcing them both to match her stride.

"We are," Tom said. "The crew will be instructed not to let either of you anywhere near the gangplank."

Maddie stared at the floating palace. Reflection from the lights on board danced on the surface of the water. Music drifted out into the night. Huge crystal chandeliers hung in the grand central rooms on both decks.

"Expensive jail," she mumbled, recalling the money Abbott had given Hammond Cutter. How much was he carrying?

"My papa would never take us on a steamboat. He says if the engines don't explode, then they are just as likely to run into things in the river. Why, my papa would just have a fit if he knew you were taking me aboard a steamboat. He says they aren't worth the time it takes to make them. The construction is terrible."

Maddie sighed. Tom turned to her. "How old *is* this child?"

"I'm almost nine." Penelope smiled.

"More like twenty-nine," he mumbled.

Maddie couldn't agree more but she wasn't about to let him know it.

# CHAPTER 18

They boarded the *Memphis Palace*, and Maddie couldn't help but stare as they climbed the stairs to their rooms. The ship's opulence was something out of another world.

She and Penelope were to share a small stateroom. Tom's cabin was right next door. He warned her he had asked the captain to inform the crew that Penelope made a habit of running off and that Maddie was in his custody. No matter what either of them said or did, they would not be allowed to leave without him when they docked.

Penelope went into their room first. Maddie stopped just outside the door.

"What makes you think I'd try to run?" she asked Tom.

"For one thing, you're headed for jail, and I'm thinking that two-thousand-dollar reward is so tempting. You'd risk taking the girl home to collect."

Penelope was her pot of gold. Maddie wasn't going anywhere without her. They both knew it.

He left them alone in their room, and as soon as the door closed, Penelope wilted. She dropped her bundle on the nearest of the two narrow beds and sat beside it. Her eyes were huge, innocent, and full of bewilderment.

"Is he really taking me home, Madeline?"

For the first time she looked and sounded eight years old and very fragile.

Maddie set her own things on the opposite bed. She hesitated a moment before she sat down beside Penelope, tempted to put her arm around the little girl's sagging shoulders.

"He's really taking you home," she said softly. "He's taking me to jail."

"What about those bad men? The ones who kidnapped me. Won't they be mad?"

Maddie wanted to deny that the twins were bad men, but couldn't. She was no better. "They can't hurt you anymore."

Penelope flopped back on the bed. "I sure hope seeing me doesn't upset Mama."

"She misses you terribly."

"How can you be sure?" Penelope looked as if she wanted desperately to believe it.

Maddie swallowed hard and hid sudden tears. "I bet all she really wants right now is to hug you and feel you in her arms again."

Penelope looked doubtful. "Maybe so. She sure misses that baby, and we hadn't even gotten used to having him around." She sighed heavily and peered up at Maddie through her lashes. "I heard Papa tell Nanny that it would be better for Mama if I wasn't underfoot."

Maddie was certain Mr. Perkins regretted ever speaking those words.

"Is that why you didn't try to get home? Because you thought your papa wanted you in Paducah?"

"Yes." Penelope stared at the ceiling and hummed for a minute, thinking. Then she sat up.

"Your father wants you home, believe me."

"Have you seen him?"

"No."

"You sure that Mr. Abbott isn't your friend?"

"Definitely not."

Penelope persisted. "Are you sweet on him?"

"Heavens, no." Maddie shook her head.

"I think you are."

"You think wrong." She frowned. She couldn't resist asking, "What makes you say so?"

Penelope shrugged. "You look at him like you're mad at him, but not really. Not deep down. Like when he dragged us onto this boat. You acted like you didn't want to be here with him, but I can tell you do. You watch him when you think he's not looking."

"That's ridiculous."

"What if we got away? You could take me to Paducah, to my real aunt's place, and then you wouldn't have to go to jail."

"I think it's time you got some sleep." Maddie didn't dare tell the girl that all she'd been thinking about was escaping Abbott.

Penelope sighed. "I'm pretty tired. Acting sure takes it out of you."

Despite the fact that all of her plans had gone awry, Maddie found herself smiling. "Does it?"

"Yes. You have to project. That means you have to shout at the top of your lungs. At least that's what Mr. Cutter says. He thinks I have a bright future on the stage." She drooped again. "At least I did."

"Maybe you should tell your parents how much you like performing."

"Oh, I don't think they'd be too happy to hear that I want to be a world-famous actress like Arabella the Magnificent."

"How do you know?"

"Well, for one thing, I heard Mama tell Papa that she knew all about his penchant for actresses, and she wasn't about to ever let him forget his promise to keep his eyes from wandering the way they had back in New York. There was just something about the way she said *actresses* that made me pretty sure she doesn't like them."

Maddie was certain the child had perfectly imitated her mother, right down to the inflection in Mrs. Perkins's voice when she warned her husband away from actresses.

"You'll just have to see how they feel about it when you get home."

"I'll have to bide my time, you mean?"

"Yes. Bide your time."

Penelope got up and started to unfold her clothing, and Maddie decided they should both get some sleep. She poured water from a tall pitcher into a washbowl on a stand between their beds while Penelope carefully set her clothes on a bench.

Moistening a washrag, Maddie walked over to Penelope. The child raised her face so that Maddie could gently wash off the stage makeup. Then she took the diamond comb out of Penelope's hair and set it carefully on the washstand.

"Let's not forget this tomorrow." She didn't mention Tom Abbott had found its mate.

When Maddie moved her own clothes, she found the red hooded cape rolled inside the bundle and handed it to Penelope.

"My cape! I love this cape." The child hugged it close. Then she looked at the garment and frowned. "How did you get this? I gave it to a little girl named Betty days and days ago."

"Believe it or not, I ran across Betty in the bayou. She was wearing it and I thought she was you."

"So *that's* how you found me."

"She confessed she snuck you into her grandfather's wagon." Maddie washed off her own face, took her hairbrush out of her saddlebag, and remembered that Tom had her skinning knife. Her anger flared as she brushed out her hair and plaited it into one long, thick braid.

Penelope insisted on chattering.

"When the old man's wagon stopped in a place called Parkville, I slipped out and started walking. I found a shortcut around the back of town and no one saw me. A little ways up the road I saw Mr. Cutter's camp, and when I read those advertisements on the sides of his wagons, I asked him for a job. He told me to audition. I had to read a piece of a play off a scrap of paper and act it out. It was the most fun I ever had in my life. He gave me the job right on the spot."

"He didn't ask about your family?"

She hung her head. "I told him I was an orphan trying to get to my aunt's on my own. I said, 'If you're headed to Kentucky, then count me in.'"

"What did he say?"

She looked up again, all smiles, hooked her thumbs under her arms, and puffed out her chest the way Maddie had seen Cutter do at the hotel. "He said, 'Why little lady, if you'll perform all the way to Kentucky, then that's where we're headed.'"

Maddie found herself laughing for the first time in a long while, but her humor was short-lived. "You'd best get out of your clothes and climb into bed," she said.

"At least all my clothes are clean," Penelope said, stripping down to her shift before she slipped under the covers. The fall night air held an unaccustomed chill.

"Arabella made one of the stage hands wash my dress. She said I smelled like a rancid old sheep."

Maddie figured she'd spent most of her own childhood smelling like a rancid old sheep.

"I hated her," Penelope said. "As far as I'm concerned, she's *not* Arabella the Magnificent. She's Arabella the Awful."

"It's time for bed," Maddie said.

"I have to say my prayers first." Penelope knelt down beside her bunk, folded her hands, and closed her eyes. "God bless Mama and Papa and my baby brother who's with the angels now. Please keep us safe here on this riverboat so we don't blow up in the night. Amen."

"Do you pray every night?" Maddie helped her fold back the bedspread and pull down the sheet.

Penelope paused and looked at her. "Don't you?"

"Not really."

"Why not? Mama says God will always take care of me. That's

why I wasn't scared to head for Kentucky all by myself. I have a garden angel too."

"A what?"

"A garden angel to protect me everywhere I go. You have one too. Everybody does."

Maddie was certain God couldn't spare any angels to watch over the likes of her.

As soon as Penelope was asleep, she planned on locking the child in the cabin and wandering around on her own. It would do no harm to explore. To be ready for tomorrow. Escape hinged on being prepared for unexpected opportunity.

Tom Abbott might think he had the upper hand, but she had never been one to give up. He was going to discover that the hard way.

"Maddie?"

"Yes, Penelope?"

"Will you tuck me in and tell me a story?"

Maddie's back was to the child's cot. Her knees nearly buckled when she heard the words that were seared on her heart.

*"Mama, will you tell me a story?"*

She closed her eyes, clutched her hands, and fought to collect herself. It seemed only yesterday her son, Rene, had asked the same thing of her.

She owed Penelope's mother this one little thing for all the suffering the woman endured. It was something she would have wanted if the situation were reversed.

Folding away the hurt, she took a deep breath and lowered herself to the side of the bed. Tucking the covers around Penelope, Maddie smoothed them gently and managed a slight smile.

"Once upon a time," she began, "there was a well-spoken man with long, curly white hair who dreamed of collecting a tribe of children."

Penelope was sound asleep when Maddie slipped out of the cabin. With a child so close, the walls were closing in on her.

Anything would be better than to be closeted with memories—
even facing the wrath of Tom Abbott.

Lamps lined the decks below, casting the world outside her
cabin door in a golden glow. Sounds from the gambling hall on
the first deck—the tinkle of glass, the lively music of a bass and
fiddle player—were offset by the peaceful lull of the river as the
steamboat slowly floated downstream. The sound of mingled voices
drifted up to her from the salons below, the words indistinguishable. She had noted the ladies and gents dressed in their finest
on the way in. She saw them staring at her black skirt and white
blouse—a servant's clothing—and at Abbott's worn clothes and
Penelope's absurd costume. She'd raised her chin a notch and stared
back. Dared them to whisper among themselves.

She knew who she was, what she was. What she didn't know
was where she was going.

Walking to the rail, she leaned against it and watched the water
slide past. If only she was on the bayou. If only she could go back to
the night the twins had kidnapped Penelope. If only she had taken
the girl home immediately she wouldn't be headed to jail.

Too late now. Too late. Life flowed on like the river, never stopping, never turning back.

A sound behind her caused her to freeze. She turned slowly and
watched Tom Abbott step out of the alcove in front of his cabin
door.

"You've been watching me." She hadn't heard the door open
and close. He had been there all time.

"You're unpredictable, Madeline, but I'm fairly certain I know
what you're thinking right now."

He walked up to the rail beside her. Stood so close their shoulders touched. Like her, he stared down into the water. She studied
his profile, his strong jaw, his furrowed brow.

"And what's that?"

"Run."

"Penelope is asleep," she said, unwilling to agree.

"And you?" He turned to face her, making her even more aware of how close he was. "Why aren't you asleep? Nightmares again?"

She shook her head. "She snores."

The truth was she could not sleep with her mind sorting ways to escape and Penelope's presence stirring up long-buried memories.

"What about you?" She tried to turn the conversation. It was too much to hope that he'd go inside and leave her in peace.

"I have nightmares of my own," he said.

"You?"

"Having a child around brings them back."

Maddie frowned. Was he making fun of her? Using her story to hurt her?

"What do you mean?"

"I was involved with another kidnapping once. A wealthy man's child, much like Penelope, only a bit younger. A boy. The kidnappers panicked. The child died needlessly."

She could see his pain as he studied her in the glow of the lamplight. They were standing too close. She was vulnerable to his nearness and knew she should go inside, but she couldn't move.

"You know since the moment I laid eyes on you, you've been a mystery to me. Who are you, Maddie Grande?"

"I'm not a kidnapper." She didn't like the speculative way he was looking at her. "I'm not that woman you are looking for either."

"You expect me to believe anything you say now?"

She had no notion how to walk away. His eyes were deep, dark, and open, drawing her in. Just now he looked as if his mind was filled with confusion as great as her own.

Was there one drop of goodness in him? Would he believe her if she told him she'd always meant to let Penelope go?

"I expected someone harsh," he said, "someone crude and cut-throat like the twins. Instead you can be charming when you want to be. You have a strength that's not merely physical, but one of spirit. It's your spirit that has kept you going despite all the tragedies life has doled out."

She was so intent upon his softly spoken words that she didn't realize he had drawn nearer until she felt his warm breath on her cheek.

The magic of the river, the soothing rocking motion beneath her feet, the smell of the fertile muddy land along the riverbank mingled with the scent of the man standing so close.

She was completely lost in the nearness of the kind of man she had always been attracted to—a man as deep and unfathomable as the river. But unfortunately, this one was on the right side of the law.

He reached out a hand. She thought for a moment he was going to kiss her.

Instead, he tucked a stray lock of hair behind her ear and whispered, "Was it worth it, Maddie? Was hiding the girl for the twins and chasing after her without me worth the years you'll spend in prison?"

She thought of all the things the twins had done. Of Terrance's mean streak and Lawrence's blind obedience to his twin. Poor Lawrence. He'd never stood a chance against Terrance.

"I was going to take her back," she whispered, almost too shaken to speak.

"Ah, Maddie. I'm sure you wish I believed that."

"Let me have her," she said. "Let me take her home and collect the reward. I'll take the money and disappear. I promise. You can say I gave you the slip. Her parents will have her back safe and sound. Isn't that what's important?"

"I can't let you take Penelope back, Maddie. I can't let you claim that reward money."

He sounded so matter of fact, so sure of himself. Whatever had just happened between them, the magic of it, was shattered into countless pieces.

"Because you don't trust me," she said, resigned.

"Because I'm a Pinkerton agent. Not only am I working with the police on this case, but the Perkinses have hired me to bring their daughter home. That's my job and I'll see it through."

"So you're determined to see me in jail?"

He stared back so intently she dared to hope he was about to say no.

"You willingly hid the girl." He reached for her shoulders, stared into her eyes. "You were willing, weren't you? Or did Terrance force you to do his bidding?"

When hadn't she done Terrance's bidding? She considered herself resourceful and independent enough to stand up to anyone, even Terrance, but with his temper, she had never defied him. She remembered the look in his eyes the night he'd kidnapped Penelope, the way he twisted her arm. She may have agreed, but she had planned to right the wrong. At least she'd planned to take Penelope home and collect the reward in the bargain.

She could see Abbott thought her as guilty as the twins.

Finally she stepped back.

"I'm sorry, Maddie."

She laughed, a brittle burst of sound.

"Sorry for what? You're just doing your job."

The sadness in his eyes unbalanced her.

"What will happen now?" she asked.

"When we get to New Orleans, Penelope will be returned to her parents." He didn't finish. He didn't have to.

"And I'll be arrested." She reached out, touched his sleeve, hoping to appeal to whatever inspired him to be near her. "Let me go. I'll disappear into the bayou."

"I wish I could."

"Who would know?"

"Penelope, for one. She can implicate you and the Russo woman, as well as your brother. And I would know. I have to sleep at night, Maddie."

"Anita?" Anita would be in as much trouble as the rest of them. "Anita is old. Can't you leave her in peace? I pushed the child on her ... I ..."

"She could have turned the girl over to the authorities. She didn't."

Maddie began to panic. She heard it in her own voice and struggled to keep her hands from shaking.

"Right after I left Penelope in her care, the storm hit and Penelope ran off. Anita didn't have time to do the right thing—"

She was unraveling. He reached for her, tried to pull her close.

"Don't." She tried struggling out of his hold. "Don't touch me."

He fell silent, gave up trying to comfort her. There was nothing more she could say. Nothing he could say that would repair the hurt he'd inflicted.

"It will be easier on you if you go with me willingly and don't cause any trouble tomorrow," he warned.

She drew a deep breath, straightened her spine, and gave him what she hoped was a long, detached once over. "Don't worry, Mr. Abbott. I won't be any trouble at all."

Maddie held herself together until she was back inside her cabin. She crawled onto the bed and pressed her back against the wall. Penelope was still snoring softly. Maddie covered her ears with her hands, pulled up her knees, and propped her elbows on them. She thought about facing the rest of her life in prison.

There was no way she could free Terrance now. As soon as she was arrested, the police could use Penelope's testimony to convict her and Terrance.

If Terrance still hadn't confessed, then Penelope was the only one except for Abbott who could accuse them. Anita would never talk.

She stared at the sleeping child. If the girl disappeared along with her, then there would be no way to prove anything. There was only Tom Abbott's word. Terrance would serve time for resisting arrest, shooting a policeman, and maybe even for killing Lawrence. But he might never confess to the kidnapping.

*"Was it worth it, Maddie?"*

Truth be told, her brothers had never done anything of worth, never owned anything they came by honestly, never thought of anyone but themselves. She was just as bad as they were.

As the steamboat continued on toward New Orleans, Maddie sat shrouded in darkness trying to see into the future. She thought about Terrance and Penelope. Mostly she thought about Tom Abbott, a man she didn't really know at all.

Tom paced the upper deck, counting steps as he walked. Easier to count how many steps it took to circumnavigate the deck than to think or to feel. Tonight he had nearly stepped over a line of his own making, a line that had always helped him keep his life on course.

He almost kissed Maddie. If he had, he couldn't have taken it.

He would give anything to take her back to the bayou and concoct a story that would appease the police—something that would explain how and where he'd found Penelope Perkins—but that would require turning his back on everything he believed in. Everything he stood for.

There was no way to erase what she had done. No way to hide the evidence.

He kept on walking. Two hundred paces. Three hundred.

No matter what he decided to do, Penelope knew the truth and she could identify Maddie. She would be asked over and over what had happened, and a child as precocious as Miss Penelope Perkins would be happy to bask in the light of notoriety and tell all.

*"Kidnapped Child Rescued: Recounts Tale of Danger and Woe."*

The desperate millionaire, the grief-stricken mother.

The newspapers fed on emotion and drama. What was better than a good kidnapping?

Maddie would be at the center of it all too. Public opinion didn't favor villains who preyed upon defenseless children.

Nor did he.

Maddie's only recourse was escape. He knew she would try to make a run for it. She had no choice. She might be able to hide out in the bayou forever if she made it back, but once they docked in New Orleans, it wasn't very far from there to the precinct station. He'd be turning her over to Frank Morgan before noon tomorrow.

She may have just promised not to give him any trouble, but he would still have to be extra vigilant in the morning. He'd deliver her to Morgan. His conscience demanded it of him, no matter what his heart desired.

# CHAPTER 19

The wharf was crowded even before the *Memphis Palace* docked. There was less commerce since the war, fewer steamboat passengers disembarking, but the riverfront still teamed with life. Laborers bent under backbreaking loads, pushing hogsheads filled with cotton bales, bags of rice, and sugar. Sailors dodged ferrymen and barge pilots. Horses, carriages, piles of baggage, harried travelers, and determined merchants all vied for space on the docks.

Maddie waited while Tom indulged Penelope. The child had demanded he tie her possessions in her cape before they stepped onto the gangway. It took all of the calm Maddie could muster for her to pretend not to care that he was about to turn her over to the police. She stood silently, watching, listening, waiting for an opportunity to escape.

There was no question she'd be taking Penelope with her. The girl knew too much for her own good. That morning while they were alone together in the cabin, Maddie had combed and styled Penelope's hair.

"What's a Pinkerton?" the girl asked.

"A detective. He hunts people down and puts them in jail like a policeman," Maddie told her. "He's a very bad man."

"Worse than those twins?"

"About the same."

"So he's not really taking me home?"

"If you want to get home, you'll have to come with me." She refused to give in and be led like a lamb to the slaughter. "It will be crowded on the dock. Our only hope is to slip away when he doesn't expect it."

She knew every inch of the streets of New Orleans. There was no one more adept at hiding in a crowd, no one better at disappearing in plain sight than a Grande. Once she got away, it would take a miracle for Abbott to find her.

"You'll have to do *exactly* as I say if we're going to escape," Maddie warned. Running with a child wouldn't be as easy.

"Then what?" Penelope wanted to know. "Then where are we going? Home?"

Maddie paused. "Do you want to go home?"

She shrugged. "You said they miss me."

"Yes, they do." Maddie's mind raced in circles and finally straightened out. "But do you really want this adventure to end so soon?"

"Will I get to act again?"

"There is every possibility."

"Then I'll stay with you. For a while, anyway." Penelope frowned up at Maddie. "Do you promise you'll take me back whenever I say?"

"Of course."

*So easy to lie*, Maddie thought. *So easy to let lies slip from my tongue.*

There came a knock at the door, and Maddie held her finger to her lips, warning the child to be silent. "We're ready." She opened the door. The Pinkerton looked haggard. Deep lines framed his full mouth. His usually intense eyes were shadowed.

*Good*, she thought. *He didn't sleep any more than I.*

Was he really haunted by the memory of a kidnapped child who died? Or had he kept himself awake, expecting her to try to escape when her only option was to jump overboard? Did he think she'd risk death rather than face jail?

He stayed close behind her as they walked down the gangway. She reached back for Penelope's arm. The girl was clutching her bundle with one hand. Tom held the other. He motioned for a carriage and immediately a hack pulled up. The driver leaned down to discuss the fare. Tom let go of Penelope long enough to dig his money pouch out of his waistband.

A second was all Maddie needed. She tugged on Penelope's arm, turned, and ran back toward the gangway. She made a sudden left, which put them behind a wagon full of sorghum barrels. There was no way Abbott would be able to see through the vehicle.

She crouched down and together they ran along beside it as it rolled slowly down the dock. If anyone noticed the two of them skulking along, they didn't care enough to say anything. The wagon made a slow circle away from the river. Maddie stayed behind it until they came to the corner of Toulouse Street, and then she broke into a run, tugging the child behind her. They darted between two buildings. Brick walls gave off the damp scent of mildew that thrived in the shade.

For a half second she wasn't certain if she was running through her nightmare or if this was reality as she clutched the girl's hand and they careened down the street.

Maddie faltered, stepped in a puddle, and kept going. When she looked back, the girl was smiling as she ran. Penelope was intelligent and quick-witted. She'd make a good partner, but there was no telling when or if she would suddenly grow tired of the excitement. No way to ensure her silence — save one.

There were no footfalls behind them, no shouts for them to halt. Maddie cut a zigzag pattern, running down one street after another, turning to double back before she ran on. Alleyways that were barely noticeable opened up for her. She took a deep breath, drank in the scents of the city that had thrived under French, Spanish, American, and Confederate flags. Through it all New Orleans had survived.

*So will I*, she decided. *So will I.*

After twenty minutes of running Penelope stopped, refusing to go on.

"I'm tired, Madeline." She was holding her side.

"We're almost there," Maddie promised.

"Can't we please walk? He won't find us now."

Maddie started again, this time at a slow trot. They entered a rundown warehouse area. Garbage littered the streets and corners.

She had found the old warehouse without hesitation. The door was so heavy on its thick iron wheels it barely rolled. The wheels protested, sorely in need of oil. Maddie managed to shove it open just far enough for her and Penelope to slip inside.

Startled pigeons flapped their wings and took flight, escaping through holes in the roof.

"What *is* this place?" Penelope walked a few feet ahead and stopped, waiting for Maddie to join her.

"An old warehouse," she said. *Home*, she thought to herself. *The place where I grew up, where I lived with my family. My tribe.*

Like one of the pigeons overhead, Maddie was poised to take flight. After a two-year absence, she saw it for what it truly was: bleak and dilapidated.

"This isn't a house." Penelope looked around with disdain. "It's like a big old dirty barn."

Maddie walked in and tossed her things on a broken-down cot. There was no clean bedding around. What there was provided fine nests for mice. The old woodstove, once vented to the outside, was still there but shoved away from the wall. No need to worry about cooking. She could beg or steal what they needed to survive.

Not the kind of life she wanted anymore, but right now her only other choice was jail.

They wouldn't be here long, she decided. Soon they would escape to the swamp and hide until she could return Penelope and claim the reward without being apprehended.

Penelope clutched her bundle and looked around wide-eyed

and as disheartened as Maddie felt. The girl stared at a bare cot before she gingerly set her things down on it.

"May I walk around?"

"Of course." Maddie was wandering herself. She walked over to a pile of wooden chairs.

*Here is where we sat when Dexter lectured.*

His favorite chair was there, near the empty bookcases in the corner. The stuffing was coming out of threadbare patches in the ripped saffron upholstery.

She lingered in the area Louie had once sectioned off as their "home." It became the quarters she shared with her son. Her children were conceived behind long draperies that divided their small space from the rest of the room and other "rooms" like theirs. The draperies had long since rotted.

The armoires were still lined up against the far wall. There were four of them, huge, dark, and overbearing pieces carved long ago by a woodworker who intended them to house goods and clothing — not to imprison small children who would emerge reborn.

Children gathered together by Dexter Grande.

She walked over to Penelope in the center of the vast, forlorn space. The child stared up at the holes open to the lowering gray sky. The warehouse had lost whatever charm it once held. Its dilapidation tarnished her memories. Time had moved on. She had moved on.

There was nothing for her here anymore. Nothing but dusty, empty space, and the sound of pigeons cooing in the rafters.

"What are we going to do now?" Penelope waited with arms akimbo, tapping her toe.

Maddie rubbed her brow. "I don't know."

"You don't *know*? I'm getting hungry and it's getting cold in here."

The sun had been out earlier that morning but now clouds gathered. Maddie glanced up. There was a reason the place was so dank. Rain fell through the holes in the roof. They would have to take shelter along the edges of the room.

In the armoires if they had to.

"Come with me," Maddie told her, leading her toward an ornately carved cabinet. "We'll put your things in here and make a nice comfortable place for you to sleep."

Tom chided himself for a fool over and over. He'd taken his eyes off Maddie for less than a second to hire a hack, and she'd not only given him the slip but she'd taken the girl.

He searched in every direction but it was almost as if the ground had opened up and swallowed them both. He ran to the water's edge, looked over the side of the dock into the water. He wouldn't put it past her to hide in the river.

The wharf was crowded with barrels and boxes, trunks and crates, bales and huge stacks of dry goods, not to mention wagons and other conveyances. Maddie and the girl could be anywhere.

Somehow she had convinced the child to leave with her. Surely she realized that the Perkins's home would be watched once he alerted the police. Returning Penelope would lead to her own incarceration if she wasn't able to ensure the child's silence.

He knew he'd never find them alone, and the longer he waited, the more impossible it would be to track her down. While scanning the streets on foot, he headed straight for the French Quarter precinct. Thankfully, Frank Morgan was at his desk. When he looked up and saw Tom standing there unshaven and disheveled, he dispensed with a greeting.

"You didn't find her," Morgan said.

"On the contrary, until twenty minutes ago, I had Penelope Perkins with me." Tom tossed his hat on a chair.

"What happened?"

"To make a long story short, Penelope had escaped before I got back to the Grande cabin and decided to head for Kentucky on her own."

"Are you serious?"

Tom nodded. "I doubled back to Langetree to have the

Perkinses identify this." He pulled out the silver comb and showed it to Morgan, then repocketed it. "They did. I went back to the bayou. Miss Grande was gone, already on Penelope's trail by then. I caught up with them both in Baton Rouge and brought them back by steamboat this morning but my luck ran out. I lost them both at the docks."

Frustration and anger had him pacing the small office. He shoved his hand through his hair.

"Sit down, Tom," Frank advised. "Would you like any refreshment?"

He shook his head, chose to stand. "What I'd like is some help before they slip out of the city. Your men can cover New Orleans, flush them out."

"Does anyone else know Maddie Grande was involved in the kidnapping?"

"Terrance, of course. Me. Penelope. A woman named Anita Russo. But Maddie will deny it. Russo will too. Without Penelope's testimony, Terrance can deny everything."

"Is she capable of hurting the girl?"

Tom knew Frank was really asking if Maddie was capable of far worse than hurting Penelope, but would she silence the child forever?

"I don't think so." He hoped not. He truly hoped not. "Has Terrence confessed yet?"

"No and I can't hold him much longer, Tom. It's hard enough to convict the guilty in this city. From what my men found out on the streets, finding Maddie Grande will be harder than you imagine."

# CHAPTER 20

Thankfully, the rain held off. Maddie stored their things in a corner and covered them with an old crate. Then she smeared dirt over Penelope's face and fluffed the child's hair into a mass of wild tangles. She folded the milkmaid apron into a ruffled shawl and tied it round Penelope's neck. People saw what they wanted to see. Maddie was satisfied no one would associate the unkempt urchin before her with the kidnapped daughter of a wealthy plantation owner.

Maddie altered her own appearance in much the same way, changing into her old clothes. She rolled up the apparel she'd been given at the hotel, made the wool skirt look like a blanket wrapped around an infant, and cradled the bundle in the crook of her arm. The authorities wouldn't be searching for a woman with an infant.

She looked Penelope over.

"I'm not sure you're a good enough actress to pull this off." She pretended to consider Penelope's ability.

Penelope tilted her chin defiantly. "Of course I am. What do I have to do?"

"We need money for food, so we're going out on the street. I want you to look as pitiful as you can. Imagine that you haven't eaten in days. Pick out a wealthy couple, tug on the lady's skirt, and beg prettily for a handout."

Penelope's eyes lit up. "Does that really work?"

"If you're good enough."

"Oh, I'll be very good."

Maddie had her act out the role a few times. The child did, indeed, have a gift.

"I'm perfect," Penelope cried. "Admit it, Madeline."

"Let's go prove it."

A million and one things could go wrong. Maddie was a bundle of nerves, but once they were out on the street she realized she had nothing to fear. No one looked at her twice as she hugged her pretend infant close and clutched the hand of the little urchin beside her. Whenever they spotted a likely couple, Maddie nudged Penelope and let go of her hand.

The child was a consummate actress. Dexter would have loved her.

Once they had more than enough coin for a few meals, Maddie ducked into a passageway and led Penelope around to the back of a restaurant on Decatur Street. The cooks were more than generous, giving them free food even when Maddie offered to pay. They were carrying the bundled food back to the warehouse when Maddie turned down a back street and Penelope bolted toward a small knot of people gathered around a long serving table.

An elderly woman was pounding a tambourine.

Maddie stepped up to the edge of the gathering. One or two people turned to look at her, but they were more interested in the covered food in her hands.

"That's my child," she said softly. "Please let me through."

Two men let her slip by. She reached Penelope and was just about to tell her they had to leave when she recognized a young woman standing on the other side of the table. Maddie hadn't seen her for at least fifteen years, but she'd never forget that face.

"Betsy—"

"Maddie?"

The missionary stared at Maddie in surprise. She dropped a soup ladle she was holding, and skirting the edge of the table, she ran around to embrace Maddie, careful not to crush the "infant" in Maddie's arms.

"Maddie! I can't believe it's you."

Maddie pulled back, stunned. "Oh, Bets. It's been so long. What happened? Where did you go?" One day Betsy had been in the warehouse with the others, the next day she was gone. Dexter simply told them that she'd moved on.

"I had to leave. I ... couldn't live that way anymore. I don't expect you to understand."

"I used to wish you'd taken me with you — "

"You were married. You had Louis."

"He's dead."

"Oh, Maddie. I'm sorry." Betsy looked at Penelope. "Is this your daughter?"

"Yes," Penelope said, executing a curtsy.

"No," Maddie said at the same time.

The missionary's smile faded when she looked closer and realized the bundle in Maddie's arms was only clothing.

The woman sighed. "Come with me."

"We really should be going." Maddie looked up and down the street. She'd already pressed her luck staying out so late. They needed to return to the warehouse before Abbott or the law found them. "I'll try to come to see you again."

"Spare a moment, that's all I ask. It's been so long."

When Betsy gave her hands a squeeze Maddie couldn't resist and followed her into the empty storefront behind them. It smelled of sawdust and fresh paint. Maddie pointed to the bench and told Penelope to sit, relieved when the girl did. Maddie pulled an apple out of the bundle.

"Eat this," she said.

"But I don't want — "

"It's all you'll get tonight."

"I saw pie out there on the table."

"Of course you're both welcome to pie," Betsy said.

"After we talk. It will just take a minute," Maddie said.

"All right then. Just for a minute." Penelope sat down on the bench and spread out her skirt. "But I want that pie."

"Betsy, I really can't tarry," Maddie told her.

"I imagine not." The woman looked her over. "Are you still living on the street? Still running games?"

"I'm just in a bind right now."

"I'm married, Maddie. I'm Elizabeth Henson now. I had no idea you were still in New Orleans, though I should have guessed when I heard the twins were still here."

"I *was* living on the bayou." She couldn't meet Betsy's eyes. "But that's a long story."

"A Pinkerton was here looking for a woman who may have been one of the tribe."

"Tonight?" Maddie was frantic thinking Abbott might be so close.

"No, it was weeks ago now. He was looking for someone who disappeared when she was a child. Her sister is trying to find her. I told him to look for the twins, that they were still in town. I told him to look for Anita—"

"Why?"

"Because the woman he's seeking might have been one of the children we cared for. One of the children that we—"

Maddie had an urge to grab Penelope and run but she feared the girl would create a fuss.

"Go get that pie. Now," she told her.

Penelope jumped up and scooted out the door.

Maddie turned to Betsy. "Dexter never told us any of their real names. Why on earth would you set that Pinkerton on our trail?"

"I thought perhaps Anita might know something that would help reunite sisters, Maddie. It's a way to ease someone's pain."

"I'm in big trouble, Bets. With that very Pinkerton."

"Then stop running and find him. Maybe he can help you and in turn, maybe you'll be able to help him find the woman he's looking for."

"That's impossible."

Tom Abbott was looking to help her all right. Help her right into a jail cell.

Betsy took Maddie's hands. "I've found my way. Now God is handing you a chance to change your life once and for all."

"God's never given me any chances before. Why should this be any different?"

The missionary turned to the window and watched her husband hand Penelope a slice of peach pie. "God's given me all I need," she said. "Now let me help you. Take my advice and contact the Pinkerton."

As Maddie hurried Penelope back to the warehouse she said, "You're to call me 'Mama' when we're on the street."

"Who was that woman?"

"A missionary. She used to be an old friend."

"I think we need a tambourine. Their money jar was full up. If I had a tambourine I'd be able to get a lot more coin out of folks." Penelope skipped a few steps ahead and then came back to Maddie's side. "It's really so easy. Just ask for it and people give you money."

"Some do, some don't. Those who do just feel sorry for you. That's all. They give you the money so you'll go away and they won't have to feel guilty for having more than you."

Penelope looked doubtful. "I think they gave it to me because they're nice. Everybody's got some good in them, except maybe those twins."

"Do you really believe that? That everyone has some good in them?"

"I do," Penelope nodded with certainty. "Sometimes you just have to wait for it to come out, but it's there."

Maddie didn't believe it for a minute.

Penelope was content with their grand adventure until twilight fell and shadows from nearby street lamps seeped through the holes in the roof and pierced the interior of the deserted warehouse. They heard the rustle of rodents scrambling through the piles of trash in the room and once in a while, the flutter of wings.

"Are those bats?" Penelope stared up at the ceiling with her hands over her head.

"Birds."

"Birds don't fly around at night."

"Owls do. They eat mice too."

Penelope looked up. "I don't see any owls."

Maddie shoved an old cot across the room for herself. She placed it near the huge armoire where she had made up a pallet.

"I don't like it in here," the child whined after she climbed in. "It's narrow and it's too hard. How am I supposed to sleep?" Her eyes grew wide and fearful. "You're not going to close the doors are you, Madeline?"

"I'm not closing the doors." Maddie had to look away.

"I don't trust you. Give me the key." Penelope held out her hand.

A frayed braided cord was still attached to the key in the lock. Maddie tugged on the cord. It was so rotted it snapped. She handed Penelope the key. "There, now get in and lie down. Please."

The child did as she was told but her hesitation proved she was not as brave as she let on. Maddie covered her with the cape before she stretched out on her own bare cot and draped her extra wool skirt over herself.

Lying there in the dark warehouse, Maddie listened to the sounds of the city outside, an occasional shout amid the clip-clop of horses' hooves, the clatter of carriage wheels against cobblestones, the shrill steam whistle from a riverboat. When she'd lived here, she barely noticed the clamor. Now she longed for the gentle heartbeat of the bayou, the mysterious sounds of the swamp to lull her to sleep.

She drifted off only to find herself trapped in the web of her nightmare, wandering through the faded, raggedy-edged world of sounds and colors that always terrified her. She awoke with a start, afraid she had awakened Penelope, but the child was still softly snoring.

Wide awake now, Maddie felt the memories oozing off the walls around her. How many children had she locked in the armoires? How many young lives had she changed? How many memories had she wiped out?

Would there ever come a day when she wasn't haunted by her own nightmare?

The next morning, Penelope woke in a foul mood. She balked when Maddie asked her to fold up her things.

"I don't want to stay here anymore." Penelope sat down on the edge of the armoire with her legs dangling outside of it and crossed her arms. Her bottom lip jutted in a pout.

Truth be told, Maddie didn't want to be here either. There was too much of the past to face, too many dark memories.

"We won't stay much longer." Despite her disguise, sooner or later a discerning individual might recognize Penelope from her likeness in the paper or one of the posters pasted up near the market stalls.

"Where are we going next, Madeline?"

"I don't know."

"You don't know? You don't have a plan? I'm a little girl and even *I* had a plan to get to Kentucky."

Maddie sighed. She stood up and started walking around the warehouse, picking through discarded items—an old boot, a walking stick, some broken spectacles. She straightened overturned barrels once used for stools. She'd always been one who'd straightened and cleaned. The only one most of the time. She thought better on her feet, sorting things out in her mind while her hands kept busy.

Glancing over at Penelope, she saw the child sitting forlornly on the cot staring at the floor. Her hands were folded in her lap, her shoulders slumped. Maddie's heart contracted. She crossed the cavernous space. Slipping an arm around Penelope's shoulders, she sat beside her.

"I really don't like it here," the child sniffed. She turned to look up at Maddie. A lone tear streaked through the dirt on her cheek. "You said this would be a wonderful adventure but it's cold and damp and dirty in here."

Cold, damp, and dirty summed up most of Maddie's childhood, but she hadn't really noticed back then. As she grew older, she had wanted more for her own children, but she had failed Rene. His childhood mirrored her own.

She tried to finger comb Penelope's tangled hair but it was useless. The child's face was still streaked with dirt. Staring down into those piercing violet eyes, Maddie saw something she hadn't seen there before, something behind the tears. For the first time since she'd met Penelope Perkins, Maddie saw true fear.

"Madeline?"

"What, child?"

"I miss Papa and Mama," Penelope whispered. "I want to go home."

Maddie closed her eyes and saw Tom Abbott's face.

*"I'm a Pinkerton agent."*

*"Hired by the Perkinses to bring their daughter home."*

No doubt he'd gone straight to the police the moment she'd disappeared yesterday morning. She was foolish to believe she could escape to collect the reward. Foolish enough to believe in the future.

*"Was it worth it?"*

She'd be lucky to escape the city with Penelope. And then what? Penelope would still identify her, and Terrance, and Anita. As long as Penelope could testify, they were all in jeopardy.

Penelope was sobbing in earnest now, slumped over with her face buried in the crook of her arm.

Maddie realized it was too late to change her own life. The reward money could have taken her a long way away, but Tom

Abbott believed her as guilty as Terrance. He wasn't going to let her get away.

With the hopeless sobbing driving her mad, Maddie began to pace the confines of the warehouse. She thought and thought but as far as she knew, there was only one way to ensure Penelope's silence forever.

# CHAPTER 21

Tom stepped into the French Quarter precinct office. Hat in hand, he waited for Terrance Grande to be brought in. He sat down, stared at the iron bars in the windows, and tried not to think of Maddie.

Impossible, given the fact she was constantly on his mind.

The way he'd seen her protect the child, the gentleness in her, her concern for the Perkins woman, convinced him Maddie Grande wasn't without a conscience. But there was still her past to reckon with, the things she'd learned and done while living with Dexter.

If she was redeemable, surely there was a way to help her. But for the life of him he didn't see any way out for her.

He heard the rattle of chains before he saw the burly, red-haired man being led into the room. The guards motioned him to sit. When Terrance recognized Tom across the table, he dropped his gaze.

"I'm sure you remember me," Tom said.

After a moment, Terrance eyed him coolly. He nodded but didn't say anything.

"I'm Tom Abbott, a Pinkerton. I sometimes work closely with Detective Frank Morgan of the New Orleans police."

"Pinkerton?" Terrance snorted. "You got no more right to hold me than they do. I didn't do nothing until you and those men jumped us."

"I'm not here about what happened the night you and your brother resisted arrest and you wounded two policemen. That's enough to put you away for a long time. Have you forgotten you killed your brother?"

"That was an accident."

Tom leaned forward in his chair and tapped the edge of the table between them. "Was it? Or did you want to ensure his silence? I know you kidnapped the Perkins girl. It's about time you confessed."

"You've got no proof."

Tom reached into his pocket and palmed the comb. He laid it on the table.

"I never seen that before in my life."

"That's funny," Tom replied. "I found it on the floor of your cabin. Under your sister's bed."

Terrance lunged to his feet. A guard shoved him back down.

"What were you doing sniffing around my sister?"

Tom shrugged. "It was easy enough to get to her. Now how about you tell me about the kidnapping of Penelope Perkins?"

"I don't know what you're talking about."

"You're saying you have no idea how the Perkins girl got to your cabin in the bayou?"

"None. You've gotta put the blame on someone and you're trying to make me look guilty," Terrance said. "I had nothing to do with it. Just ask Maddie."

In chains, Terrance Grande had lost some of the bravado he'd exhibited in the saloon, but Tom feared he wasn't willing to confess anytime soon.

Tom played his only card. He knew with the political climate in the city the testimony of a former slave would never keep this man behind bars on kidnapping charges. Penelope's word was another matter.

"You willing to let this all fall on your sister? I found her, along with Penelope Perkins. The child can identify all of you."

"If Maddie had the girl, then it was all her own doing. She's been a bit teched since her boy, Rene, died. I wouldn't put it past her to steal a child for herself," Terrance said. "She tell you what she's good at? She tell you how she can make a child forget its own name?"

Shaken, Tom imagined reaching across the table, taking the man's throat between his hands. What kind of a coward sold out his sister?

"If that's all you have to say, then the guards might just as well take you back to your cell." Tom started to push up out of his chair. Terrance got up and shuffled toward the door. When he reached it, he hung back and turned to Tom.

"What's in it for me if I confess to something I didn't do?"

"You did it and you know it. Confess and maybe you won't hang for killing your brother. Maybe you'll just rot in prison for the rest of your life and think about how Lawrence died. You're not going anywhere for a long, long time. The least you could do is help Maddie out."

Terrance stared at Tom a heartbeat or two. Finally he said, "It ain't Maddie's fault, you hear? None of it was her doing."

Here was the glimmer of hope Tom never thought to see.

"I made her keep the girl. She wasn't for it. Madeline told us to take her back, but I thought it would be easy money."

Terrance slowly nodded. "You write it all out on a paper and put in that it weren't Maddie's idea. I'll make my mark on it."

# CHAPTER 22

L angetree's just down that lane yonder."

Maddie looked at the child asleep beside her on the high seat of a buckboard wagon. She'd cleaned the girl up as best as she could, placed the single comb in her hair.

Figuring Tom Abbott wouldn't expect them to return to the riverfront, Maddie had headed back and found someone willing to take them up the river road. It had taken her no more than five minutes to appeal to a driver with a load of furniture bound for a plantation five miles north of Langetree. He agreed to let them ride along.

"I could carry you on up to the house," the driver offered at the end of the tree-lined drive.

The plantation house was far enough away that it wasn't even visible from the road. It was still early afternoon and a number of carriages and wagons had passed them on the river road. Maddie was counting on someone headed back in the opposite direction to come along and take her back.

"Thank you kindly, but you've done more than enough. We appreciate it."

She gently shook Penelope's shoulder. The child awoke, rubbed her eyes, and looked around. "Where are we?"

"Home." Maddie climbed down and reached up to help her down.

Penelope leaned against Maddie as they stood side by side in the road watching the wagon roll away.

"Can you find your way from here?" Maddie asked.

"Aren't you coming with me?"

Maddie stared down the long wheel-rutted lane bordered by oaks. A wide green lawn spread out on both sides and rolled all the way to the river. It was an idyllic setting. This child lived in a world Maddie could never even imagine.

She thought of the reward. Money the Perkinses could easily afford to spend.

Still, there was a price to be paid for freedom.

"I don't think that would be such a good idea," Maddie said.

"'Cause your brothers kidnapped me."

"That. And other things."

"I promise I won't tell anybody about what happened."

"They're bound to find out." Sooner than later, she thought. Tom Abbott was never far from her mind and probably right on her trail. The police might even be watching the place, hoping she'd walk into a trap.

"Nobody will find out." Penelope looked longingly toward the house. "Not if I don't tell."

"You best get going," Maddie said, clutching her own bundle close. If she wasn't careful, someone might drive up the lane and see them together. "Will you be all right?"

"I almost made it across the Mississippi, didn't I?" It was a warm afternoon. Penelope slipped off her cape. "Come with me, Maddie. I want to show you my room. You can meet Mama and Papa. I'll tell them you're just a kind stranger who found me and brought me home. You know I can make them believe it. I am a talented actress, after all."

In the distance, a shiny carriage was approaching, headed back toward New Orleans. With any luck, the occupants were going all the way to town.

Maddie looked into Penelope's upturned face, into her wide, trusting eyes.

*I've taught this child how to beg and how to lie. I can't let her lie to her own parents.*

Maddie knew the sooner she was on the road, the better. She would head directly back to the bayou to warn Anita and then move on. Eventually, Tom Abbott and the police would be coming for her, but with any luck at all she'd have a head start.

Penelope began walking down the lane alone, then suddenly turned and came running back. She grabbed Maddie around the waist and gave her a hug.

"I'll never forget you, Maddie."

"I'll never forget you either."

"Thank you for bringing me home." Penelope pulled away and smiled up at her. Now that she was almost home, her eyes sparkled with not only tears but mischief. She gave Maddie one last hug.

"Who knew getting kidnapped would be so exciting?"

Maddie was pulling out of her embrace when the small black carriage suddenly turned off the main road and onto the lane. It was shiny and new, sporting black lacquer and fine-tooled leather.

An urge to run hit Maddie but there was nowhere to hide on the wide-open lawn. The carriage door opened before the driver had completely stopped the vehicle a few feet from them.

"Mama!" Penelope ran toward a woman in black silk who nearly tumbled out the door in her haste to reach her daughter.

Mrs. Perkins knelt in the dusty road and clutched Penelope to her. She didn't make a sound. Her shoulders heaved as silent tears ran down her cheeks.

Maddie could feel the woman's relief and joy and ached so intensely with it that she had to look away. She started to hurry toward the main road but the driver, a powerfully built black man, climbed down from the high-sprung driver's seat and blocked her way.

"Mama, it's all right. I'm home now. Please don't cry anymore," Penelope gently patted her mother on the back.

Mrs. Perkins cupped Penelope's face between her hands and studied her closely.

"Are you truly here, darling?" the woman whispered.

"Yes, Mama."

"Are you all right? Did they hurt you?"

"No, Mama."

When the woman slowly turned to Maddie, Maddie's heart nearly stopped. She waited in silence, watched the other woman lean on Penelope as she got to her feet.

Penelope led her mother over to Maddie and grabbed Maddie by the hand. "Mama, I got clean away from the bad men and this nice stranger offered to bring me home," she said. "She found a ride for us too, and she was just going to leave when you drove in." Penelope squeezed Maddie's hand with all her might and winked. "Isn't that right, *ma'am*?"

Maddie couldn't take her eyes off of the woman smiling through her tears with such unbridled gratitude.

"I'm Mary Perkins." The woman's lips trembled as she spoke the words. "I owe you everything I have. *Everything*. I thank you for your kindness from the bottom of my heart."

*This*, Maddie thought, *is the glorious joy I will never know. No matter what else I've done or what part I played in the kidnapping, I have given this woman her child back. I have given her something I will never have, the pleasure of holding my children close again.*

*At least I have done this.*

"I ... I'm happy to have helped," Maddie finally managed to say. Penelope continued to cling to her hand.

"You must come up to the house with us," Mary Perkins invited. "My husband is doing business at a neighboring plantation, but he'll want to thank you properly. Besides ..." She looked down into Penelope's upturned face and smoothed her palm over her daughter's cheek. "There's the matter of a reward."

Maddie took a deep breath. A few days ago she would have done anything for the money. This was her chance to tell Mary

Perkins the truth, to confess the part she'd played in the kidnapping, but her courage failed her.

She had brought Penelope home. It was all the goodness she could muster for one day.

"I have to go," she whispered. "I have to get home."

The other woman tried to protest. "But the reward—"

"I did nothing to deserve it," she said softly.

"You escorted my daughter safely home."

"I must go," Maddie insisted. She gave Penelope's hand a squeeze and the child finally let go.

"I don't understand," Mary Perkins said. "You brought our daughter back to us. You *deserve* the reward."

Maddie shook her head. "No, Mrs. Perkins. I don't. Please, consider this a gift. From one mother to another."

# CHAPTER 23

Tom handed Terrance Grande's confession over to Frank Morgan. The police contacted the *Times Picayune*, and the editor agreed to run a story about Penelope Perkins being sighted near the wharf. Messages were sent to the authorities near Clearwater to be on the lookout for Maddie Grande, the child, and Anita Russo.

Though he wanted to believe Maddie had been bullied into hiding the child, he was no fool. Terrance might have confessed just to keep Maddie out of jail. Since stealing children was routine for the Grandes, he wasn't completely convinced of her innocence.

Terrance claimed she wasn't an accomplice in the kidnapping, but even knowing Tom was a Pinkerton, she had abducted the child right out from under him. What he couldn't figure out was why. It was insane of her to believe she could still collect the reward. Her only option was to hold Penelope for ransom.

Maddie Grande was digging her own grave.

He hadn't slept in two days, but he had taken time to return to his apartment, clean up, and change into respectable clothing. It was with a heavy heart that he rode up the oak-lined lane to the Langetree mansion again.

Once again, a Langetree servant met him in front of the grand manor and took his horse. Tom noticed the black mourning draperies were still at the windows, but they'd been drawn open. As before, he was ushered into the house, told to wait in the formal drawing room.

Penelope's ornamental comb was in his pocket. Though only a sliver of silver, it weighed heavy as his heart when he saw the portrait of Penelope above the mantel. Now he knew that the image didn't do her justice. It did not capture her intelligence nor her stubbornness, though there was the familiar pluck and confidence in her smile.

He heard footsteps behind him and dreaded facing the Perkinses—until he saw Mary Perkins sweep toward him with a bright smile on her face.

"Mr. Abbott, I was wondering when we'd see you again. My husband is in his study; he'll be right down."

Tom marveled at the change in her. There were still telltale smudges of violet beneath her eyes, but her color was high and her face wreathed in a smile. Now he could see Penelope had inherited her beauty from her mother.

He wanted to wait to explain until Peter joined them. He didn't relish repeating the story. Thankfully, Peter Perkins entered almost on his wife's heels. He extended a hand in greeting, pumped Tom's with a wide smile of welcome.

"It's good to see you. I can tell by the confusion on your face that you haven't received my letter yet," Perkins said. "I had a servant take it to New Orleans just this morning."

"Letter?" Tom feared he sounded as dumbfounded as he felt. No doubt Perkins had fired him, but that didn't account for all the smiles.

"Would you like something to drink? Coffee? Whiskey?" Perkins indicated a nearby wing chair. "Have a seat, Abbott. Have a seat."

"Sir, I want you to know that I am, along with the entire New Orleans Metropolitan Police, still doing my best to find your daughter."

Peter quickly looked at his wife poised near the wide doorway with her hands demurely folded. They were still pale against her black mourning gown, but her cheeks were bright, her smile undimmed.

"So you don't know yet?" Perkins held out his arm. His wife crossed the room and slipped into his embrace.

"Know what, sir?"

"Our prayers have been answered. Our daughter is home. Returned to us filthy, but other than that, she seems to be just fine."

"She's . . . here?"

"She is indeed, and telling wild tales of traveling with a troupe of actors as she tried to make her way to Kentucky on her own. Under other circumstances I'd be in shock, but to tell you the truth, Abbott, we're just so happy to have her home safe and unharmed that I wouldn't care if she told me she'd ridden an elephant across Louisiana."

"She's here?" Tom repeated. He shook his head in disbelief. "I'm not a drinking man, Mr. Perkins, but if you don't mind, I think I'll take you up on the offer of whiskey. Just a shot."

Peter walked over to a small butler's table covered with crystal decanters and poured Tom a liberal dose. Tom took a drink, winced, and set it down.

"What did she tell you about the kidnapping?"

"She said two men abducted her and that she was frightened to death at first. Then she was able to escape them and met up with the acting troupe. She begged them to take her to her Aunt Gail's in Kentucky—the poor little thing had taken it into her head that she was a burden to us."

"Did she say who else was involved?"

Perkins nodded. "No. Just the two men. Twins, she said."

Tom's mind was spinning. Had Penelope implicated Maddie at all?

Just then Mary Perkins said, "Here she is now. Darling, say hello to Mr. Abbott. I'm afraid you gave him a merry chase."

Tom turned and there was Penelope in the doorway. Dressed

in a navy gown with a starched white collar, fresh white stockings, and ankle-high shoes, she had a huge white bow pinned atop her head. She looked the picture of angelic innocence as she obediently stepped into the room.

She was smiling until she recognized him. Then she froze. "What's *he* doing here?"

Her mother reached for her hand and drew her close. "Why, this is Mr. Abbott, dear. He's the detective we hired to find you."

Penelope shook her head. "He's a bad man. Worse than those twins who kidnapped me."

Peter Perkins's smiled finally dimmed. He turned on Tom. "What's she talking about?"

Penelope spoke up before Tom could answer.

"He said he was going to bring me home but he lied. He really wasn't going to do anything of the sort."

Mary led Penelope to the settee and sat down. The girl remained standing. Mary took both of the girl's hands in hers and looked up into her daughter's eyes.

"How do you know Mr. Abbott, dear?" Mary asked softly.

Penelope threw a dark glance at Tom.

"He found me in Baton Rouge and made us get on a steamboat." She turned to her father. "You always say how dangerous steamboats are, Papa. He made us ... I mean *me*, get on one."

"You found her in Baton Rouge?" Perkins demanded. "Then how did she wind up asking a stranger to bring her home yesterday? How was it she ended up alone again?"

Tom explained as precisely as he could exactly how he found the Grande twins, which led him to the cabin on the bayou and Maddie Grande. He pulled the silver comb out of his pocket and handed it to Perkins.

"I found it in the Grande's cabin, but when I returned after you identified it for me, your daughter had somehow escaped. Maddie Grande was on her trail. I caught up with both of them in Baton Rouge—"

"Where *I* was the star of the Phoenix Rising Theater Troupe," Penelope added proudly. " 'Out of the ashes of the South comes live theater!' "

"She was indeed performing with a troupe of traveling actors," Tom said.

"*They* were kind enough to take me along to Kentucky," the child added.

"After I recovered her—"

"*Stole* me from them, he means."

"After I recovered her and had Maddie Grande in custody, I felt a steamboat was the fastest way back to New Orleans. Not only that, but I could keep them both confined aboard. I'm sure you've noticed your daughter is very resourceful for her age, Mr. Perkins."

"You were *never* bringing me home," Penelope argued. "Maddie said so."

"Maddie Grande is a liar," Tom said softly.

"She is *not*," Penelope shouted.

Peter Perkins anchored his hands on his hips. "Just who is this Maddie Grande?"

"The kidnappers' sister. They left the girl in her care, but Penelope gave her the slip. Which led to the chase. I was intent on delivering both of them directly to the precinct station in the French Quarter, but as soon as we disembarked, Miss Grande managed to escape and took your daughter with her. The police have been scouring the city for two days. I came out here this morning to tell you that I had found Penelope and that she was fine the last time I saw her, but that she was missing again."

Tom stared at Penelope. "Do you know where Maddie is now?"

"No." Penelope walked over to her father's side. "Papa, I learned how to beg for money. I was quite good at it."

"Oh, Peter," Mary sighed, but she was fighting back a smile. "Can you imagine?"

Peter Perkins laughed. "Actually, I can. I wouldn't put anything past our Penelope."

"How did you get home? Did you run away from Maddie?" Tom asked.

"I didn't have to run away. She brought me home," Penelope said.

Mary Perkins gasped. Penelope glanced warily at her mother.

"Penelope, was Maddie Grande the woman with you yesterday?" Mary asked.

"Yes."

Tom gaped at Mary Perkins. "You saw Miss Grande?"

"Why, I even spoke to her," Mary admitted. "I tried to convince her to come to the house and wait for Peter to return. I told her she deserved the reward."

"She didn't take it?" Tom was stunned.

"She refused," Mary confirmed.

Peter Perkins explained, "Penelope showed up yesterday afternoon with a woman and convinced Mary they had just met."

Perkins paused to smile lovingly at his wife. "I'd finally talked Mary into getting out in the fresh air, and her carriage was on the way back up the drive when the driver saw Penelope and the woman standing there."

He hunkered down in front of his daughter. "Do you know where this Maddie Grande is, dear? Do you know where she was going?"

Penelope tapped her toe impatiently and glanced over at Tom before she turned to her father again. "Why?

"Because Mr. Abbott needs to find her."

"I'm not telling if he's going to put her in jail."

"Where did you stay in New Orleans?" Tom took a step closer.

"A smelly old place with bats and mice and rats." She tried to turn the topic. "Do you know how easy it is to get money from perfect strangers, Papa?"

Her mother reached up and straightened Penelope's bow. "Darling, please. Fooling people out of their money isn't something to be proud of. You are a very lucky girl to have always had more than you need."

"You say you hid in a big empty building?" Tom persisted.

Penelope turned on him, her face pinched into an angry frown. "You pretended to be sweet on Maddie when all the time you only wanted to turn her over to the police. You are *not* a nice man."

"I never pretended to be sweet on her." Tom's collar suddenly felt too tight.

"Do you know what she's talking about, Abbott?" Peter Perkins was watching him speculatively.

"I have no idea where they might have been holed up in the city, but we'll find the place and I'll find Maddie Grande," Tom promised. "If it's the last thing I do."

Suddenly Penelope grabbed hold of her father's coat. "Papa, *don't* let him take Maddie to jail. She's my friend. She took good care of me and brought me home. She didn't do anything wrong."

"She may have been coerced into hiding Penelope, but she failed to tell me where the girl was when she had the chance."

"She didn't kidnap me. *They* did. Maddie was nice to me from the start. I never saw those men but once," Penelope cried.

"One of the twins is dead. The other is in jail for other crimes, but he's finally confessed to the kidnapping," Tom told Perkins. "According to her brother, Maddie Grande was forced to shelter the girl."

"Please, Papa. Tell him to leave Maddie alone." Penelope tugged on Perkins's jacket. He hunkered down on one knee. She cupped her father's cheek and smiled into his eyes. "Do it for me, Papa?"

"The woman did bring Penelope home," Mary reminded him. "She seemed jittery yesterday and now I know why. Surely she took a terrible risk bringing our daughter back and she refused the reward. Isn't that all we wanted, dear? To have Penelope home safe and sound?"

"She led Abbott on a merry chase across Louisiana. As far as I'm concerned, she doesn't deserve to get off without consequences," Perkins said.

"Perhaps not, but she doesn't deserve to go to prison."

"Please, please, Papa?"

Perkins finally nodded reassuringly to his child and got to his feet. He sighed, all seriousness when he turned to Tom.

"Do you think this woman poses a threat to other children?"

*"A mother's heart can't bear losing a child."*

*"Maddie brought me home."*

*"Did she tell you she can make a child forget its own name?"*

"Abbott?"

"No, sir. I don't believe she is."

Perkins looked to Mary, who nodded in agreement. She urged Penelope to join her on the settee. Penelope watched Tom, for once quiet but wide-eyed with hope.

"Mr. Abbott, Maddie Grande did bring my daughter home safely. She did not try to con us out of the reward money, nor did she demand a ransom, though I would have paid any amount, even if I had to beg, borrow, or steal it."

Penelope huffed. "If I'm not allowed to beg, Papa, is that just a figure of speech? I'm really good at begging, if you ever need money."

Perkins crossed the room and stood before Tom.

"I won't press charges against Maddie Grande, Mr. Abbott, now or in the future. I'd like you to pass that along to the New Orleans police. Call off the dogs. I'll see the twin who has confessed prosecuted, mark my words." A muscle twitched in Perkins's jaw. "You be sure to tell the authorities that I'll make certain that man does the time for the kidnapping, no matter what it costs me."

"I will, sir."

"I'll be contacting Pinkerton personally to let him know that you helped put Penelope's kidnapper behind bars and escorted her safely back to New Orleans."

"Thank you, sir." Tom was just relieved that Penelope was safe and that the case hadn't ended in tragedy. He felt Perkins was giving him far more praise than he deserved, but he couldn't waste time protesting.

Right now monetary reward was not in his mind. He was still

trying to accept the notion that Maddie had somehow redeemed herself enough to win her own freedom.

He bowed to Mary Perkins and Penelope and bid Peter Perkins good-bye. Perkins shook his hand and thanked Tom again. Tom was letting himself out when Penelope tugged on his coat sleeve.

"You'll keep your promise, won't you? Or do you still want her arrested?"

"I never wanted her arrested, but I had to follow the law."

"Will you let her know I didn't tell on her? I kept our secret as long as I could?"

He nodded. "I will if I ever see her again."

As long as Maddie thought she was still wanted, she was perfectly capable of staying hidden.

"Oh, you'll see her again," Penelope assured him. "You're sweet on her, no matter what you say. I think she's sweet on you too."

He took his leave convinced that in a few years, Miss Penelope Perkins would have a lot more men than just her father dancing to her tune.

Tom turned his thoughts to New Orleans and explaining the situation to Morgan. The official hunt for Maddie would be suspended. If it wasn't for the case that had led him to the Grandes in the first place—his search for Megan Lane—he could move on and forget all about her. But something Terrance said had haunted him since yesterday.

*"She tell you what she's good at? She tell you how she can make a child forget its own name?"*

She may have not only known Megan Lane, but she may have had a hand in turning her into a loyal tribe member.

Outside, Tom mounted up for a last ride down the alley of oaks. The kidnapping case was closed, but his heart was wide open. He saw Maddie's dark hair in the color of the rich southern soil. He heard her voice in the breeze rustling through the trees. The sunlight on her face reminded him of the warmth of her smile.

He hated to think about her running scared, but she was used to dodging the law to survive. She needed to know she was free, that Terrance had confessed. No matter what she'd done, he didn't want her on the run for the rest of her life.

It wouldn't take long to return to her cabin to give her the news. Then perhaps he could find out what she knew about the children taken in by Dexter Grande. With any luck, there might be a record of the children's former identities.

He could only hope she had returned to the bayou.

If she hadn't, he had no idea where to look next.

# CHAPTER 24

Frank Morgan was both surprised and relieved to hear Penelope was home. He promised to call off the search for Maddie and the girl and would contact Peter Perkins about pressing charges. There was nothing more for Tom to do but wire a report to Alan Pinkerton and await payment for services rendered.

He paid his rent, bathed, and changed into respectable clothing, and quickly read his mail. There was nothing of any urgency. He'd received a cordial letter from Laura Foster in Texas informing him that she had recently married and was now Mrs. Brand McCormick. She hoped every day brought him closer to a clue that might lead him to her sister.

He wasn't about to give Laura false hope, not until he found Maddie again and settled things with her. Only then could he pick up the thread that had led him to Maddie in the first place. She had nothing to lose. If Maddie knew where to find Megan Lane, why wouldn't she tell him? If she was Megan Lane, why not admit it?

Seated at his secretary desk, he took pen in hand and replied.

*Dear Mrs. McCormick,*

> *Congratulations on your recent nuptials. Searching for your sister may have inadvertently helped me solve a kidnapping case. I remain hopeful that eventually I will prove successful, though*

*after so many decades, the trail is quite cold. If and when I have
something new to report, I will contact you again.*

*Until then, I remain your humble servant,*

*Tom Abbott*

He folded the letter and carefully impressed a brass stamp with his initial in the warm sealing wax. He packed a clean shirt in his saddlebag, donned his concealed weapons, grabbed a hat, and made his way to the livery near the wharf. There, he found his horse and the one he'd bought to replace the mare comfortably stabled after their trip downriver.

After paying the livery owner, he had but one final errand before he left town. As he rode through the streets leading the spare horse, his gut told him Maddie was no longer there. He had nothing to go on but a hunch that she would return to the bayou before she moved on. If there was anything he'd learned during his years as a detective, it was to follow his hunches.

Tom reined in before a small shop off of Jackson Square. The windows were lined with furnishings and items women were fond of. He found what he was looking for, and within twenty minutes was on his way.

Maddie paced the interior of Anita's cabin while the older woman scalded a mixture of pickling to pour over a ham. The scent of molasses and allspice flavored the air but did nothing to whet Maddie's appetite.

"I'm not runnin'," the older woman insisted. "You do what you have to do, but I'm not guilty of nothing and I'm too old to up and move again."

"I can't leave you here on your own, Anita. It's 'cause of me that you're in this fix. I'll do what it takes to get us set up."

Maddie paused at Anita's shoulder, absently watched her stir the boiling ingredients. She'd skirted New Orleans on her return from Langetree and headed straight here.

"I owe you for the mare," Maddie added. "When I get some money together—"

Anita cut her off. "That old nag wasn't worth anything. Don't fret yourself over it. If Terrance gets out and comes asking for you, what should I tell him?"

"The truth. I don't know where I'm going."

Anita knew her well enough to know what she wasn't saying.

"I've known that boy since he was child. I believe it's high time you were shed of him anyway," Anita said.

"He's a man, Anita. Not a boy."

A man without honor. A man like Dexter. She'd realized that over the past few days; the rock that had been the foundation of her world had crumbled into dust. Tears burned and she quickly wiped them away, but not before Anita saw.

"It's time you moved on, Madeline. I've seen your desire to get out since long before Rene died. It's time to bury all your heartache, child, and make a new life for yourself while you're still young enough."

"Do you think I can?" Maddie whispered. "Do you really think I can start over?"

"I know you can. Deep down, you know it too. You can do anything you set your mind to."

For a good hour, Maddie tried to talk Anita into leaving, but to no avail. She knew the longer she tarried, the greater the risk of discovery. Anita walked her out to the dock.

"The Clifford cabin is deserted—least ways, that's what I hear," Anita said. "It's a good four miles up the bayou. You could be there before nightfall, go to ground, and hide for a few days. Now that the girl is safe, I'm willing to bet the police stop searching for you. They've got Terrance. That ought to hold them for a while."

"Terrance will never confess to the kidnapping, and Tom Abbott will never give up. If Penelope's word isn't enough, he'll need me to help charge Terrance with kidnapping."

Though she tried to put him out of her mind, it was impossible to forget and just as impossible to believe he would ever stop searching for her. His sense of honor wouldn't let him. No matter how long it took, he would see her behind bars.

She couldn't shake her fear of imprisonment anymore than she could forget him.

# CHAPTER 25

Hands on hips, Maddie stood in the middle of the cabin and studied the pile of things she'd stacked on the table — a pile she'd already culled by more than half. What remained wasn't much. A small bag of rice and one of red beans. Her skinning knife, a rope, and some cord. Two boxes of buckshot. Her oilskin. Three pair of stockings. A faded sunbonnet and a dark gray sweater at least one size too small but warm. She'd rolled up one of Lawrence's wool jackets along with a pair of his long johns in case the weather took a turn.

She had no money, possessed nothing of any value save the skills she'd acquired over a lifetime. She vowed if she made good on her escape and established herself elsewhere, she wouldn't use the tricks Dexter had taught her. She would have to rely on her hunting and trapping expertise — limited at best — and her housekeeping skills. Looking around the shack, she figured that was pitiful collateral.

She glanced out the window. Long shadows warned her the afternoon was slipping away. She had to hurry if she was going to leave before dark. Sorting through her meager possessions again, she reminded herself that she'd been lucky so far, but she couldn't depend on her luck holding forever. Hopefully, she hadn't lingered too long already.

She made a trip outside with her stack of clothes to load them in the pirogue.

She walked back in to get more, closed the front door, and gasped when she swung around and found Abbott standing inside the back door holding a large box. Her hand flew to her heart.

"You!"

Frantic, she scanned the room. Her shotgun was propped against the wall within Tom's reach. They both saw it at the same time.

Her shoulders sagged. She stared at him from across the cabin. They both spoke at once.

"I knew you'd come," she said.

"I thought you'd be long gone." He looked at the table. "You're packing to leave."

She nodded. There'd be no running now.

He stepped into the room, ignored the shotgun, and held out the box. She hesitated before accepting and then set it on the table. "Open it," he said. "It's for you."

"I don't want anything from you." Afraid of losing herself in his stare, she tried to look away but wound up focusing on his lips.

"It's a gift."

"Unless it's a key, it won't do me much good in jail," she said softly.

"You're not going to prison, Maddie."

"You're willing to let me go?"

"Terrance confessed. Said he forced you to hide Penelope. Since you returned her of your own accord, you're in the clear."

Afraid her legs would give out, she felt around for a chair. Suddenly Tom was beside her. He tossed his hat on the table, drew out a chair, and helped her ease into it.

"I'm not wanted?"

He smiled. "You know how convincing Miss Penelope Perkins can be. She pleaded your case. Fortunately for you, she has her father wrapped around her little finger."

Maddie wound her own fingers together in her lap, trying to believe there was no reason to run anymore. Save one.

"What's going to happen to Terrance?"

"There will be a trial in a few weeks. He shot a policeman and kidnapped a child. I doubt he'll be free for years."

"Years," she whispered. "Are you certain?"

"He shot Lawrence. We'll never know if it was accidental or not."

Thankful she was already sitting down, she shook her head. "He shot Lawrence? You never said so before."

Tom shrugged. "I figured you had enough to handle."

"Lots of men get set free these days." New Orleans was notorious for its corrupted legal system. That was something Dexter always counted on. "No matter what they did."

"Stop your worrying. Mr. Perkins might be a Yankee, but he's got a lot of wealth and power behind him. He'll see that Terrance pays for what he did."

She could live the life she'd started here, this time alone. She could stay close to Anita, help out as the woman grew older.

Or she could trap and hunt and save enough money to leave with a free conscience. She could start over where no one knew who or what she was. The choice was hers.

While she sat silently contemplating, Tom reached around her, picked up the box, and set it on her lap. "Open it," he urged.

She looked up at him curiously before untying the thin piece of cord around it. When she lifted the lid, she saw a finely crafted oil lamp nestled deep in excelsior. The chimney, fluted and rimmed by decorative glass beads, was packed beside the lamp bowl.

"It's lovely," she said softly. He held the box for her while she drew out the lamp pieces and set them on the table. "Far too pretty for this place."

He was so close his arm brushed her shoulder as he reached around her to set the box down. Seconds passed in silence as Tom stared into her eyes.

"You're the most beautiful thing in this room, Maddie."

Before she could say anything, he lowered himself to one knee and took her hands in his. It was impossible to pull away as she stared into the dark depths of his eyes.

"I was convinced I was a loner, that there was no place in my life for a woman, but I'm afraid I'm falling in love with you, Maddie Grande."

For the second time that afternoon, tears filled her eyes. She blinked furiously and pulled her hand free to wipe them away.

"You don't know me," she said. "You think you know who I am, what I've done, but you don't know the half of it."

"I know you've lost two children—"

"My husband was knifed in an alley in New Orleans over a stolen watch."

She looked at the ceiling for a moment before she could meet his gaze again.

"He died over a gold *watch*. Louie was a thief. Just like me. Just like all of us." A tear streaked down her cheek. "We were so proud of our son, Rene." She shook her head in disbelief. "We were proud because he had a knack for stealing. By five he was following in Louie's footsteps—"

"Stop." Tom pressed his fingertips to her lips, then ran his knuckles along her cheek. "I don't care about your past."

"You should," she protested. "You are a Pinkerton. A man of honor. A man who tracks down thieves and cutthroats like me and puts them behind bars and I—"

"You are a woman who deserves a second chance at life. You deserve to love and be loved again."

"Yesterday you were going to turn me in to the police."

"I had to do my duty. That doesn't mean it wasn't killing me. Now you're free to start over and be the caring, nurturing woman I know you are."

She was speechless. He believed in her when she could only doubt. He believed there was goodness inside her. She thought of Betsy and her strong faith. She remembered what Penelope had said.

"Do you think everyone has good in them, Tom?"

He thought about it for a moment, searched her eyes. The light in his own eyes dimmed. He shook his head no.

"I've seen too much bad in the world to believe there is good in everyone, but—"

"I agree. Which is why this is crazy. I won't deny that you and I are attracted to each other, but you don't really love me. You love the woman you want me to be. What if all I'll ever be is a thief and a liar?" She looked down at their hands. "You are a man of honor," she whispered. "I have none."

He got up, pulled over another chair, and sat down beside her. She glanced out the open back door. Night was fast approaching.

"You should go," she told him.

"I won't give up that easily," he said.

"Believe me, I know that."

"Why did you refuse the Perkins's reward?"

"Right up until the moment I saw Mrs. Perkins's face, I wanted that money."

"I think you took Penelope home because you cared about her and because you knew her mother was suffering."

She bit her bottom lip to keep it from trembling. "You have no idea what I've done."

"You can't help the way you were raised, Madeline."

She searched his face as the past rose up to haunt her. Needing to move, she got to her feet, walking across the room. Flushed and obviously more than a little angry, she heard him close the distance between them. When she tried to bury her face in her hands, he took hold of her wrists. She fought to pull away but he wouldn't let go.

"Look at me, Maddie," he said softly. "Whatever you were, whatever that man forced you to become, is not your fault."

Seeing the warehouse again had brought it all back and stripped away all but the ugly truth. Dexter wasn't a revered father who'd created a close-knit tribe of urchins and molded them into a family, but a heartless monster who played at being a god.

"I'm no better than he was."

"He preyed upon defenseless children—"

"And I helped him." She didn't try to look away or hide her shame this time. This man thought he loved her. He surely wouldn't once the whole dark truth was out.

"Make up for what you did by helping me now. I'm looking for a woman who may have been taken into the tribe as a child twenty-three years ago."

She paused. "You met a missionary in the city. Her name used to be Betsy—"

"Mrs. Henson."

She nodded. "We were close once, like sisters. I saw her when I had Penelope with me. She told me a Pinkerton had been questioning her."

"I spoke to her before I knew of the kidnapping. She had mentioned the twins. I put her information together with what the police knew. Tracking the twins led me to you and Anita. I think both you and this Elizabeth, or Betsy, know more than you're saying about the tribe members. What's important now, Maddie, is that families be reunited."

She laughed at the idea. "Reunited? Who would want any of us now?"

"You might be surprised. Did Dexter keep a list of the children's birth names or where they came from?"

"Of course not." She brushed her hair back off her face. "Not that I know of, anyway. Everything he had is long gone now. There's nothing at the old warehouse. We made it so the children didn't even know their own names."

"How is that possible?"

"It can be done. Betsy did it and because I was Dexter's favorite, she taught me how to 'change' the children he brought into the tribe."

"What do you mean, 'change'?"

She closed her eyes. Her fingers tightened around his.

"Whenever Dexter brought a little one into the tribe, it was up to me and Betsy to 'change' them into one of us." She had to swallow before she could go on. "We put them in armoires, locked them in. Kept them in the dark for weeks, gave them little food and water. We convinced them bad men were after them, men who had killed their parents."

"Dexter kidnapped all those children?"

"No. Not all. He said some were given to him by their parents, people too poor, too hungry, to keep them. Some had been orphans living on the streets and came to us. Those we didn't have to change. It was just the little ones Dexter brought home."

"Did someone change you?"

The idea was abhorrent and terrifying. To even think that once she might have belonged to a real family broke her heart. It would also mean that her entire life had been built upon Dexter's lies.

"I wasn't changed. My parents were friends of Dexter's when they died of yellow fever. They asked him to raise me."

"Do you remember them?"

"No."

"How old were you?"

"I'm not sure. Three, maybe."

"How old are you now?"

"I ... I'm not sure. Twenty-six, I think."

"You're certain you weren't changed?"

"Yes. Betsy would have told me the truth; if not back then, she would have told me when I saw her the other night. She was my closest friend."

"And the twins?"

"I changed Terrance. She changed Lawrence."

"Do you remember their real names? Before they were changed?"

She heard the disgust in his voice. The disbelief.

"No."

"Is Madeline your real name? What was your last name?"

"Stop it, Tom! Is this what you do when you interrogate some-one? Keep going round and round? Trying to catch them in a lie? Of course it's my name." She tried to walk away but he followed her across the room.

He lowered his voice. "The families of those missing children deserve to know what happened to them."

"But they were *not* kidnapped." Even as she protested, she realized she could not be completely certain. She was used to parroting what Dexter had told her. She would never know the truth now.

Before she could protest, she found herself enfolded in Tom's embrace. He'd moved quickly, smoothly. He was braced for a struggle, she could feel it, but all of the fight had gone out of her.

She melted against him and went so far as to rest her head on his shoulder. If only life was as easy as simply saying yes to the love he offered, as simple as believing in new tomorrows.

She sighed and closed her eyes. His shoulder was warm and solid beneath the fabric of his jacket. She rubbed her cheek against it, inhaled his clean, spicy scent. He stroked her back, ran his fingers through her hair.

His silence was a gift. His embrace a comfort and a temptation.

She didn't deserve Tom Abbott's love. She would never deserve him.

Maddie took a deep breath and lifted her head. She stared into the depths of his eyes, touched the crisp curl on his forehead. She held her breath, knowing what was sure to come.

He leaned close and kissed her. Softly, gently at first, and then with an intensity that matched her own. She kissed him back knowing it was good-bye and that she would never kiss him again. Then she pulled away and folded her arms across her midriff, little comfort against her pain.

"Please go now," she whispered.

"But Maddie—"

She saw the confusion in his eyes and was sorry for the kiss. It was one more selfish transgression to add to her long list.

"Go. You're only torturing yourself."

He looked at her possessions piled on the table. "Are you still leaving?"

"I don't know." She knew she couldn't stay. He would dog her and never give up trying to win her heart. "I guess it's my life to do with as I please now."

"You know I'll find you again, Maddie. No matter where you run. Finding people is what I do and I'm good at it."

"Please. Just go and leave me be."

*Before I lose my resolve. Before I beg you to stay.*

She could see he was angry as he turned on his heel, walked over to the table, and picked up his hat. He walked out without bidding her good-bye.

Maddie went over to the table. She started to reach for the glass chimney of the new lamp, but her hands were shaking too hard to trust and so she left it there. Tom Abbott not only knew about Dexter and her past, but now he also knew her darkest secret and what she was capable of. No one outside of the tribe knew of the "changing."

Any idea of love he thought he had for her would soon fade once he had a chance to contemplate what she'd told him.

Broken, she sank onto a chair and let her tears fall.

# CHAPTER 26

As confused as he was angry, Tom decided that if this was what came of being in love, then he was lucky he'd never fallen before. Until now he had convinced himself that marriage was out of the question. He loved his work and felt there was no room in his life for marriage and a family. Maddie had changed all of that. There was no denying the passion behind their kiss before she demanded he walk out of her life. But there was also no denying the pain.

He stood beside his horse, furious at himself for walking out, furious at her for turning him away. He was sick to death of doing the right thing. Seeing her suffer for what she'd done in Dexter's name, he found himself searching for words of comfort, but nothing could express the depth of his sympathy. That so many innocent children had suffered along with her was incomprehensible.

Seeing Maddie in such despair made it easy to forget he sought justice through law and honor. Right now he was just thankful that Dexter Grande was beyond his reach.

Twilight was upon him, yet in this primeval world where only scant sunlight filtered through the lush, interwoven branches of the treetops, there was little difference between night and day. He turned and stared at the dark interior of the cabin, thought of the woman sitting there alone.

He'd been shocked when he heard that she didn't remember her own past. She still furtively clung to the idea that she had not been "changed" simply because Grande assured her she hadn't been, but Tom suspected she had been victimized like the others. Claiming her parents had left Maddie in his safekeeping was a very convenient story from a man who collected children. What caring parents knowingly turned their child over to a master thief and confidence man?

If Dexter had lied to her, who was she? Where had she come from? She appeared to be in her late twenties, but she could be younger or older. Megan Lane would be thirty-two now. What if Maddie was the woman he'd been searching for all along?

*Impossible*, he thought. *Insane. But what if?*

Surely there were stranger coincidences in life.

As the fog crept in off the water, he warned himself to take care. He thought of Laura McCormick in Texas, of Maddie. And of himself. He was in danger of breaking so many hearts — but if Maddie turned out to be Megan Lane, not only would he have reunited the sisters, but he would give Maddie the gift of knowing who she really was along with a family and a new start.

He watched a small flame flare, and then the yellow glow of lamplight filled Maddie's shack. Her silhouette passed by the window. He went back to the open door without making a sound. Inside, Maddie was carrying a mug to the table. She hadn't heard him, hadn't seen him yet.

"Megan?" His voice carried across the room.

He'd expected her to turn and tell him to leave again. He hadn't expected her to drop the mug. It shattered and spilled coffee on the floor. Color drain from her face, and she turned pale as chalk. She stared at him with red and swollen eyes.

"What did you just say?" She trembled violently, her hands fisted at her sides. She watched him warily as he crossed the room.

"Megan."

She flinched again, as if he'd slapped her. He crossed the room, took hold of her arm.

"Does the name mean something to you?"

"No."

"Then why are you shaking?"

"You frightened me. Isn't that enough?" She shoved away, went to get a dishrag. He picked up the remains of the mug.

"There's something more."

"It's just a name." She shook her head and knelt to mop up the puddle of coffee.

When she finished, he reached out and pulled her to her feet. She came willingly, too distraught to fight him. He smoothed her hair back off her forehead, tipped her face toward the lamplight. Her brows were perfectly matched, evenly arched.

"Let me go," she whispered.

He did. She walked outside.

The fog hugged the water but could not silence its gentle slosh against the pilings. The night air was cool and damp. Maddie hugged herself as she stood at the very end of the crooked dock, staring down into the mist.

Tom walked up behind her, tempted to draw her into his embrace, but did not dare.

She surprised him, suddenly turning her back on the water. They were face-to-face now, inches from each other.

"Who is Megan?"

Impossible, he thought.

Perhaps he held the key to the door to a new life for her, a life that would take her far away from him.

"Tom? Who is she?"

"You have no idea?" He'd found his voice, but not his courage.

"Yes. I'm afraid she's the girl in my nightmare," she whispered. "One of the children I changed. I don't know why else the name would frighten me so."

He ran his hands down her arms, took hold of her right hand,

and led her to a low bench outside the front door. She sat down, leaned against the wall of the shack.

Seeking confirmation, he said, "Tell me about your nightmare."

After a hesitation, she took a deep breath. Her voice took on a far-away quality as she spoke.

"I'm always a child again, running, always running through the streets of New Orleans, trying to keep up with another little girl. She pulls me along, refusing to let go of my hand." She paused, closed her eyes but only for a second. "There's a man with us, a tall man—"

"Dexter."

She shook her head. "No. Definitely someone else. I never see his face. He's tall and much thinner, like a scarecrow. His back is to us. He's in a hurry, dragging her along. She's tugging on me. We form a chain of three. I can't break free."

He could see the telling was painful, but she went on.

"She won't let go. Once I asked Dexter about the nightmare, fearing he'd lied to me and I had been changed like the others, but he swore I wasn't. He said when I was small, I got lost in the market stalls and screamed for Betsy. He said that's all the nightmare was—a memory of my terror that day."

"What does she look like, this girl in your dream?"

Maddie frowned. "I don't know," she whispered. "She hasn't any face. When she turns to me, she *has no face*, Tom. That's what is so terrifying. There's *nothing* where her face should be."

"The name Megan Lane—"

"Is it her name? Is it the name of the faceless girl?" She looked as terrified as she was hopeful that he could put an end to her nightmares. "Who is she?"

Not once since he'd known her had she been this fragile. He might have the knowledge to put the pieces of her life back together, to make her whole. But did he have the courage to tell her when the truth would take her away?

Because he loved her, there was only one choice he could make.

"Based on your reaction, I think it's you, Maddie. I think *your* name is really Megan Lane."

"That's impossible," she whispered. "I'm Madeline. Madeline Grande."

"Your name may have been Madeline, but not Grande. Think, Maddie. If your parents gave you to Dexter, you would have had a name other than Grande at one time."

"We were all renamed Grande."

"It's very possible Dexter lied about your family." He took a deep breath, told her about Laura Foster McCormick's search for the sister she hadn't seen in over twenty years.

"Laura's name was Lovie Lane back then. Does that mean anything to you?"

Tears welled up in Maddie's eyes. "I've never heard it before but ..." She grabbed his hands, held on tight. "I feel as if I'm coming apart inside and out."

Her fear was palpable. No longer able to watch her suffer, he wrapped her in his arms and rocked her gently, shushing her with whispers and kisses against her temple. In the state she was in, he doubted she was even aware of what he was doing or she would have never allowed it.

Maddie was very aware of the warmth of his embrace, the comfort of Tom's strong arms around her, his lips against her skin. He placed each kiss with tenderness and care.

Even if she was someone else, what difference did it make now? What relation would want to claim her? She had been Maddie Grande for too long. Her soul was tarnished. She was not worthy of his love.

Tom's lips were moving near her temple. He whispered, "Surely you know better than anyone that Dexter was a confidence man, a master manipulator. Didn't you ever catch him in a lie?"

Sadness filled her heart, like the fog that crept slowly along the bayou. Sadness and humiliation not of her making.

"After Dexter died, Anita told me that my marriage had been a sham. Dexter had sensed I was changing, that I wanted out, so he brought Louie into the tribe. As he planned, Louie and I fell in love. We believed him when he claimed he had the power to marry us. He was so proud. We would be the first of his tribe united in marriage. It was only after Dexter died that I learned he hadn't any legal right to perform a marriage ceremony. We were little more than children ourselves. How could we have known any different? He was in complete control of our lives. We believed everything he told us."

She remembered how furious Anita was when Dexter pronounced them man and wife. Anita knew the truth. It was all a sham. But Maddie wanted to believe in the lovely lie, for it was, after all, her wedding day.

"My children were illegitimate," she sighed. "At least Louie never knew." It was another pound of shame added to the burden she already carried.

Now that her initial shock had passed, she found the strength to raise her head and meet Tom's eyes. They were shadowed by more than the darkness of the night. There was worry there, and deep concern.

She sat up straighter, but didn't pull out of his embrace.

"If this is all just some story you've concocted to keep me here . . ."

"I was looking for Megan Lane before I connected the twins to the kidnapping. Elizabeth Henson told me to talk to Anita Russo. That would have led me to question you eventually, even if there had been no kidnapping."

His arm was still draped around her shoulders. She leaned back against the wall, folded her arms around her waist, and stared out into the dark. The fog had dissipated. High overhead, the sky was spattered with stars. In the distance, a bullfrog croaked. Then there came a loud splash and the sound was silenced.

"There is only one way to find out, you know," he said. "Laura Foster McCormick."

"Laura McCormick." The name called no face to mind. "What does she look like?"

"We met years ago, during the war. Long before she moved to Texas. She's beautiful. Blonde. Blue-eyed. Looks a bit like your friend, the missionary."

"Nothing like me."

"She describes Megan as having brown hair, brownish eyes, and fair skin. Her parents were Irish. That describes one of a million women in New Orleans." He paused. "I think you should go to Texas and meet her. Perhaps she can identify you."

*Texas.* The idea was daunting, not to mention insane. "I don't have the money to get to Texas."

"I'll take you, of course."

"I can't let you do that."

"Mrs. McCormick will pay the expenses. Hopefully she can put all doubt to rest once she sees you."

"You're grasping at straws, Tom. You want me to be more than I am. Turning me into this Megan Lane is the most convenient way."

He shook his head and took her hand.

"Believe me, Maddie, there's a part of me that hopes you are *not* Megan Lane, because that would open up a world of opportunity for you. You'll have family, and if I know Laura, you'll have a home too. One that's miles and miles from here."

It was insane to even consider there was a chance, and yet, what if the woman in Texas proved to be the faceless girl of her nightmare? The girl who once promised *"I'll watch out for you. No matter what."*

What if that girl *had* been searching for her for all these years?

"If she is my sister, she surely won't want someone like me in her life."

"Why not give her a chance to make up her mind?"

Maddie knew she'd get no sleep this night. Just then Tom's stomach rumbled.

"Sorry," he apologized.

It served as a good excuse for Maddie to let go of his hand. She was amazed to discover she had the strength to stand.

"You must be starving. I've some turnip pie."

"I don't want to put you out, but if you're eating, I'll take some."

She shook her head. "I'm not hungry, but let's not let it go to waste. Besides, you can eat by the light of the lovely lamp you gave me."

Tom followed her inside, both of them thinking of everything he'd just told her, neither willing to speak of it again just yet. He pulled out a chair and sat down after Maddie refused his offer to help. She dished up a huge slice of thick-crust turnip pie.

She didn't eat a bite but was content to sit nearby and watch. Neither of them said much, but their unspoken words hung heavy on the air.

"It's getting late." He leaned back in his chair.

"Too late for you to leave now."

Their eyes met and held. Her cheeks flushed and she looked away.

"If you don't mind, I'll bed down in the shed again," he offered.

Relieved, she nodded her assent and went to collect some blankets and a pillow off one of the twins' cots. She walked him to the door, handed him the bundle. The night was cool but dry.

It had been a long time since she'd known a man's touch, the feel of a man's hands on her. It was the first time she'd been tempted since Louie died. But Tom was a man of duty and honor and she . . . She wasn't certain who or what she was anymore.

"Think about everything I said tonight," he urged as he stood in the doorway again.

"As if I will be thinking of anything else." She almost smiled.

"Tomorrow we'll make plans to leave for Texas, but only if you want."

Maddie watched him walk alone down the narrow path toward the shed. She might not have known who she was, but she knew what she wanted: a man she didn't deserve.

# CHAPTER 27

Maddie gave up trying to sleep and rose long before dawn. She stoked the fire in the stove and mixed up a batch of biscuits. The table was set when Tom knocked on the back door. Despite a determined effort not to react, her heart jumped when she saw him standing there with water droplets glistening in his hair. His shirt collar was damp. A night's growth of stubble covered his jaw, which was both masculine and tempting. She could almost feel his rough beard against her cheek.

He looked as if he hadn't gotten any more sleep than she. His gaze roamed over her, and her knees went weak.

"Come in." She stepped aside and he walked past her. Thankfully he didn't bring up the subject of Texas until he'd polished off two helpings of everything and plenty of coffee.

Silence lengthened in the cabin as the minutes ticked by. Finally, Tom casually linked his arm around the back of his chair and studied her closely.

"Have you made a decision, Maddie?"

At least she tried to smile. He didn't even make an attempt.

"What if I go to Texas and this woman, this Laura Foster McCormick, wants to find her sister so badly that she's ready to believe I'm the one ... even if I'm not?"

"I'm willing to bet she wants to be as certain as you."

It was impossible to ignore him. His presence filled up the cabin the way thinking of him filled up the empty spaces in her heart. She took a deep breath, drummed her fingers against the tabletop. "She may not want anything to do with me once she finds out about my life."

Unable to sit still any longer, she walked over to the stove, picked up a pot holder, and moved the coffeepot off of the front burner.

Texas was a world away from everything she knew; her old life in New Orleans, her love of the bayou. If Mrs. McCormick proved to be her sister, if the woman offered her a place in her life, would she miss Louisiana? Would she think of Tom Abbott and find herself wondering what might have been?

If she truly was Megan Lane, would she miss Maddie Grande?

There was only one way to find out.

She turned to Tom. He was still waiting for an answer.

"I won't need to take much, I guess," she said, looking around the cabin.

Tom waited without comment, his expression closed.

"When should we leave?"

He slowly stood, carefully pushed the chair beneath the table. His hat was on the closest cot. He picked it up, dusted it off with his cuff. "As soon as you can be ready. I have a bit of business to attend to first. A day in New Orleans should do it."

"How long will the journey take?"

"I'm not sure, exactly. We'll go by train whenever we can."

Her things were packed. "I can be ready in a quarter hour," she said.

"I'll wait outside, give you some time alone."

"There's one more thing. I almost hate to ask."

"Anything."

"I need to see Terrance. To ... to tell him good-bye before we go."

She could see that he was less than happy with her request.

He straightened his jacket collar. Fiddled with a button. Finally he said, "I can arrange it if that's what you want."

"I do. I need to see him. He could have let me go to prison for the kidnapping too, but he didn't."

"I understand, but I'm going with you. You'll not face him alone."

She nodded. "Thank you." He started for the door. She stopped him. "Tom?"

"Yes?"

"This is impossible, you know. I'm not the one."

"We'll see, won't we?"


He apologized for the state of his apartment. Maddie didn't know why. The place was larger than her cabin and he lived there all alone. On the second floor of a building with a lovely walled garden, light poured through double-glass doors that opened out onto a balcony that overlooked the street below. The apartment mirrored the man himself; well kept, organized, with few personal touches to give any hint as to the nature of the person dwelling there.

He found lodging for her with his landlady, Mrs. Matthews. The woman was more than happy to have her stay in her spare room. Tom went to make arrangements for their journey and left Maddie uncomfortably settled with the talkative widow. She pretended to listen to a stream of idle chatter while sipping café au lait.

An hour later, there came a knock on the door and Mrs. Matthews ushered in an elegantly dressed woman accompanied by a young mulatto girl in her teens carrying large bundles wrapped in muslin.

Mrs. Matthews smiled and looked over at Maddie with new regard. "Miss Grande, this is Madame Bouchard." Mrs. Matthews's excitement was more than evident. "She is *the* most well-known seamstress in New Orleans."

The lean, sophisticated woman in a lovely pearl-gray gown gave a slight bow and spoke in a pretty French accent. "I am here to help you with your travel wardrobe, mademoiselle." She turned to Mrs. Matthews. "You have a room we can use, I suppose?"

Mrs. Matthews led the way as Maddie followed the short procession down the hall. Her concern grew with every step. The moment the bedroom door closed, the young girl began pulling an assortment of expensive gowns out of muslin bags.

"I'm afraid there's been some mistake," Maddie began. "I can't afford any of these things, madame." She glanced back and forth from the seamstress to the gowns. Any other woman would be captivated by the pile of fine fabrics and ruffles in raspberry, navy, and a stunning emerald-green wool. Maddie worried.

Madame Bouchard was in the process of shaking out the emerald piece, a hip-length hooded cape with silk frogs for closure. She handed the cape to her assistant.

"Let's not speak of money, mademoiselle. Mr. Abbott assured me that he wants you to have the best, and so only the best is what I have brought with me. Such short notice, though. I'm afraid you will have to choose from ready-made things." She leaned closer and lowered her voice secretively. "Lucky for all of us that the woman who contracted these items is close to your height and measurements. She will never know that I remade her order."

"But . . ."

"*Non, non.* Remove your blouse and skirt, mademoiselle. We both know they have seen better days. Besides, Mr. Abbott is anxious to begin the journey tomorrow. To Texas, is it? We've no time to waste."

Maddie stood her ground.

"My things are perfectly suitable, madame."

Madame Bouchard's gaze took in Maddie's black skirt and white blouse. She stepped closer and met Maddie's level gaze, her accent suddenly gone.

"Look, Miss Grande, we both know your things may be serviceable for doing housework or however else you are accustomed to spending your time. But they are not at all suitable for traveling across the country in the company of a gentleman like Mr. Abbott. Not at all. I think you would do well to choose all of the garments I've brought along today if for no other reason than *not* to embarrass him."

Maddie doubted her appearance would embarrass Tom Abbott. When he'd boarded the riverboat with her and Penelope, he wasn't in the least embarrassed to be seen with them and they had all been the worse for wear.

No, she knew exactly what his intentions were. He wanted her to eradicate the image of Maddie Grande before he introduced her to her *supposed* sister.

Maddie thought about walking out of the room, but Madame Bouchard remained insistent, waiting impatiently for her to undress. Her assistant was close to tears. It wasn't the seamstress's fault that Tom wanted her to appear more presentable. The woman was only trying to do her job.

Maddie sighed and began to unbutton her blouse, instantly drawn into a flurry of fittings as the seamstress and her assistant marked and pinned the clothing for immediate alteration. She chose two demitrained skirts suitable for travel with matching spencer-waist blouses. Nothing with tiers of ruffles or sculpted bows would do. The plainer the better, she insisted. The seamstress tried to talk her into more. Maddie refused. The items she chose only needed hemming.

The stunning green cloak with a gathered hood was by far her favorite. She insisted the cape was all she really needed. Her own clothing could be hidden beneath.

Madame Bouchard *tsk*ed and shook her head. Her heavy French accent had returned. "Take two more gowns, mademoiselle. Any other woman would take them all."

"I am not any other woman, madame."

Tom Abbott had offered her his heart and she'd refused it. She had no right to cause him considerable expense, even though this wild-goose chase to Texas was his idea.

Madame Bouchard and her assistant worked tirelessly and at the end of three hours pronounced the pieces ready.

"Now that I know your size, I will send over a night dress for you. Something in the finest cotton with a yoke and full sleeves." Madame Bouchard looked well-satisfied as her assistant packed the more formal gowns Maddie had obstinately refused.

Maddie had never had one single article of clothing that was new, not even a simple nightgown. She found herself blushing, picturing Tom Abbott going over the receipts and discovering he had paid for a nightgown. She made a silent vow to pay him back no matter how long it took.

As soon as Madame Bouchard left, Maddie went straight to Mrs. Matthews. She set aside the shame of her illiteracy and explained that she needed the woman to kindly pen Tom's name and address for her. She had no idea what might come, but at least she would know where to send payments to Tom when she had funds to spare.

Though she appeared curious, Mrs. Matthews obliged without question and handed Maddie a slip of paper with the information on it. Maddie carried it to her room and safely tucked it away.

Tom spent the afternoon wiring Alan Pinkerton and Laura Foster McCormick, then made plans for the trip. He procured tickets for the New Orleans Opelousas and Great Western Railroad departing for Braeshear City early the next morning. Located at the port on Berwick Bay, Braeshear was the end of the rail line across southern Louisiana. From there they would board a steamer headed for Galveston and, upon arrival, continue by train up to Dallas.

It was hard enough knowing he might never see Maddie again. Planning the journey, aware that he would be in her company across southern Louisiana and up the length of Texas, had him doubting his own sanity.

By the time he returned to his apartment, he was convinced that he was a masochist of the first order, but he couldn't very well send Maddie off by herself. Nor could he trust her to meet Laura McCormick on her own. He was prepared to escort her all the way to Glory even if it killed him.

What he wasn't prepared for was her ire when he returned home and stopped in at Mrs. Matthews's apartment. He could tell Maddie was furious the minute his landlady ushered him inside. At least Maddie waited until Mrs. Matthews excused herself before she turned on him.

"The seamstress you sent over arrived." Maddie crossed the small parlor, keeping distance between them.

"She was accommodating, I hope? Did she have anything to your liking?"

"My liking? Everything she brought was to my liking, but all too terribly expensive. I tried to send her away—"

"Why?"

"Because I'm not some charity case, Tom. I am what I am. If this Laura Foster or McCormick—or whatever her name is—is so shallow that my appearance matters, or if it helps to persuade her I'm her sister, then she's not someone I want to be related to. And if you are too embarrassed to travel with me the way I am—" She held out the sides of her brown serge skirt and let it fall. "—then I beg you let me go back to the bayou and forget this whole thing."

He walked close enough to touch her, but didn't.

"I don't care what Mrs. McCormick thinks of your clothes." Before she could walk away, he reached for her hand. She tried to tug free but he wouldn't let go. He pulled her closer, lowered his voice. "You don't know me very well if you think you would ever embarrass me. No matter what you were wearing."

"But, Tom—"

"I thought you'd be pleased," he said softly. "I thought all women liked new clothes. I didn't mean to insult you, Maddie."

He could see his reasoning surprised her. She stared into his eyes, searching for the truth. She must have found it, for he felt her relax.

"It will take me forever to repay you."

"They're gifts."

"Gifts I can't accept."

"You willingly lived on stolen goods, no doubt, but you won't accept gifts?"

"That's a terrible thing to say." She looked away and then admitted, "But it's true."

"I didn't say it to hurt you." He tried to pull her closer but she wouldn't budge. "I wanted you to see that you are changing, Maddie. Whether you know it or not."

He wished she realized she was not merely a thief unworthy of love. How long would it take for her to see that?

She raised her chin a notch and promised, "I'll repay you."

Her unwillingness to accept anything from him was irritating. "Don't worry," he said coolly. "Your sister will compensate me."

It was a false promise. Maddie's clothing was his gift to her.

"And if I'm not Megan Lane?"

"Consider the debt paid. I've always wanted to see Texas."

It was a warm evening. The doors to the balcony were open. The splash of the fountain in the garden below drifted upstairs along with the scent of jasmine. He longed to pull her into his arms, to kiss her—but she'd made her wishes quite clear at the cabin. He let go of her hand.

"We leave at dawn tomorrow," he said. "Right after we pay a visit to Terrance."

She took a deep breath, steadied herself. "I'll be ready."

He wished he could say the same.

# CHAPTER 28

Closeted alone in the small room where she would face Terrance, Maddie wished she hadn't asked Tom to wait outside. Despite pleasant weather, the first floor of the old precinct building was cool and damp. When she heard the rattle and slide of chains in the hallway, a shiver ran down her spine. She knew it wasn't from the cold.

Terrance walked in, shackled at the wrists and ankles. He balked when he saw her, pinned her with an ice-blue stare, then continued into the room. She saw the slight upward curl of his lip, knew that this meeting would not bode well for her. Unwilling to let him intimidate her, she sat up straighter and pressed her palms against her thighs beneath the table.

The guard with Terrance pulled out one of two empty chairs, and Terrance sat down opposite her. The guard stepped back. For a moment, she and Terrance exchanged a silent stare.

"Fine new clothes you've got on." His voice was low and hoarse, but she heard the smirk in it. "You must be keepin' that Pinkerton happy."

There was nothing she could say to defend herself. Not anything he would understand anyway.

"What'd you come for?" he demanded. "To gloat?"

"I came to say good-bye."

"Unless you know somethin' I don't, I'm not going anywhere."

"I am. I'm going to Texas."

"*Texas*?" It was the first time she'd ever seen him this shocked. "What in blazes you gonna do in Texas?"

She shrugged. "Maybe start over."

He snorted. "You'll never change. We can't change who we are any more than a gator can stand up and walk on two legs. You'll see."

Her gaze shifted to the empty chair beside him.

"Do you miss him?"

"Who?"

She knew he would show no emotion that he considered a weakness. Even she hadn't really allowed herself to grieve over Lawrence. In the tribe people came and went. That's the way it was.

"Lawrence. Do you miss him?"

"He was always too soft. Too slow. I had to do all the thinking for him." Terrance shrugged. "Now I got less to worry about."

She thought back to her first memory of the twins. It was night. Dexter had walked into the abandoned warehouse on Canal Street with a sobbing, identical four-year-old boy on each hip. She was seated on the floor with her back to the wall tossing dice with Betsy.

Betsy looked up expectedly. Until that night, Dexter had given all the new recruits into Betsy's care, but this time he said, "Here you go, Madeline." He lowered one of the terrified boys onto her lap. "Time you learned our initiation ritual."

"Good luck, Maddie," Betsy said. "You seen me do this often enough you know how. But if you need help, just ask."

Maddie looked at the sobbing child on her lap and gave him a shake. "Hush," she whispered in his ear. "No crying. It's dangerous. Be still now."

"I want my mama." The boy's breath caught. He shuddered and nestled close.

Maddie had watched and learned carefully. She was twelve, and now it was time to prove herself to Dexter. She looked forward to his praise. Confident, she carried her twin to a rickety cupboard where Dexter kept a glass jar filled with hard candies. She popped one into the boy's mouth, set him down, and then led him by the hand to one of four huge, intricately carved armoires positioned around the warehouse. She turned the key, opened the armoire, and indicated the empty space with a wave of her hand.

"Get in. You'll be safe there."

"I want my mama ..." The terrified twin stared into the armoire and then up at Maddie. He grabbed hold of her skirt and wadded it into his grimy little fist.

She knelt before him, held his tear-stained face between her hands. "Listen to me and listen well. Your mama is dead. You have no one left in this world but us."

"But—" His eyes widened. He glanced toward the huge sliding door of the warehouse, then he searched the open spaces. Betsy had already tucked the other boy out of sight. The child opened his mouth as if he were about to wail. Maddie put her hand over his lips and leaned close.

"Bad men are after you. It's lucky Dexter found you or you'd be dead already. Now get in and stay there. When it's safe, I'll let you out. You speak to no one but me. Trust *no one* but me."

When she lifted her hand away from his mouth, the boy was still terrified but no longer wailing.

"I'm scairt of the dark," he whispered.

"You should be more scared of what those horrible men will do if they find you. Now get in."

He climbed inside.

"Sit," she commanded.

He slipped down the inside wall and hugged his knees to his chest.

"Keep quiet no matter what you hear. I'll bring you food when it's safe."

She quickly slammed the door before he could protest. Betsy

watched from across the room, her own ward already safely locked away. The older girl nodded as Maddie turned the key in the lock.

Within five minutes both boys were pounding on the doors, screaming to be let out. They cried until they grew hoarse and their screams subsided.

Maddie covered her ears until the only sounds issuing from the cupboard were hiccups and an occasional weak moan. Finally she tapped on the armoire door.

"You'd best be quiet, boy," she whispered. "The bad men are right outside."

She and Betsy went back to tossing dice.

"Wonder what he'll name them," Betsy said.

From a broken-down armchair beside a low table stacked with baskets full of gold pocket watches and ladies' reticules, coin purses, and silver snuff boxes, Dexter heard them and smiled. He wore a velvet tailcoat and a saffron brocade vest. A shoddy tricornered hat, one of his abundant collection of hats, was within reach.

"I was thinking of naming them Terrance and Lawrence," he said. "How does that sound?"

Betsy shrugged. "Why not?"

Maddie thought the names were as good as any. She liked how they rhymed.

She heard a small, desperate thump on the door of the armoire where her twin was hidden, but there were no more wails.

Betsy's twin was deemed ready to be released a day short of three weeks later. He didn't even ask what happened to his brother. Dexter named him Lawrence.

After forty-one days in the dark cabinet—long days and nights during which Maddie was the only person to speak to him, the only one to bring him food and water, or to change his slop pot—the boy renamed Terrance finally stopped asking for his mama.

When he was at last allowed to emerge, blinking like a wary mole at the light that filtered in through the warehouse windows, he answered only to Terrance. Though he was immediately drawn to his twin brother and tickled by their likeness, he had to be reintroduced. Neither had any memory of their former life.

Maddie's first "changing" was a much-celebrated success, though the process eventually began to haunt her. With Betsy's disappearance shortly after Maddie was trained, Dexter depended upon Maddie to turn child after child.

Some of the tribe joined the band of their own accord, but they were usually a bit older, between eight and eleven. Some were white, others free children of color. More straggled in after the war left them adrift and homeless. They found life with the tribe easier than having to scrounge for themselves. Life with Dexter offered them protection and something they all craved: family.

Terrance shifted on the hard chair. The chains rattled, bringing Maddie's thoughts back to the narrow, windowless room.

"You come to say anything in particular other than good-bye?"

"I wanted to thank you for telling the truth about my part in the kidnapping." She wondered if perhaps he had done it because there was an ounce of good in him somewhere. At least she hoped so until he leaned forward and spoke in a low whisper.

"You think I did it out of the kindness of my heart? Think again. I figured with you on the outside, I'd stand a better chance of finding my way out of here someday—if you know what I mean."

The guard stepped up, grabbed Terrance by the shoulder, and forced his back against the chair.

"But with you in Texas, I guess I can forget the notion of you breaking me out of here. Just don't be a fool too long, Madeline. You'll never be anything but a thief and a liar. You'll never be able to hide who you really are, not even under a hundred fancy dresses and hats."

"Did you kill Lawrence?" She asked him point blank.

"I shot him, if that's what you mean."

"Did you kill him to keep him quiet?"

Terrance's stare never wavered. He leaned closer. The guard

was there again, nudging him back into his seat. Reminding them they were not alone. Terrance lowered his voice to a whisper.

"What do you think, Maddie? You're the one who made me who I am. You're the one who taught us how to survive. What do *you* think?"

# CHAPTER 29

To Maddie's way of thinking, nothing changed between her and Tom during the long journey to Texas. He was polite, albeit distant. He purchased a new carpetbag for her things, one that complimented a small hat trimmed with curled emerald ribbons and little blue feathers that Madame Bouchard had tucked in as a *lagniappe*, an unexpected little extra given by New Orleans merchants and vendors. He made certain she was comfortably settled whether aboard the train or the steamer across the gulf.

It should have been an exciting journey full of promise.

From the moment they boarded the train in New Orleans she tried to convince herself she should be happy. But riding beside Tom, sitting shoulder to shoulder with him, reminded her that they might soon part ways.

Passing bayous and rivers, fields of waving cane, the cypress forests, tupelo, gum, and water oak on the way to Breashear Bay, she found herself wondering why she'd ever agreed to this. How did she think she could walk away from the only home she'd ever known? How naïve she'd been to think she could spend days in Tom's company and not be tempted to give in to her longing?

Then she would remember why she was here. If Laura McCormick was her sister, she could be one step closer to the life she'd always wanted, a real home, perhaps even family.

*You should be happy.*

Tom kept his distance when he could. She should have been grateful, but that only made her anticipate the times she could be near him. He was ever solicitous while escorting her from her cabin to the dining room aboard the steamer. Sitting beside her on the long train rides, he made certain she was comfortable. He saw to their meals and hurried her along when they disembarked during the brief stops at depot restaurants.

He was confident and organized, caring and committed to her safety. On the rare occasions when he would let down his guard, they would converse and even laugh about something they saw along the way. They were so close, so companionable, that Maddie was tempted by the possibility that they might very well make a fine life together—until she remembered who she was and what she had done.

Most of the time Tom remained distant. He never tried to kiss her or hold her hand. He was so expert at masking his emotions that she began to wonder if his feelings had changed since the night she told him she would never love him.

She should have been happy but she wasn't.

As they neared their destination, she found herself hoping that the McCormick woman would take one look at her and announce that she couldn't possibly be Megan Lane. At least then she'd be free to go back to Louisiana.

After they left Galveston to board the train to Dallas, the land opened up with each mile away from the Gulf. They crossed high tableland broken by a series of hills and valleys. Herds of cattle were scattered across land so open and unbroken, so dry, she wondered how they survived the elements. She found herself longing for the lush, fertile land and humidity of Louisiana, for the Spanish moss and deep forest shadows of the bayou.

She knew nothing of Texas. The land didn't speak to her the way the bayou did.

Now, as they sat shoulder to shoulder crammed into the jolting, brightly lacquered Concord stage on the last leg of the trip to Glory, she wasn't happy in the least. She was not only scared spitless, but afraid the swaying motion of the stage was about to bring up her hastily downed breakfast.

She snuck a glance at Tom and caught him staring at her. When they'd met outside their hotel rooms in Dallas that morning, she noticed he was freshly shaved, wearing a clean white shirt beneath his black coat and vest. He was a striking man. She'd seen more than one woman openly admire him along the way.

A shiver ran down her spine as he leaned close and whispered in her ear.

"You look a little green. Are you all right?"

She nodded, afraid to speak.

"Are you sure?"

"I'll be fine."

Both of the wall seats as well as the bench seat down the middle of the coach were filled. A plain-featured woman with a toddler asleep on her lap sat on her right. Maddie tried not to stare at the child though she ached to hold him. Her gaze kept drifting to his angelic expression.

The woman's husband was on the opposite seat beyond the center bench. He, too, was sound asleep, head back, snoring with his mouth open. Maddie wondered how anyone could sleep through the series of jolts and spine-bruising bumps.

A young soldier in full uniform sat next to the window staring forlornly across the plain. A lawyer from Houston occupied the bench seat directly across from Maddie. He apologized each time his bony knees connected with hers.

"Is it much further?" she asked Tom.

The lawyer pulled his watch out of his waistcoat.

"We should be there in about twenty more minutes," he said, snapping the watch closed.

She thanked him, looked across at the toddler and out the window.

*Only twenty minutes to Glory?* There was absolutely no sign that they were anywhere near a town.

She could hold on for twenty more minutes. She brushed at the dust on the skirt of her new traveling ensemble. That morning, for the first time, she had donned the lovely raspberry skirt and blouse from Madame Bouchard. The pieces fit perfectly, and she found the contrast between the deep purple hue and the emerald cape stunning. Each time she recalled the admiration on Tom's face when she had stepped out of her hotel room, she blushed all over again.

Peering around the ruffled edge of her little silk hat, she took the opportunity to study his profile as he stared out the window on his side of the coach, apparently lost in thought. Either he was worried that she wasn't Megan Lane or he was as loath to say good-bye as she.

He turned without warning, caught her staring. She blushed but didn't look away.

"They do know we're coming?" she asked.

He nodded. "I sent a telegram early this morning before we left Dallas. Told them we'd be on the afternoon stage."

"You think she'll be there to meet us?"

"We'll find out soon enough."

Not in the least embarrassed at eavesdropping, the lawyer added, "We're running late."

They fell silent. The stage bounced and swayed so violently she was convinced the driver was aiming for every pothole.

She concentrated on the view and then, as if it had suddenly popped up out of the ground, the town of Glory appeared. The stage slowed as they passed a small park with a tiny white church and church hall, then entered one end of an extremely wide street, apparently the only one in town. It was lined on both sides by false-fronted shops and stores. Most were one story, but there was an occasional second story here and there. She saw the livery and a land office. The *Glory Gazette* newspaper was housed in its own building. There was a small milliner's shop and a butcher shop next door.

The stage finally stopped outside the dry goods and mercantile. Maddie leaned closer to the window. The boardwalk was empty.

Passengers in the center seat piled out before Tom took his turn. He offered her his hand. Maddie realized she'd not only grown accustomed to his gentlemanly manners, but craved his touch, no matter how fleeting. He always offered her a hand in and out of conveyances. His palm rode possessively at her waist whenever he ushered her along.

*I'll miss this. I'll miss him.*

The realization came swift and hard as he let go of her hand as soon as she was safely on the boardwalk. She didn't allow herself to think past this minute. Courage in place, she shook out her skirt and gazed around.

They were in the middle of town with the wide-open sky visible all around. Glory was barely two blocks long and nothing like New Orleans. There was nowhere to hide. No anonymity here.

She waited until the residual rocking motion stopped before she moved. The guard atop the stage was tossing baggage down to a storekeep who'd appeared from the mercantile. The clerk was tall and thin, his hair carefully parted down the center and well oiled. As he lined up the baggage on the boardwalk, he nodded to passengers and called a greeting to the driver, then took the mailbag the guard handed down.

The weather was brisk and cool, though the sun was shining. The passengers collected their baggage and wasted no time milling around on the boardwalk. A buckboard arrived and a rancher collected the young family. The soldier headed down the street. Maddie watched him pass through the swinging double doors of the Silver Slipper Saloon. The lawyer hurried toward the land office. Within minutes, only she and Tom were left.

"I'm Harrison Barker." The storekeep introduced himself, hooking his thumbs in his vest. He nodded toward the store. "I own the Mercantile and Dry Goods. Welcome to Glory. Anything I can help you with, don't hesitate to ask."

Tom introduced them both. "We need directions and a ride to the McCormick place. Is it far?"

Barker shifted the bag of mail and nodded down the street. "No need for a ride. You see that big house at the very end of Main? Grandest house in these parts. That's Foster's Boardinghouse." Then he cleared his throat. "Actually, it hasn't been a boardinghouse for nearly a year now. Not since the owner married the preacher and he and his children moved in."

*Preacher?*

*Grandest house in these parts?*

Maddie stared at the house as Barker continued. "You're out of luck if you were fixin' to stay there—" Harrison suddenly stopped and looked them over. "Why, you must be the pair Mrs. McCormick's been waiting for. Special guests, she said. I nearly forgot all about it."

As Tom collected their carpetbags, Maddie stared at the mansion again.

*Special guests?*

"Something you need, miss?" Barker asked. "A drink of water or a bottle of sarsaparilla after that long ride?"

"No," she said absently, then forced a smile. "Thank you, though."

"Well, you two enjoy your visit," the storekeep said. "Stop by if you need anything at all."

"We'll do that." Tom thanked the man. Holding both carpetbags, he extended his elbow. Maddie slipped her hand into the crook of his arm, and together they started down the street.

"I can't do this," she mumbled.

"Maddie—"

"She's married to a *preacher.*"

"It will be fine. You'll see." He didn't sound so sure.

"She's not my sister."

"Don't be so afraid to believe you deserve something good."

"She's rich, Tom. She's married to a *preacher*," she repeated, then halted so abruptly the tug on his elbow caused him to drop her bag.

She had stopped in front of a building with gold script lettering on the window that read *The Glory Gazette* and in smaller print *Editor in Chief and Publisher, Hank Larson*. There was an empty bench below the window. Tom picked up Maddie's bag and nodded toward the bench.

"Sit a minute, Maddie."

He figured she would do anything to forestall the inevitable. He was right. She sat. He heard her sigh as she continued to stare at the imposing house at the far end of the street.

"This is no time for cold feet," he said. Still, he couldn't blame her.

"You're not afraid of gators," he reminded her, trying to lift her spirit.

"Alligators are predictable. Besides, I won't be walking in there with a shotgun."

"You weren't afraid to take off through the countryside alone, to camp alone at night, or to lead me on a chase through the bayou. You can certainly find the courage to walk two blocks to meet a woman who might be your long-lost sister."

She turned on him. "You said you were *confident* she *is* my sister."

"I'm very confident." So much so he wished he wasn't.

"What if I am Megan Lane? What wealthy, preacher-marrying woman in her right mind would want to claim me as her sister?"

He wanted to say, "Let's forget I started all of this nonsense and go home." But since he could not make her love him, the best he could give her now was a chance at happiness.

A small bell just inside the newspaper office tinkled, drawing their attention as the door opened. Together they watched a man in a checked suit and bowler hat step outside. He appeared to be near Tom's age. Tom noted his ink-stained fingers and, when he turned, the brass sheriff's star pinned to the lapel of his coat.

"I saw you folks through the window. I'm Hank Larson." He extended his hand to Tom.

Tom stood and introduced himself and Maddie. The men shook hands.

"You're editor in chief of the *Gazette*," Tom said.

"Have we met?" The man's smile was warm, his expression curious.

Tom indicated the window behind him. "It says so right there in big gold letters."

Hank Larson laughed and Tom liked him immediately.

"It doesn't say anything about you being sheriff, though," Tom added.

"That's because it's only a temporary position. If you're moving to Glory, maybe you'd be interested in taking over the job."

"I'm definitely not interested." Tom added, "We've come to visit the McCormicks."

"That's a shame," Hank said, then quickly added, "Not about the visit, about you not moving here. We're always looking for new folks to grow the town. The land office is offering some great real estate in the area in case you change your mind." The editor looked at them each in turn. "Laura and Brand are good friends of mine and my wife, Amelia. I'd be happy to walk you down to the house."

Tom felt Maddie's hand tighten on his sleeve.

"We'll be fine. But thank you."

Hank pulled out his watch and checked the time. "You'll have to excuse me," he said, apologizing. "My wife is expecting me. Tell Laura and Brand that we'll be there for Sunday supper tomorrow." He paused a moment as realization dawned. "I expect you two have something to do with it being a special occasion."

Tom could tell from Maddie's panicked expression that the sooner he got her delivered to the McCormicks's the better.

# CHAPTER 30

As soon as Hank Larson walked away, Tom picked up the carpetbags and offered Maddie his arm again. She hesitated but accepted. As they walked down the boardwalk she tried to concentrate on surroundings that were vastly different from everything she knew. A knot of cowpunchers rode down the street on spirited horses. A heavy wagon rumbled past. The driver whistled and gee-hawed to his team. A tumbleweed danced out from between two buildings and rolled across the street.

The air was cool and yet so dry she imagined the summer heat would surely bake the life out of a person. Living out on the edge of the world would take great strength of will. Despite her trepidation, she knew she was strong enough to weather anything. Still, Texas was so big, so raw, that it was overwhelming.

They reached the corner much too soon. They crossed the street and at the McCormicks's place they passed a long curved drive leading to a carriage house in back.

Maddie's attention was drawn to a side garden with a birdbath surrounded by a circle of rosebushes near the porch. A wooden swing beckoned beyond the white porch rail. She tried to imagine Laura McCormick sitting on the swing watching the birds.

Since Tom's hands were full, Maddie opened the gate in the low picket fence and stepped aside as Tom carried the bags through.

They exchanged a smile. She was certain he meant to reassure her before they climbed the steps together.

The house looked freshly painted. There wasn't a single chip in the high-gloss black on the trim and shutters. The white clapboards were pristine against the black woodwork. A shiny oak front door sported an oval window draped with an intricately woven lace curtain. The brass hardware gleamed.

Without warning, Dexter's voice rang in Maddie's head.

*Lucky Maddie. Play your cards right and you'll be set for life. This woman is looking for a long-lost sister, so oblige her. Give her what she wants. No harm in that. You'll be doing her and yourself a favor.*

She remembered what Betsy had said, *"God is handing you a chance to change your life once and for all."*

Had Betsy known all along she was Megan Lane? Was that why she had urged her to contact Tom?

Surely Betsy hadn't been encouraging her to pretend to be someone she wasn't.

Tom set down the bags and reached for the bell.

"Wait!" She grabbed his hand. "How do I look?"

"Beautiful."

She closed her eyes, shook her head. "No, Tom. Really."

"You look beautiful. And excited. And nervous."

"I shouldn't be nervous." She wished it was so. "I'm either her sister or I'm not. We'll know in a moment."

"You're right. So smile."

She tried to silence Dexter's voice and pasted on a smile.

Tom rang the bell. Holding her breath, Maddie waited.

He rang it again a few seconds later. Suddenly they heard the sound of running footsteps inside accompanied by a child's high-pitched voice. "I'll get it, Sam!"

"No you won't! I'll get it." Another child.

There came the distinct sounds of a scuffle before the hem of the window curtain lifted, and Maddie saw two small faces peering up at them. Then came scrabbling for the doorknob. Finally the door whipped opened to reveal a girl and a boy who appeared to be around eight and ten years old.

"Is your mother here?" Tom inquired. "We've come to see Mrs. McCormick."

"She's not our mother. She's our stepmother," the boy informed them.

"But we love her anyway." The little girl planted her hands on her waist. She wore a starched pinafore. One strap had slipped off her shoulder. Her braids bobbed as she looked them over. "I'm Janie McCormick and this is my brother, Sam."

"Could one of you tell Mrs. McCormick we're here? Now?" he added when neither child moved.

Maddie gave Tom credit for his patience.

The boy, Sam, stepped back and hollered at the top of his lungs, "Laura! Pa! They're here!"

Maddie looked over their heads into the entry hall furnished with a table, a hall tree with a fine beveled mirror, an umbrella stand full of umbrellas and a lovely lace parasol. The walls were covered in a dramatic pink-and-burgundy cabbage rose paper. A thick tasseled carpet runner hid most of the hardwood floor.

Suddenly a handsome man well over six feet tall with blond hair and a ready smile hurried into the entryway from a side room.

"Let them in, children. Move. Please." He hustled them back so that Maddie and Tom could step inside. He reached for their bags and Tom handed them over.

"Welcome. Welcome to our home. I'm Brand McCormick. Reverend Brand McCormick, actually." He stepped back and looked Maddie over from head to toe. "You must be Maddie."

She found herself holding her breath. Was he searching for some likeness to his wife?

"I am," she said, slowly warming to the sincerity in his kind smile. "This is Tom Abbott," she added.

"Of course." The preacher set the bags off to the side of the hall and shook Tom's hand.

"Papa?" The little girl tugged on his pant leg. "You said they were special guests. They look pretty ordinary if you ask me."

"Janie, mind your manners." Brand McCormick rolled his eyes. "They were told we've been expecting special guests, but not the nature of your visit." He turned to Maddie. "My wife, as you can imagine, is very excited to meet you."

Maddie couldn't find the words to describe her own emotions. Brand McCormick seemed to understand. He wasted no time in graciously ushering them through the wide pocket doors into the sitting room.

"Please, have a seat, both of you. I'm sure such a long journey couldn't have been easy."

Maddie chose a tufted settee and Brand quickly stepped aside so that Tom could sit beside her. No matter how at ease Reverend McCormick tried to make her feel, she was still thankful Tom was there.

"We've seen a lot of your state on the way up from Galveston," Tom said.

"There's nowhere on earth like Texas."

Maddie found it hard to concentrate on the conversation as the men chatted. Tom spoke of being from Michigan. Brand hailed from Illinois.

"I'm sure Laura will be right down." Brand glanced anxiously toward the stairs.

"She's getting all gussied up," Sam announced. Both children were hovering in the doorway.

"Son, Laura always looks beautiful—" Brand began.

"But she's a nervous wreck," Janie piped up.

"Janie . . ."

"She said so, Papa. I ain't making it up."

"You're *not* making it up."

"I *know*." Her braids bobbed as she nodded.

Hearing that Laura was nervous put Maddie a bit at ease. Despite the lush surroundings and expensive appointments, there were no airs about the reverend and his children, no critical perusal of her appearance.

Brand turned to the children. "We were supposed to offer refreshments," he reminded them. "We've fallen derelict in our duties."

"We made some Mexican wedding cakes and Texas tea sandwiches and sugar cookies and lots of other stuff. You want some?"

"I'd love some," Tom said.

Maddie wished she was comfortable with Brand McCormick and the children, but her heart was in her throat.

"I'm sorry we've nothing stronger than tea in the house," Brand apologized.

"Tea is fine," Tom assured him.

There came the rustle of silk and a floorboard squeaked on the stairs.

"Here she is." Brand walked over to wait at the bottom of the staircase. Even over the pounding of her own heart, Maddie recognized the love and admiration in his voice, saw the devotion in his eyes.

Beside her, Tom rose. If he hadn't taken her hand and urged her to stand, she most likely would have remained frozen in shock.

She tightened her grip on Tom's hand as Laura McCormick descended the stairs.

Barely medium height, Laura was full-figured with thick, curly blonde hair that defied an intricately upswept style. Her teal silk gown was gathered into a low bustle edged with a cascade of ruffles. The fabric shimmered as she walked through a beam of light pouring in through a side window.

Laura never once took her eyes off of Maddie as she swept gracefully across the room. Maddie, feeling like a faded brown wren beside her, could only stare. When the woman halted in front of her, Maddie realized she was a good four inches taller.

Laura's eyes were swimming with tears. "Megan," she whispered. "I've dreamed of this day for so long. I never, ever gave up hope, not even through the darkest hour." Laura reached up and cupped Maddie's face between her palms.

*Shouldn't I feel something?* Maddie wondered.

There was no rush of recognition, no overwhelming relief for Maddie. No wellspring of joy or remembrance.

Tears began streaming down Laura's porcelain cheeks. She let go of Maddie long enough to draw a lace-edged handkerchief out of her sleeve and dry her tears before she sank onto the settee, drawing Maddie down beside her.

Maddie was vaguely aware of Brand inviting Tom to join him in the dining room.

"We'll let the women chat." He spoke as if the unfolding drama was an everyday occurrence.

Maddie felt Tom hesitate. She wanted him there, but it was important she and Laura talk alone. Besides, she had no right to depend on him. Maddie gave him a slight nod, although as he followed Brand out of the sitting room, she was tempted to run after him. Once the men were gone Maddie turned her full attention to Laura.

"You don't remember me, do you?" There was bittersweet regret in Laura's voice. She sounded more resigned than sad. She smiled through her tears, and two dimples appeared in her cheeks. She reached out and tenderly tucked Maddie's hair behind her ear. "It's a miracle that Tom found you."

Maddie didn't doubt her sincerity but wondered how deep was Laura's desire to find her sister. They looked nothing alike.

"How can you be sure I'm your sister?"

Laura's eyes continually searched her face with wonder.

"Because you look exactly the same, just all grown up." Laura reached toward her hair, then paused, her hand arrested in the air. "May I?"

Maddie nodded and Laura brushed aside her hair. She gently touched the end of Maddie's right eyebrow.

"That very faint scar at the end of your brow," Laura said.

There was no way Laura could have seen it. She had to have known it was there.

"What about it?"

"Do you recall how you got it?"

"No."

"You fell aboard the ship and hit your head on a cleat. There was blood all over. Ma was frantic. Surely you remember."

"I'm sorry. I don't even remember ever being on a ship."

"We sailed from Ireland with our parents. Is there nothing you recall? Our parents?" Laura appeared to be trying to come to terms with the truth.

"No. I'm sorry." Maddie truly was sorry that Laura was so convinced.

Finally Laura relaxed a little and settled back against the settee. "Tell me all about your life. Tom wired that he would leave the details to you."

"My life?" Maddie dropped her gaze to their linked hands. Laura's were soft and dove white, her nails clean and evenly shaped. She wore a simple gold wedding band, but her pearl drop earrings were worth a small fortune. She appeared perfectly comfortable in her fine teal silk gown, unlike Maddie, who felt like a complete imposter in her new finery.

She tried to imagine her ragged nails as smooth and even as Laura's, her skin pale and soft, and a closet full of lovely silk gowns, and again heard Dexter's voice in her head.

*Be what she wants. Play your cards right and you'll be set for life.*

*Impossible. It's impossible to hurt this woman, Dexter. I won't. I can't.*

In that instant Maddie realized Tom was right. She was changing. Maddie Grande, the old Maddie, would have passed herself off as the long-lost Megan. The old Maddie Grande would play on Laura's weakness and take advantage of this grand home and guileless family.

*Tell me all about your life*, Laura had said. Maddie refused to hurt this kind, caring stranger.

"I'm so sorry. I'm afraid you're mistaken." Maddie was on the verge of panic. "Tom's wrong. Mr. Abbott, that is. He's been wrong from the start. I'm not your sister. I'm so sorry we've done this. If you could just get Tom, I mean Mr. Abbott, we'll be on our way."

She knew she was breaking the woman's heart, but to let things go any farther would be beyond cruel.

Maddie tried to stand but Laura's hands tightened around hers. When Laura spoke again there was a strength of will and authority in her tone that Maddie would never have suspected the woman possessed.

"Megan — or Maddie, if you like — please listen." The sparkle disappeared from Laura's eyes, her smile faded. She lowered her voice, glanced toward the hall. "I've known Tom Abbott and of his reputation for years. He would *never* bring you here on a whim. He wouldn't do that to me, nor to you. If you aren't comfortable talking about your past yet, I completely understand. Your life may not have been ... perfect ..." Laura stumbled and stopped.

"Perfect?" *If only you knew how far from perfect*, Maddie thought.

"But neither was mine," Laura said, "as you can imagine."

Seeing Laura McCormick surrounded by a wealth of the finest things money could buy, Maddie found that hard to believe.

"No, I can't imagine," she said.

"I'll never forget the day we were separated." Laura's gaze took on that faraway quality again, as if she could see into the past. "I prayed you were spared my fate, but I'm not fool enough to believe it."

*Spared? The day we were separated?*

Images from Maddie's nightmare flashed through her mind. The long narrow hallway lined with gas lamps. The screams.

Laura's fingers tightened around Maddie's. "What is it? You're as white as a sheet."

"It's nothing," Maddie whispered.

"It's something. Tell me."

"I've had a nightmare. The same one over and over for as long as I can remember."

"Go on," Laura nodded. There was such sincerity in her touch, such hope and understanding in her gaze, that Maddie was moved enough to continue.

Slowly she began to relate the dream, the race through the streets of New Orleans, the gangly man, the tall double doors. A crimson-lined hallway. She took a deep breath and shuddered, picturing it as she spoke.

"A faceless girl is constantly tugging me along behind her, demanding I keep up. I know I must. I know that if I don't, I'll anger the man. I wake up so terrified."

Laura was weeping again. Not the way most women cry, not the way Maddie did, turning red-faced and blotchy. Laura McCormick managed to look beautiful even as slow, perfectly timed tears streamed down her cheeks.

And through her tears, Laura smiled triumphantly. "I was certain the moment I saw you, surely you must believe it too. I'm *not* crazy."

"I never thought you were crazy," Maddie began.

"Oh, I saw it on your face. But I know now, beyond a shadow of a doubt, that you are my sister. The man in your nightmare is our uncle, Timothy. He and his wife took us in after Ma and Da died, but they had two boys of their own and little to spare. Not enough for all of us anyway. He came home one night and told our aunt that he'd found a home for you and me. A grand place where we'd have everything we could ever desire."

"But—"

"It wasn't a grand place, you see. It was a brothel," Laura whispered. She fell silent while the full import of what she said sank in.

Maddie shook her head no. "I've never been in a brothel. That much I know. I may have done many terrible things in my life, but I never whored."

The minute the words were spoken Maddie saw how deeply

she'd wounded Laura. Haunted shadows dimmed the sparkle in the woman's eyes.

"I'm so sorry," Maddie said. "I'm sorry."

"There's no need to apologize," Laura assured her. "I know what I was, as does nearly everyone in this town. I was a prostitute from the age of eleven. It's something I can put behind me, but I'll never forget. I'm not proud of my past, but I've come to terms with it. I survived and that's what's important."

Maddie could only gape. "But ... you married a *preacher*."

"I married a kind and loving man full of forgiveness, understanding, and unconditional love. A man who practices what he preaches. If only there were more on earth like him." She smiled a small, secret smile. "Oh, not that I didn't try to convince him to walk away, but Brand isn't one to give up. But that's a story for another time."

Maddie sat in stunned silence while Laura continued.

"The morning our uncle took us away, I tugged you along behind me. He said we were going to a new home where we'd have plenty to eat and fine clothing, but he delivered us to a brothel in the French Quarter. We were taken inside together, led upstairs. When we reached the second-floor hallway, a man came toward us. I had no idea what would happen next. He tried to pull you away from me.

"I had promised Mama I would keep us together. I swore to her on her deathbed that I'd watch over you. But the stranger carried you away." She closed her eyes, remembering. "He had a mane of thick, curly white hair stuffed beneath an odd crumpled hat. His hair was wild, and very, very long. When he hoisted you over one shoulder, you fought like a wild cat. I was helpless. All I could do was start—"

"Screaming," Maddie finished. "You screamed and screamed."

Laura nodded slowly. "You did too. He carried you down the hall, and I was taken into a room where I was, indeed, given a fine new dress. My cheeks were powdered and my lips rouged. I never saw you again."

"I'll never forget the sound of those screams," Maddie whispered. "I've dreamed that scene over and over nearly every night of my life."

She tried to equate Laura's lovely face with the one missing from her nightmare. After hearing Laura tell her nightmare in detail, Maddie realized it all had to be true. Yet it was almost too much to comprehend. She didn't remember their parents, her uncle, or being sold to a brothel.

*"He had a mane of thick, curly white hair stuffed beneath an odd, crumpled hat. His hair was wild, and very, very long . . . He hoisted you over one shoulder."*

A chill had run down Maddie's spine when Laura described Dexter perfectly. One of the two men that Maddie couldn't identify in her nightmare had been Dexter. Her mentor. The man she looked up to. The man she considered her father.

Laura whispered, "Please forgive me, Megan. I couldn't save you." She looked at her hands. "I couldn't even save myself."

If Dexter had taken her from the brothel, there was one and only one reasonable explanation as to why she couldn't connect the scene in her nightmare to her life with the tribe. She still refused to believe.

"How did you come by the name Maddie?" Laura wanted to know. "That was our aunt's name too."

Before Maddie could admit she didn't know, she nearly jumped out of her skin when Janie McCormick suddenly slid the pocket doors open without warning and burst into the room. The girl curtsied prettily and announced, "Tea is now being served in the dining room."

She held out the hem of her plaid taffeta dress and made another low bow and then rushed over and draped her arms around Laura's neck.

"What's wrong, Laura?"

"Nothing at all, dear. I'm just so happy to see Miss Grande." Laura patted her cheeks with her handkerchief and then fluffed her hair.

Brand appeared in the doorway, took one look at his wife, and steered Janie toward the door.

"Sorry, ladies. Don't hurry. Join us whenever you're ready."

"Why don't we join them?" Laura suggested, taking a deep breath. "I'm in the mood for a good strong cup of tea right now and I'm sure you are too." She studied Maddie carefully. "In fact, you look very pale. Have you had anything since breakfast?" .

Maddie was still too stunned to move or to think. There was so much more she needed to know, so much to tell Laura, before all of this was settled. How would food ever pass the lump in her throat?

But Laura was already on her feet. "Come, Maddie. The children have worked hard preparing treats for this afternoon. We'll have all the time in the world to talk now, won't we?"

Maddie tried to smile but failed miserably as she followed Laura out of the sitting room and across the hall.

# CHAPTER 31

As much as Tom enjoyed talking with the affable Reverend McCormick, he was preoccupied with how Maddie was faring in the next room. When the two women suddenly appeared in the doorway, he took one look at her face and knew: not very well.

Her freckles stood out in copper relief against her pale skin; her eyes were huge and more green than brown. Laura McCormick was in the process of tucking a hankie into her sleeve, her own eyes still bright with tears. Unlike Maddie, Laura glowed with happiness.

Tom and Brand both stood as the women entered. Tom saw Laura nod to Brand and exchange a smile. Brand's relief was measurable.

*So, it's true.* The usual elation Tom experienced after he solved a case was missing. Maddie was Megan Lane, Laura's long-lost sister.

Looking dazed, Maddie paused near the expansive dining table covered by what seemed an acre of lace and silver. A crystal compote heaped with fruits and flowers adorned the center of the table. The children were excited and ready to begin serving the adults.

Tom pulled out the chair next to him, but Maddie appeared too distracted to move as the children and Brand McCormick bantered back and forth. When she finally met Tom's gaze, her tremulous smile of relief upon seeing him warmed his heart. She wasn't willing to accept his love, but apparently she valued his companionship.

As Maddie rounded the table to sit beside him, Janie McCormick chattered on about how she and her brother had made all the food from Laura's special collection of boardinghouse recipes.

When Maddie turned his way, Tom leaned closer and whispered, "Are you all right?"

She nodded but couldn't speak. Seated at the end of the table, Laura began to pour tea from a sterling teapot. Sam, wearing his Sunday best, walked around the table carrying a small silver plate. He presented it to Tom.

"Would you like some?" he offered. "We made three kinds, so don't take too many of these or you'll be too full for the rest."

"Sam," Brand laughed, "our guests can take as many as they like."

"Still, Papa. You said we can't hog all the cookies, so they shouldn't either."

Tom took two sugar cookies for himself and one for Maddie. He set a cup of dark, steaming tea in front of her before he accepted one for himself.

"Anything else? Sugar?" he asked her.

She gave the slightest shake of her head, then picked up a teaspoon and absently began stirring the tea. Before she set the spoon down, she studied the delicate pattern on the tip of the handle.

Tom had already noticed the silver pattern. The lines were simple and clean, not ornate in the least. Imprinted on the end of the handle was a single shamrock inside a circular ring.

Tom looked up and noticed that Brand and Laura were watching Maddie closely. Laura had paused with her hand resting on the handle of the sterling teapot.

"Maddie," Laura gently urged. "What is it?"

Maddie blinked, looking around as if she had no notion of where she was.

"It's nothing, really," she said at last.

"Please, tell me," Laura urged.

Maddie stared at the spoon handle, then at Laura.

"This is very pretty." She lifted the spoon. "But looking at it makes me feel as if ... as if ..." She shrugged, unable to put her feelings into words.

"As if you've seen it somewhere before?" Laura prodded.

Maddie remained silent and rubbed her temple.

"I don't know what's wrong with me." She turned tear-filled eyes to Tom and whispered. "I feel like I'm coming apart again."

He wished he'd never brought her here. Wished he'd left her alone on the bayou. At least then she wouldn't have this tortured confusion in her eyes.

"Maddie?" Laura said. "Please. Look at me, Maddie."

Maddie turned to the woman at the head of the table.

"My mother — " Laura stopped, cleared her throat and corrected. "*Our* mother possessed only one thing she valued almost as much as her family. It was a small brass pendant, a circle that she said represented eternity. Inside was the shape of an Irish shamrock. She wore it around her neck on a rawhide string."

Maddie set the spoon down on the fine Belgian lace and slowly traced the shamrock design with her fingertip.

"What happened to it? The pendant?"

"Our Uncle Timothy sold it for whiskey. Do you remember it, Maddie?"

Tom found himself waiting for Maddie's answer as if the rest of his life hung in the balance.

"I don't," Maddie said slowly, her gaze never leaving Laura's. "But for some reason, looking at it makes me feel very, very sad."

Tom's heart ached for her when he saw the tears in her eyes. He reached for her hand, drew it into his lap, and held it tight beneath the table. Her eyes widened at his touch, but she didn't even try to pull away.

After tea Maddie wanted nothing more than to escape outside into the fresh air. Laura must have sensed her discomfort, for she suggested Brand take the children to the church with him to prepare for tomorrow's service. Tom declined an invitation to go with them.

"If I'm not needed here, I'll just go and see about my lodging," he told Laura.

Maddie longed to ask him to stay or, at the very least, to take her with him. She wasn't ready for any of this any more than she was ready to reveal her past to Laura. She certainly wasn't ready to contemplate the future or Tom's leaving.

"Nonsense," Laura said. "We have more than enough room, and we've been looking forward to having you both here. It's been far too long since I've been able to cater to guests. Your things are already upstairs. Just follow the hall to the last door on the right."

"I don't want to be any trouble," he told her.

"Nor do I," Maddie quickly added.

"I'm sorry." Laura appeared crestfallen, looking to each of them in turn. "I didn't imagine you'd want to stay anywhere else. Not that there *is* anywhere else to stay in Glory. There is a new hotel going up, but it's not even fully framed yet. The Silver Slipper has rooms above the saloon, but given its reputation, I doubt you'd be comfortable there, Tom."

"If you're certain . . ."

"Quite certain," Laura nodded. "We'll love having you both here."

Tom went upstairs to his room, leaving the two women alone. Laura took Maddie into the kitchen, where she introduced her to Ana and Rodrigo Hernandez, the help, then led her over to a long window near the back door and pointed out the Hernandez cabin beyond the backyard.

"Brand's adult son, Jesse, lives in a room in the carriage house," Laura said, nodding that way. "The younger children adore him, but they tend to be a handful. He prefers having his privacy out there."

Maddie wished she felt as comfortable in her newfound role as Laura appeared to be at accepting hers.

"Would you mind if I went outside and walked through the garden?" she asked.

"Not at all," Laura smiled. "In fact, I'll come with you if you'd like."

Unwilling to be rude, Maddie tried to find a polite way to decline Laura's company, but words failed her. This woman, her sister, watched her with such hope and sincerity that Maddie couldn't deny her anything.

Thankfully, Laura was perceptive enough to notice her hesitancy.

"On second thought," Laura said, "there's no doubt you need time to let things sink in."

Laura bid her wait while she went and collected her cape. "There's a chill outside. You'll need this." Laura handed over the emerald wool garment. "Be sure to button up."

Maddie was used to being the caretaker. To be nurtured was a blessing, but it would take some getting used to. She thanked Laura and stepped out onto a wide veranda that wrapped around the house. In the yard beyond, rosebushes lined the drive. The Hernandez cabin at the edge of the property sported buckets of huge red geraniums beside the front door. A tidy vegetable garden had been planted alongside. Four horses grazed in a corral surrounded by a split-rail fence. Above and beyond stretched endless blue sky with a few high clouds drifting overhead. The house faced Main Street. There was nothing beyond the back fence except the open plain that rolled out like an endless sea.

Maddie took a deep breath of cool, dry air. Laura was right. There was a slight chill in the breeze. She tucked her cape close, went down the steps, and headed along the path toward the corral. She was intent upon circling the drive and walking to the front of the house.

Perhaps she would even try the porch swing.

Laura McCormick seemed like a perfectly intelligent woman

and not given to hysteria. Nor did she appear to be in such desperate emotional need that she'd claim just anyone as her long-lost sister.

The fact that Laura had described Maddie's nightmare in detail was most telling. Dexter had explained the dream away, but no doubt Dexter had lied to her. Now he was dead and the secret would have been buried forever—if not for Laura's determined search, and if not for Tom's hunch.

Her nightmare was the only scrap of memory left of her former life as Megan Lane. As much as she was loath to believe it, she had to have been changed like the others. She bit her lips together, tried not to dwell on how she must have been shut up in the dark and held captive, threatened until every last memory of herself, her family, even her own name, was gone.

Had Dexter known her aunt's name was Maddie? Or had he bestowed the name on her in jest because it belonged to a woman who had condoned the sale of two little girls to the highest bidder?

Would Anita tell her the truth if asked?

# CHAPTER 32

The breeze gusted a bit stronger as it whipped across the open land to tease the hem of Maddie's cape and play havoc with her hair before it died down. She tucked her hands in her deep pockets, unaware of the sound of footsteps until someone was nearly upon her.

Hoping it was Tom, instead she found herself facing a striking young man well over six feet tall. At first glance, she assumed he was related to the Hernandezes. She took in his fringed buckskin boots, glossy black hair that fell to his shoulders, and the lethal-looking blade sheathed at his waist. A six-shooter hung low on his hip.

It wasn't until he gave her a slight half smile that she realized his features mimicked those of Brand McCormick, but in an exotic way.

"I'm Jesse Langley," he said.

"Brand's son." Maddie smiled in acknowledgement as well as surprise. "I'm Maddie Grande."

"I can see they didn't tell you much about me."

"No. I thought ... are you a McCormick?"

"I'm half Cherokee. Jane and Sam are my half sister and brother. I'll let Brand tell you the rest of the story someday if he's inclined," Jesse said. "I can see you have other things on your mind."

He gazed out over the corral area. When she remained silent he added, "If it's any reassurance, I've only known Laura a little over a year, but she's one of the best people you'll ever want to meet. If you are related to her, you should consider yourself lucky.'"

"Do you know ..." Maddie suddenly stopped. Perhaps Jesse knew nothing about Laura's former life.

"I know all about Laura. I also know how much finding her sister means to her. I wouldn't want to see her hurt after what she's been through in this town."

"I don't intend to hurt her." *That much is true*, she thought. It appeared there was much about her sister that she didn't know. Much they still had to share with each other. So many lost years. A lifetime of details.

"You take care walking around out here," Jesse advised. "It's not too late in the season for a rattler to come along."

She saw a teasing glint in his eye and liked him all the more for it.

"Do you hunt, Jesse?"

"I do, ma'am."

"Please. Call me Maddie."

"I hunt everything there is that puts food on the table."

"How about muskrats?"

"Can't say as I ever shot one."

"I'm a muskrat trapper myself. I can catch just about anything in the bayou that puts food on the table." She'd tried to shock him but he accepted it without a blink.

"You use a gun?" He sized her up.

"I'm a fair shot," she said. "Mostly I trap and sell the pelts."

He looked her over with a new appreciation. "You don't look like a fur trapper."

Suddenly Tom spoke from behind them. "She's quite a good hunter, actually. She totes a shotgun when she's on the lookout for gators."

Jesse Langley's eyes widened. "You hunt alligators?"

"They live around my place." She pictured the cabin, missing it.

Maddie introduced the two men. Jesse studied Tom and tugged on the brim of his own hat.

"I'll leave you two to yourselves. Have a nice stay," he told them.

Tom waited until Jesse was out of earshot. "How are you holding up?"

"I feel as if all the pieces of my life have shattered and are lying on the ground around me." She thought of Laura again. Found herself wishing she remembered her older sister. "She's beautiful, isn't she?"

He nodded. "A fine-looking woman."

Maddie recalled that he had met Laura during the war. Now she couldn't help but wonder about the circumstances.

"Where did you meet her?"

"At a social gathering. I was undercover."

"As a Pinkerton?"

"As a spy for the Union. She had the confidence of a lot of wealthy Southern politicians."

"Did you know she was a ... she was a ..."

"Prostitute? Yes. She was also a Union sympathizer willing to pass along information. She went by the name of Lovie Lamonte back then. When she wrote to me last year, she explained that she had moved to Texas and was posing as a wealthy widow. Naturally, I've kept her past confidential."

"Even from me."

"She asked me specifically not to tell you. Besides, it's my job to keep secrets, Maddie. You know that."

Of course she knew it. She couldn't fault him. He had promised Laura he would keep her confidence and he had. A man of honor could do no less.

But had she known, she wouldn't have embarrassed Laura the way she did—and she might have been a lot more at ease meeting her.

"She's convinced you are Megan," he said.

"You two spoke of me?"

"Just now. There's not a doubt in her mind. She asked what I knew of your past, and I told her that it was up to you to tell her."

Again, the most honorable thing.

"Knowing Laura's history should make it easier to tell her about my past," she sighed. "It should be easier, but it won't be."

"Because you are ashamed? Or do you think it will change her opinion of you?"

"Both."

They reached the edge of the property and stopped beside the split-rail corral. He turned toward the house. "You've nothing to be ashamed of. You were both sold into lives you didn't choose. You were only children. If anyone understands, it will be Laura. Besides, there's far more between you than the missing years. You're sisters. There is a bond of blood there."

"Yet I have no memory of her or our parents. Only of the night we were separated."

"Your nightmare."

She nodded, stared out over the undulating plain. When the wind suddenly blew something into her eye, she cried out and ducked her head.

"Here," Tom said softly. "Let me help." He placed his hand beneath her chin and tilted her face up. His hands were warm and sure. "Hold still." He gently held her lid, touched the tip of his little finger to the corner of her eye.

"A small grain of sand, that's all." He brushed something away.

He was so close his image wavered in her tears. Her heart raced, spurred by his touch. He cupped her cheek. His gaze searched her face and paused on her lips. His arm slipped around her, drawing her closer.

She knew he was going to kiss her and she couldn't bring herself to stop him.

Maddie was in his arms. Warm and pliant and willing. For days Tom had wanted nothing more than to taste her sweet lips, to hold her close and never let her go, and now she was in his arms. Then he reminded himself she was no longer Maddie Grande and stepped back so abruptly she was caught off balance. He steadied her with a hand beneath her elbow.

"The game has changed, Maddie," he said softly.

"This isn't a game, Tom. This is my life."

"You're not Madeline Grande anymore. You can have a new beginning. No one here will ever know about your past; they'll only know you as Laura McCormick's sister."

She touched her heart. "In here I'll always be Maddie Grande. I have to live with who I became and what I've done."

"Maybe in time you'll remember. As for what you've done, look at your sister. She hasn't let her past stand in the way of her happiness."

"I'm not even sure I like it here." Lost, she looked around and shivered as the wind gusted again.

He took her by the arm, turned her toward the house. Together they started down the drive. As they neared the back porch, Maddie ignored the steps and followed the drive around to the front.

"I want to sit on that porch swing," she told him. "I want to see what it's like."

He found himself smiling. He'd thought the same thing when they'd walked up the front steps.

He also found himself thinking of Reverend McCormick and the obvious pleasure Brand took in his children when they babbled on about cookies and tea sandwiches. McCormick supported his wife's search for her long-lost sister and seemed to take it all in stride. The man's gaze constantly strayed to his lovely Laura.

Somehow McCormick balanced his calling and his family. Tom had no doubt that Brand was as committed to his faith and his flock as he was devoted to his family.

For the first time in his life, Tom found himself wondering if he could be both a Pinkerton and a family man. Would it be fair to put himself in danger if he had a wife and possibly even children depending on him?

"After you," he said, indicating the swing after they climbed the front porch stairs.

A hint of a smile crossed Maddie's lips. She sat down, folded her hands primly. He sat beside her, stretched his arm out along the back of the swing, casually rested it against her shoulders.

They began to rock slowly back and forth. The chain on the left creaked with each move. A carriage passed by, drawing their attention. As they watched it roll past, the occupants, a man with a full beard and a woman in a sunbonnet, both waved.

He and Maddie waved back and Tom chuckled.

"You don't see that in New Orleans. Strangers waving at one another."

"People can hide in a city," Maddie observed. "You walk down the street and no one really sees you. That's what makes thievery so easy."

"I imagine here it's just the opposite. Everyone knows who you are and what you're doing."

"I suppose."

He wondered if living in a small town would grow tiresome, or if she would come to appreciate the advantages. He thought back to her life on the bayou, the solitude, the silence. Perhaps living in Glory would help her find middle ground.

He heard her sigh. Found her staring down at her hands.

"I *want* to tell her, Tom. It's a burden that grows heavier with every passing second. I *have* to tell Laura about myself, and I should do it before Brand and the children come back."

"Tell me what?" They looked up to find Laura standing just outside the front door.

Tom wished he could come to Maddie's rescue, but all he could give her was time with her sister. He stood up, straightened his jacket, and gave them both a slight bow.

"If you ladies will excuse me, I think I'll go for a walk. Have a look around town."

"The church is at the far end of Main," Laura said. "If you see Brand and the children—"

She paused. He knew exactly what she was thinking.

"I'll ask them to show me around," he said.

# CHAPTER 33

Tom went inside to grab his hat off the hall tree and was back out and off the porch in seconds. Looking up at Laura, watching her watch Tom leave, Maddie was reminded that the two of them had met during the war. At a social function, Tom had said.

She imagined Laura dressed in high fashion, covered in jewels, surrounded by rich and powerful soldiers, politicians, entrepreneurs. Men who would be so lost in her dimples and her stunning eyes that they would have no idea she was milking them for information. She would be a hard woman for any man to resist.

Now her biggest concerns appeared to be tea cookie recipes and correcting children's manners.

"Come with me," Laura said.

Maddie left the swing and followed her into the house where Laura entered the sitting room and opened a barely noticeable narrow door in the far wall. She let Maddie enter first and she found herself inside a small room with only one window. The walls were lined with bookshelves filled from floor to ceiling with books. Two comfortable armchairs flanked a low butler's table.

"Have a seat," Laura invited. "I'll have Ana fix us some café au lait." She hurried away, leaving Maddie alone to marvel at the collection of books.

When she returned, Laura sank into the empty chair and tucked her feet up under her.

"I've never seen so many books in one place," Maddie said. "Have you read them all?"

Laura laughed. "Not yet, but I've read a good number of them. Books were my hiding place when I could not bear my life. I escaped into them. You can borrow any that you like."

"I can't read." Maddie colored with shame but kept her head high.

Without hesitation, Laura smiled. "Then I'll teach you."

Ana slipped in, served the café au lait, and slipped out. Maddie closed her eyes and savored the scent and the taste. She smiled with her eyes closed.

"I missed New Orleans terribly." Laura's expression was full of such understanding that Maddie found it impossible not to open up to her.

"How hard was it for you to become accepted here?" She asked out of concern for Laura but also wondered about the challenge of making a life here.

"When I moved here, I posed as a wealthy widow named Laura Foster. About four years later, Brand set his sights on me and refused to take no for an answer. I tried to dissuade him. I feared for his position if anyone found out about me—as they were bound to—and very shortly, they did."

"Was it terrible?"

"At the time it seemed like the end of the world, as all crises do. I ran away but Brand came after me. His faith and love gave me the strength to face my past and his congregation." She studied Maddie's face and said quite earnestly, "You really don't have to tell me anything, you know."

"I can't have it between us."

There was a comforting silence in the house with the men and children gone. Tantalizing aromas escaped the kitchen as Rodrigo prepared the evening meal. It was a serene moment with just the two of them tucked away in the library.

Maddie took a deep breath. "The man who took me away that night—"

Maddie heard Laura catch her breath. The high color quickly faded from Laura's rosy cheeks. Her hands gripped the arms of her chair.

"It's not what you think," Maddie quickly assured her. "He never hurt me physically. In fact, he treated me like a daughter."

Laura grabbed her hands. "Oh, Maddie! I'm so relieved. That night, after ... after what happened to me ... all I could imagine was that you were somewhere in that house suffering the same pain and humiliation. I would have never believed that anyone there would have anything other than perversion on his mind. To think that he raised you as his own. Why, it's a miracle."

Maddie's heart ached for this woman she barely knew. Her sister must have suffered very deeply for a long, long time.

"I wasn't the only child Dexter Grande 'acquired.' Are you familiar with the name? He had to have known the owner of the brothel. Did he ever cross your path?"

Laura shook her head. "Not that I recall."

Maddie went on to tell her of the warehouse in New Orleans and the tribe.

"Dexter used us all. Taught us to beg, steal, gamble, pick pockets. He taught one of the older girls and me to lock up the young ones he brought home. We kept them imprisoned until their memories were erased and they became dependent on us and each other.

"Until now I refused to believe it happened to me. I asked him once and he denied it. I asked him about my nightmare and he explained it away. Even knowing what Dexter was capable of I believed him, but you have proved that he destroyed my past exactly the way I did to so many."

*"You're my favorite, Maddie."*

*You're a liar, Dexter.* She wished she could say it to his face.

"You'll never forget what happened, but you must try to put it behind you now," Laura urged.

Maddie closed her eyes for a second. Saw Louie, Rene, Selena—the tiny lifeless babe so cold in her arms. She shook her head no.

"Some things I don't wish to forget." She opened her eyes and found Laura brushing away a tear. Maddie said, "I was married, Laura. At least I believed I was."

She described Louie, explained how he was killed. When he died.

"How old were you then?"

"I don't know. I ... I really have no idea how old I am now."

"You are nearly thirty-two," Laura smiled. "Your birthday is next month."

"So old," Maddie whispered. "I thought I was no more than five and twenty."

Laura's laughter was an uplifting sound despite the pain in the room. She said, "If you think that's old, then I'm ancient. I'm two years older than you."

"We had two children." Maddie went back to her story. "Our daughter, Selena, died at birth. My son, Rene, died five years ago. He was the age your Sam is now. Do you and Brand know how precious, how irreplaceable, your children are?"

"I can't imagine losing a child," Laura whispered. "I'm not sure I would survive."

"I hope you never have to."

"And Dexter Grande?" Laura's color was back.

"Dead."

"Good." Laura's fierceness shocked Maddie. "How did Tom ever find you? He had no more than a name to go on."

Maddie flushed. "He heard of Dexter and the tribe and was looking for me only because I was a Grande and might be able to help him."

"He wrote and said the search for you inadvertently helped him solve a kidnapping case."

"My brothers stole a little girl from a wealthy family."

"Brothers?"

"Brothers in the tribe. I'd moved to the bayou with them a year ago. Dexter had died; the rest of the tribe had disbanded and drifted apart."

"Where are your brothers now?"

"One of them was killed. The other will be in prison for a very, very long time. Tom insisted I meet you. He had no proof that I was your sister. He was just going on a hunch and I thought he was crazy."

Laura gazed out the window toward the white church steeple in the distance.

"I've learned not to question why things happen the way they do. Not anymore," she said.

Maddie found herself thinking how lovely it must be to have faith.

"How long have you and Tom been in love?" Laura asked without warning.

"What?" Maddie bobbled her cup and saucer.

"It's obvious he loves you a great deal. You have noticed, haven't you?"

"He admitted as much before we came here." Maddie was amazed at how easy it was to talk openly with this woman she'd just met.

"Don't you return his love?"

"He's a Pinkerton. I'm a thief."

"A former thief." Laura smiled. "Or should I hide the silverware?"

Maddie found herself smiling. "No. Of course not. But—"

"At one time I never thought marriage to Brand was possible."

"A life with Tom is not for me," Maddie said.

"You don't love him enough, then, is that it?"

Maddie thought back to the love she'd once felt for Louie. She'd been so young. Every minute had been new and exciting. They shared the same lives, the same experiences.

She couldn't deny her physical attraction to Tom, the way his combined gentleness and strength made her feel. He was courageous, intelligent. An upstanding citizen and man of his word.

All reasons why she couldn't give into her feelings.

"No." It was a little lie uttered very softly. "No. I don't love him."

The truth was she loved him too much. She loved him enough to let him go.

# CHAPTER 34

That night at dinner the McCormicks assumed Tom and Maddie would go to Sunday service with them the next day. Maddie declined, but no matter how hard Brand and Laura tried to change the subject, the children relentlessly wanted to know why not. When Tom agreed to go, adding that he was interested in hearing Brand speak, Laura assured Maddie that her absence was still all right. Jesse would be at home too.

Maddie realized she had no excuse not to join them save one: the only time she had been inside a church was to steal from the donation box.

For the first time in forever, Maddie slept without suffering her nightmare. The beautiful weather held, and the next morning, she decided to accompany them. They arrived at the church early and found Hank Larson's wife, Amelia, the new choir director, already there. Amelia took the children to the back room to await the others.

Brand stationed himself at the front door eager to greet his flock while Tom escorted Maddie and Laura down the center aisle of a church that wouldn't fill the first floor of Laura's home. A crowd soon gathered in their seats, and a hush fell over the congregation when the choir finished their opening hymns and Brand took his place behind the lectern.

With Tom beside her, Maddie studied the people around them.

These were definitely not soft city dwellers. The ruggedness of their lives showed in their sunburned, weathered features and the lines etched into their faces. No one else appeared to be as well off as Laura. Comparing Laura to the citizens of Glory, it dawned on Maddie that her sister was even more out of place than she.

After church, Laura gathered the family for Sunday supper and included Hank and Amelia Larson. Amelia, the town apothecary, was the closest thing Glory had to a doctor and Laura's closest friend. Amelia even mentioned that Laura had planned and hosted the Larsons's wedding.

Hank plied Tom with questions. When he discovered Tom was a Pinkerton, he relentlessly tried to persuade Tom to become Glory's sheriff.

Once supper was over, before Ana Rodriguez brought out her husband's special flan for dessert, Laura tapped her spoon against her water goblet and called everyone to attention. Silence descended over the table.

She looked at each one of them in turn.

"I've told you about how my mother and father sailed over from Ireland to Louisiana to find a new life and how they both died far too young, leaving us behind. We were separated when I was a child of about your age, Sam."

Noting how young and vulnerable Sam appeared, Maddie wondered how she and Laura even survived at all.

"For years I've been searching for my sisters," Laura said.

Maddie caught her breath. Her gaze fell to the handle of her spoon, to the shining shamrock within a circle.

"Sometime back, I hired Tom to find Megan. She and I were closest in age. She was the one I'd seen last. So my search began with her."

Maddie looked up to find all eyes upon her.

"... and he has found her. Her name is Maddie Grande now,

but she is my sister all the same." Laura lifted her goblet. Around the table, everyone lifted water and wine glasses in a toast.

"Welcome home, Maddie," Laura said. "This is your home with us for as long as you wish. If I had my way, it would be forever."

Cheers went up from the children. Brand winked across the table at Laura, who blushed beautifully.

Slowly a hush fell and Maddie realized they were all expecting her to say something. Beside her, Tom nodded encouragement, though he wasn't exactly smiling.

When Maddie finally turned to Laura, she said the one thing that was on her mind.

"We have *sisters*?"

Later that evening, after the house was dark and silent and everyone was asleep, Tom heard a faint, creaking sound and went downstairs. He found Maddie on the porch swing, gently gliding back and forth. She had wrapped a patchwork quilt around a plaid wool robe.

"Can't sleep?" He settled beside her.

"No."

"Me either. I thought I heard the swing."

She immediately stopped. "Do you think it's disturbing anyone else?"

He started it up again. "I could barely hear it."

Somehow Maddie had made it through dessert, watching as the others all had second helpings of Rodrigo's flan. She followed everyone to the sitting room, but as soon as the Larsons left, she claimed exhaustion and retired to her room.

"I'm still trying to fathom that I have two others sisters somewhere. Laura said Katie and Sarah would be twenty-eight and twenty-six now, if they survived." She paused a moment and then asked, "Have you been searching for them too?"

"I had no idea there were more sisters. After you went upstairs Laura told us that your uncle spoke of taking them to the Ursuline orphanage, but it was closed by '53. There were plenty of other institutions, though."

"What if he lied and sold them too?"

"That's what Laura and I both fear."

Maddie fell into a deep, thoughtful silence.

"I know what you're thinking," Tom said. "If Dexter did have them, you're not responsible for anything that happened. He used you, Maddie. As much as it pains you to admit it, he used you."

"Do you think it's possible one or both of them were brought into the tribe? That I may have been responsible for changing my own *sisters* without recognizing them? That I lived with them and didn't know it?"

"I don't want to believe that's possible. Besides, you said there were not many girls." He tried to sound encouraging, but he wasn't sure of anything anymore. He forced himself to consider the facts.

"Not all the adoption and orphanage records were destroyed during the War. I may find a lead eventually." He was tempted to hold her hand but didn't. "You were very quiet at dinner."

"It's all so overwhelming."

"Say the word and I'll take you back to Louisiana when I leave," he offered.

She was silent for so long he thought she hadn't heard.

Finally she asked, "Back to what?"

"The bayou. Your friend Anita. You don't have to stay here if you don't want to." He hoped she'd say yes. She might not want his love, but at least she would be close enough for him to visit if he ever felt like torturing himself between cases. Maybe, with time and persuasion, she would change her mind and accept his love.

"Laura was devoted to finding me. I can't leave so soon. I can't hurt her."

He felt like a miner, stooping to pick up a nugget of hope. She hadn't said she intended to stay on forever, but chances were, the more settled she became, the more ties she established, and the closer she grew to Laura, she would never go back to Louisiana.

His words echoed on the night air, breaking Maddie's heart.
    *"Say the word and I'll take you back to Louisiana when I leave."*

He was going back. He had stopped trying to convince her they belonged together. He was moving on.

This afternoon Hank Larson had been so hopeful Tom would agree to become sheriff of Glory that she'd let herself imagine they might both be starting new lives here. But deep down she knew he'd be leaving. Just as she knew she had to let him go.

"Thank you again for offering to take me back, but I'm looking forward to getting to know my sister. I've dreamed of a new life for so long that I'd be foolish not to stay."

*At least for a while*, she thought. *At least until I'm no longer in love with you.*

Clutching the quilt, she rose, intent upon returning to her room. She knew she wouldn't be able to sleep, but if she stayed with him any longer she might be tempted to change her mind.

She walked to the porch railing to stare up at the stars crowded in the clear indigo sky. She heard Tom move up close behind her and was sorely tempted to lean back against him. More than anything she longed to feel his arms around her again.

As if he read her mind, she felt him step even closer. His warmth drew her into him. His arms went around her waist, and she relaxed against him with a sigh. Together they stared up at the heavens until, without warning, he let go and stepped away. His footsteps rang loud and clear against the porch. The door opened and closed, and when she turned around he was gone.

Tears filled her eyes and through them she watched a falling star streak across the sky. It was so bright and near she wondered if it had crashed to earth on the open plain or if it burned out before it reached the ground.

She would never know the fate of that star.

Just as she would never know what might have been had she accepted Tom's love.

# CHAPTER 35

Sleep evaded Maddie until just before dawn when she fell into a restless slumber and didn't awake until after nine. She dressed and hurried downstairs, where she found Laura lingering over coffee in the dining room.

"Good morning, sleepyhead," Laura greeted her with her ever-present smile, but she wore a look of concern as well.

"Is everything all right?" Maddie asked.

"Is everything all right with you?"

"Yes, of course," Maddie said. "Where is everyone?"

"Brand has already gone. He has a church board meeting every Monday morning, and he likes to walk the children to school beforehand." Laura waved Maddie into an empty chair and went into the kitchen for a moment.

She returned and settled into her own place again and folded away the copy of the newspaper she'd been reading. A moment or two later, Ana came in with a breakfast plate piled high with scrambled eggs, a thick steak, biscuits, and gravy. It was enough for three and smelled delicious but Maddie wasn't hungry. She took a bite of the fluffy eggs, fingered the shamrock on her fork before she set it down.

"Has Tom been down yet?" She wondered if he'd been able to sleep.

Laura avoided Maddie's gaze a second, then sighed.

"I thought you knew he was leaving on the early stage to Dallas."

"No. I . . ." Stricken, Maddie's heart stumbled. Her hand went to her throat.

He hadn't said a word last night. He'd left her on the porch without so much as a good-night, let alone a good-bye. She closed her eyes against a rush of tears. Laura was on her feet and beside her in a second.

"Oh, Maddie. I'm so sorry. I thought you knew."

"He's really gone?" Hands shaking, she wove her fingers together in her lap.

Laura reached into the pocket of her apron and pulled out a letter. "He left you this."

Maddie's hand shook as she took the letter. She stared down at the letters that formed her name. Those she recognized.

"I can't read it. He left me a letter that I can't even read."

"He wanted me to wait and give it to you when you were able to read it for yourself. He asked me not to give it to you until then, but seeing you this way—"

"That could be months," Maddie whispered. "Years, even."

"I think he knew that. I don't think he wanted you to have it until then."

"Why?"

Laura pulled out the chair beside Maddie and sat down. "Maybe he didn't want to influence you."

"Why are you giving it to me now?"

Laura smiled through her own tears. "Because you're my sister and your heart is breaking, and maybe this will help."

"Read it to me." Maddie handed it back.

Without hesitation, Laura broke the seal and quickly scanned the page. A hint of a smile lifted the corners of her lips.

" 'Dearest Maddie,' " she began. " 'Congratulations on learning to read. I knew you could do it. By now you have settled into your new life in Glory, and I am no doubt still doing the work I was meant to do.'

" 'I'm sure there will be times that I try to convince myself that you chose to stay in Texas so that I would have the life you think I wanted. Just as I left you there so that you can have a bright future with a family that loves and cares for you. A family that can give you everything.'

" 'I wonder how often I will ask myself if perhaps we didn't love each other too much. If you had asked me to stay with you, to give up my work as a Pinkerton, I would have. But I could have never asked you to give up your chance at a new life for one that included me—a reminder of your past.'

" 'I hope by the time you read this letter that our lives have unfolded and that we are both content, if not happy, with the choices we've made for each other. One thing I do know for certain, Maddie Grande. I will always love you. Sincerely, Tom.' "

Laura handed her back the single page. Maddie looked down at the jumble of words. Tom's bold writing was soon blurred by her tears.

She felt Laura's arm slip around her shoulder.

"You know that no matter where you go or what you do, you'll always be my sister." She forced Maddie to raise her head and slipped a kerchief out of her pocket with a laugh. "I've found that with children around, it's a good thing to keep a lot of hankies at the ready."

She dabbed away the tears on Maddie's cheeks and looped Maddie's hair back behind her ear.

"Go after him, Maddie. There's still time, but you'll have to hurry. If there's one thing certain about the stage to Glory, you can always count on it being late."

"But—" Maddie searched Laura's eyes. "We've just found each other."

"Are you staying because you truly want to, or for me?"

Maddie tried to picture Laura as a child, a helpless big sister screaming as they were separated, a big sister who had lived with the guilt of breaking a promise to their dying mother.

A sister who loved her so much that she deserved the truth. Laura, above all people, deserved the truth.

"For you," Maddie felt a sadness of a different sort. "I'd be staying here for you. I don't want to break your heart."

Laura hugged her close and said, "My prayers have been answered just knowing you're alive and knowing where you are. I can't ask you to sacrifice your love for Tom. You know where I am. Come home anytime you want."

Home. She knew that no matter where Laura was, she would have a home if she wanted one.

"But—what about the children? And Brand?" Maddie was already on her feet, already wondering if she should take time to collect her things, throw them in her bag, or just run out the door. "Will you tell them good-bye for me? Will you explain?"

"Of course," Laura assured her. "Of course I will."

Her sister was crying but her cheeks were bright with color, and she was smiling through her tears.

"Hurry," she said. "Run upstairs and get your things. The carriage is hitched up. I'll get Jesse to drive you down the street."

"Will you go with me?" Maddie hated to leave her so soon. She couldn't bear telling Laura good-bye yet.

Laura's dimples deepened and she laughed.

"Oh, Maddie, I wouldn't miss this for the world."

Earlier, as Tom wandered around the Mercantile and Dry Goods store awaiting the stage, Harrison Barker dogged his steps.

"We've got a nice assortment of moustache cups." Barker waved a feather duster over a row of the aforementioned ceramics when Tom stopped to stare at them. "If you're thinking about growing one, that is."

"Not really," Tom replied, moving on to the aisle where rows of men's western style boots were on display. He wasn't thinking of anything at the moment but Maddie and whether or not she'd be shocked to discover he'd left without so much as a good-bye.

Taking the coward's way out didn't sit well with him, but he was afraid that if he tried to tell her good-bye he wouldn't be able to leave. He'd find himself accepting the job of sheriff and spend the rest of his life if it took that long trying to wear Maddie down, trying to convince her they belonged together.

He found the telegraph office opened early, so he took the time to wire Allan Pinkerton that he was headed back to New Orleans. Hopefully there would be a case waiting for him when he arrived. Something, anything, to take his mind off of Maddie.

"We've some very affordable boots." Barker was still at his elbow.

Money wasn't a problem. Laura had written him a very generous bank draft for a job well done. He tried to turn it down but she insisted he accept. As he pocketed the check, he found himself wishing he'd ignored his hunch and never brought Maddie to Texas.

Outside there came the sound of hoof beats as the stage pulled up.

"Would you look at that?" Harrison pulled out his watch. "First time in a year they been ahead of schedule." He turned to Tom, extended his hand. "Well, Mr. Abbott, it was nice meeting you. Too bad you're not staying in town."

If he wondered why Maddie wasn't leaving with him, Barker didn't say. Then again, Tom remembered, this was a small town. Between the Larsons and the McCormick children everyone probably already knew that Maddie was Laura's sister and that she'd come to stay a while.

Tom walked to the front door, picked up the bag he'd left on the floor, and went outside. He was the only passenger waiting to board and discovered he had the entire stage to himself.

The driver held the door and waited for Tom to hand his bag up to the guard. Tom adjusted his hat and couldn't resist a last glance down Main toward the McCormick's house. There was no sign of anyone on the porch. He wondered if Maddie was still asleep or if she had learned that he was gone.

He mounted the coach step and the stage sank on its springs. The driver closed the door, climbed up onto the box. He cracked the whip, the team pulled in their traces, and the coach lurched forward as they headed away from the McCormick house, away from Glory.

# CHAPTER 36

Maddie hadn't wasted time in putting up her hair. It lay loose and wild about her shoulders in a tangled fall. She didn't care. She'd thrown her clothes in her bag, dressed in the black skirt and white blouse from Baton Rouge, and donned her cape. At the last minute, she grabbed her gay little hat, anchored it with a hat pin, and was ready.

She glanced in the mirror on the way out of her room. Her hat was already askew but she couldn't take time to right it. Flying down the staircase, she nearly tripped and fell headlong before she caught herself.

*Break your neck, Maddie, and you'll never see him again.*

Despite the near accident, she found herself excited and almost happy for the first time in a long, long while. All she had to do was get to the Mercantile before the stage left.

"Are you ready?" Laura was at the bottom of the stairs in a stylish waist-length fitted jacket and a wide-brimmed hat with a sweeping ostrich feather that bounced when she moved.

"Ready." Maddie studied Laura's face, searching for a sign that her sister was upset about her decision, but Laura was all smiles.

"I'm truly happy for you," Laura assured her. "Follow your heart, Maddie."

If there was nothing else to convince her they were sisters, there would still be Laura's uncanny ability to know what was on her mind.

She reached out and gave Laura a quick hug. Then she took a deep breath and tightened her hand on her satchel.

"Let's go," Maddie said, heading for the front door.

"This way," Laura grabbed her arm. "Jesse has the carriage at the back door."

It took them longer to climb into the carriage and get settled than it did to drive down the street to the Mercantile. Maddie breathed a sigh of relief when she saw the stage wasn't there, but Tom wasn't waiting out front.

"He's probably inside," Laura told her. "I'm sure Harrison is bending his ear."

Maddie didn't wait for Jesse to come around and hand her out. She climbed down on her own and Laura tossed down her carpetbag. Jesse tied the carriage horse to the hitching post and was reaching for Laura's hand when Maddie turned around and nearly bumped into Harrison Barker as he strolled out of the store with a feather duster in hand. He took one look at her bag and his brow crinkled into a frown.

"Thought you were staying on." He looked over her shoulder and called to Laura, "Heard this young lady is your long-lost sister and that she was going to be stayin' on."

Laura stepped onto the boardwalk and let go of Jesse's hand. Brand's son stood by in stoic silence, arms folded across his chest, leaning against the carriage.

"She was, but now she's not. Not that it's any of your business, Harrison." Laura stood beside Maddie. "Is Mr. Abbott inside?"

Maddie thought Tom had surely heard them. The fact that he hadn't come out yet didn't bode well for her.

Harrison reached up and ran his fingers along the part that divided his hair down the middle and smiled at Maddie.

"I'd be happy to show you around town, at your convenience, of course," he offered.

Maddie found herself at a loss for words.

Laura didn't. "Harrison, please. Where is Tom Abbott?"

"Oh, the stage has already come and gone. Can you believe it? Ahead of time." He addressed Maddie again. "You'll have to wait for the afternoon stage to come through."

*He's gone.*

*Tom's gone.*

Maddie didn't hear what else Harrison Barker had to say. The stage had come early. The stage that was usually late. And Tom was gone.

*Maybe we're not meant to be together. Maybe it's best I let him go.*

*"One thing I know for certain, Maddie Grande. I will always love you."*

It didn't matter that he'd gone or why he'd left her. What mattered was that he loved her. That he would always love her. No matter what she'd been in the past, no matter that she'd turned him away.

Laura had a hold of her arm and was saying something.

Maddie blinked, suddenly aware Harrison was staring at her. So was Jesse, with his crooked half smile. Laura was watching her, too, expecting her to say something.

"What?" Maddie said.

"I asked what you want to do now," Laura said.

"I suppose we should go back to your house. I'll wait there and then take the afternoon stage to Dallas."

"I hate for you to go all the way to Dallas alone," Laura said.

Jesse stepped forward, hands on hips.

"Make up your mind, ladies. I ain't got all day."

By the time Tom realized he'd made the biggest mistake of his life, Glory was miles behind him. Alone in the stagecoach, he was reminded of the journey with Maddie beside him. He missed her nearness, her smile, her touch. It was one thing to leave her behind thinking that it would be easier than seeing her every day, but it didn't take long for him to decide he'd rather be with her than without her.

He tried to stand up and pound on the roof to get the driver's attention, but the wheels hit a pothole and he was knocked back onto his seat. He pulled off his boot, tightened one hand around the window frame, and started banging the boot heel on the roof.

He heard the crack of the driver's whip and the coach picked up steam. The wheels kicked up dust and rocks as the stage bounced along the only road across the middle of nowhere.

Tom plopped back down and shoved his boot on, then took off his hat. He grabbed hold of one of the swaying handles dangling overhead, stuck his head and shoulders out of the open window as far as he dared, and started whistling and shouting to the driver and the guard.

The bouncing jarred his teeth as he hung half in and half out of the window. He'd given another sharp whistle, hoping he wasn't wasting his breath, when the guard's face suddenly appeared above him.

Tom shouted, "Stop!"

The guard pulled back and disappeared but a few seconds later the driver reined in the team and they gradually rolled to a stop. The driver climbed down as Tom opened the door and stepped out of the coach. He winced, his ribs bruised from the jarring they'd taken in the window frame. It took a minute to regain his balance once he was on steady ground.

The driver, his white moustache stained red-brown, spat a stream of tobacco juice into the dirt and eyeballed Tom with a hard squint.

"This better be good," he said.

"I changed my mind. I want to go back," Tom told him. "I'll pay extra."

The man threw back his head and guffawed. "I'm ahead of schedule for the first time in years and you wanna go back? Are you plumb crazy?"

*Crazy in love,* Tom thought. *Crazy for taking no for an answer. Crazy for thinking I can live without Maddie.*

"No, sir," he said with a smile. "For the first time in a long time I'm pretty sure I'm not crazy."

"Well, I'm not going back, not for all the tea in China. Best I can do is let you out right here."

Tom looked around. He was miles from nowhere. The plain undulated into valleys sliced by creeks and washes, over hillsides covered with last summer's dried grass. There was no sign of any cattle, no ranch houses, no humans. Nothing but miles and miles of land that stretched far and away in every direction.

But he was on a main road. Surely someone would be coming along sooner than later.

"You armed?" The driver looked him up and down skeptically. Tom wasn't dressed like a westerner. He looked more like a city slicker in his matching coat and trousers than a man able to handle danger.

"I'm from New Orleans," he assured the weathered driver. "I don't go anyplace without a sidearm, a Bowie knife, *and* a derringer."

"Well ..." The driver spat again. "That settles that. I won't feel too bad about leaving you alone out here. You sure?"

"I'll stay." He'd made up his mind before he had taken off his boot.

"Could be a long wait." The driver grabbed hold of the side handle and climbed aboard again. "Could be you'll sit here till another stage comes along."

"When's that?"

"Could be this afternoon. Could be tomorrow."

Tom sighed. He never came by anything of worth easily. Maddie was worth however long it took to get back to her. "I'll walk and hope sooner or later I get a ride back to town."

The guard, cradling a rifle across his arm, leaned over to Tom's side of the road again and shook his head. "Consider yourself lucky the renegade Comanche ain't stirred up any trouble in these parts for a few months now."

"*What* renegade Comanche?"

Before the man could answer, the driver cracked his whip, whistled to his team, and the coach was off in a thunder of hooves and the rumble of wheels.

When the dust settled, Tom pulled off his hat and wiped his face with the back of his coat sleeve. Then he picked up his bag and started walking to Glory.

# CHAPTER 37

"I'm so sorry, Laura. I never meant for you to be on this wild-goose chase." Seated on the edge of the backseat of the elegant carriage, Maddie clung to the seat in front of her. Jesse's hands were sure on the reins as he pushed the mare to a near breakneck speed. It had been his idea to try to catch the stage.

"We're on a mission in the name of love," Laura assured her before she turned to the young man beside her and nudged his shoulder. "Jesse, slow down," she told him. "I want to reunite Maddie with Tom in one piece, not at her funeral."

Jesse snorted but drew back on the reins a bit. The carriage crested a rise. Maddie strained forward, squinting against the sun.

"Is that the stage in the distance?" she asked.

"Looks like it." Laura leaned forward and hung on tight to the front of the carriage. The stagecoach was almost too far away to make out what it was.

Jesse said, "I never thought we'd really overtake 'em."

The stage disappeared in seconds. As they sped up again, Laura still had a death grip on the carriage. Maddie's hat was slipping toward her right ear. Jesse was the only one smiling.

"I ... think ... we ... should turn around." Maddie's teeth rattled as they jolted along. "I can telegraph ahead ... and reach ... Tom in Dallas."

Tom was a man of order and routine. He would no doubt stay at the same hotel where they'd lodged on the way. He'd be easy enough to find—if he wanted to be found. He had no reason to hide from her.

"Will you look at that?" Jesse squinted at the road ahead and then shook his head in disbelief.

"What is it?" Laura was holding her handkerchief over her nose, fighting dust.

*What now?* Maddie wondered.

"Looks like somebody in the road," Jesse said.

Maddie leaned forward between them and scrunched up her eyes. Sure enough, there was a lone figure silhouetted in the middle of the road. A man, by the looks of his hat and trousers.

Laura reached back and grabbed her hand and squeezed it.

"It's him, Maddie! I just know it's Tom."

"What's he doing out here?" Jesse wanted to know. "That fool is just lucky we came along."

Within a few more yards they were close enough to see that it was Tom. Maddie couldn't imagine what he was doing alone in the middle of nowhere, but she didn't care. She reminded herself to breathe as they quickly closed the distance.

When they were a few yards away, Tom waved his hat over his head, signaling them to stop.

Laura touched Jesse's sleeve. "Stop back here, Jesse. Let's give them some privacy."

Maddie started to climb out of the carriage even before it rolled to a full stop. She caught the hem of her petticoat on the wheel, and once she hit the ground, she gave it a hard tug and heard the rip of tearing fabric.

She turned toward Tom, took one step, and then with no control over her legs, she started running. She ran until she was close enough to launch herself at him and threw her arms around his neck. He lifted her up and twirled her around and around before he set her on her feet and planted kisses on her cheeks, her lashes, and along her temple.

She cupped his face and claimed his lips in a kiss that went on until, breathless, she pulled away. "What are you doing out here?"

"I hope the same thing you are," he said. "I was on my way back."

"You were walking back to Glory?"

"Honey, I was going to crawl back to Glory if I had to." He took hold of her shoulders, held her at arm's length, and said, "Maddie, this time I'm not walking away."

"This time I'm not going to ask you to." She stared back into fathomless eyes that no longer hid his feelings. She saw all the love she'd been afraid to claim there. "I'll never lie to you again, either."

"Will you marry me?"

She could feel the tension in his hands, as if he was braced for a refusal.

"Yes." She answered without hesitation. "Come what may, I'll marry you, Tom Abbott."

When he pulled her close and kissed her under the endless Texas sky, she lost herself until the soft, slow plod of hoofbeats and the creak of carriage wheels brought her back to reality. Tom pulled away first but kept his arm around her waist. Maddie felt herself blushing with embarrassment when she looked up and saw Laura and Jesse watching from the carriage.

"Are you two about ready to go home?" Laura was all smiles.

Maddie looked to Tom.

"We're ready," he said.

"Then grab your bag," Laura told him. "I can't waste any more time out here. I've got a wedding to plan."

# CHAPTER 38

Somewhere in the darkness where the land met the midnight sky, a lone coyote howled at a milk-white sliver of Texas moon. Nestled in the quilt again, with one foot tucked beneath her on the porch swing, Maddie wondered how close the scavengers would come to Glory. There was another howl, this one farther away.

She relaxed and had just set the swing in motion again when the front door opened and Tom stepped out onto the porch of her sister's fine home.

"I had a feeling I'd find you out here." He walked over and sat beside her. "Are you all right? No nightmares?"

When he draped his arm across her shoulder, Maddie leaned against him and smiled, truly content.

"No more nightmares," she said softly. "Not since Laura and I were reunited." She reached for his hand, turned it over, and traced his palm. "Thanks to you."

"Brand would say it was meant to be. Just as we're supposed to be together."

She found herself smiling, hopeful and confident of the future for the first time in forever. She was still in awe of all that had come to pass.

"I can't believe we'll be married tomorrow. Right here. By a real minister."

"Your sister is an amazing woman," he said. "She can move mountains when she puts her mind to it."

"She knows me so well."

"She's determined to make our wedding a day you won't forget."

Come morning, they would be married by Brand in Laura's elegant sitting room. The only ones in attendance would be the McCormicks, as well as the Larsons, who would stand witness. Maddie refused a new gown, but had agreed to wear one of Laura's. Ana had been working for two days making the alterations.

Maddie turned to Tom, studying his profile in the dark, wishing she could see into his eyes. "You don't feel rushed, do you?"

He turned her way, cupped her cheek. "Do you?"

"I asked first."

He leaned closer, slowly kissed her, and then raised his head. "Tomorrow morning seems like years and years away."

Maddie nestled her head against his shoulder. They sat in contented silence, slowly rocking the swing back and forth, listening to the sounds of the night. It was enough for now, only because they were so close to the promise of tomorrow and so many tomorrows to come.

"I'll tell Hank that I'll take the job of sheriff," Tom said, breaking the stillness, "if you want to stay in Glory. Just say the word."

She tried to imagine life in Glory with Tom sworn to uphold the law, tried to imagine him wearing Hank's shiny brass sheriff's badge. No one but Laura and Tom would ever know of her past, but she couldn't help wondering if she would ever fit in.

*The wife of a sheriff.* She shook her head and bit back a smile.

"What about being a Pinkerton? Would you miss it?" she asked.

"I'd still be doing what I love to do, though I doubt there's much crime here in Glory."

"It's definitely not as dangerous as New Orleans." At least that was one advantage to having him uphold the law in this one-horse town.

"Tom?" She traced his hand again, stroked his palm.

"Hmm?"

"I really want to go home," she whispered. "I want to go back to Louisiana. To New Orleans." She would do that for him; she would live in the city again. She would live wherever he was, wherever he wanted.

"Wouldn't you prefer the bayou?" he asked.

She sat up, squeezing his hand.

"Could we?"

He was quiet for so long she was sorry she asked. Then he shrugged.

"Why not both? I'll find a bigger apartment in the city—"

"Your apartment is big enough—"

"We could keep a cabin on the bayou closer to town."

"Are you sure?" She was almost afraid to hope it could be that simple.

"I'll need a place in the city for business," he said. She could tell he was thinking aloud. "My contacts are there and most of the cases I'm given are centered around New Orleans. We can use the bayou house as a retreat. It'll be perfect." He stopped suddenly and turned to her. "Unless you mind living in New Orleans part of the time. You must have so many bad memories . . ." His words drifted away.

She reached for his face, ran her thumb along his jaw and over his lower lip, and then kissed him. "We'll make new ones," she whispered. "We'll make new memories of our own."

"We should go in. Get some sleep before tomorrow," he suggested.

Neither of them moved.

"Are there any women in the Pinkerton Agency?"

He laughed. She didn't.

"One or two. Why?"

She shrugged. "Who better to catch a thief than another thief?"

He drew back, took a long look at her.

"You're serious."

"What am I going to do while you're out solving cases?" She

couldn't imagine sitting alone in his apartment day after day waiting for him to return, knowing he was on the hunt for criminals, searching for clues, combing the streets in one disguise or another.

"I thought of getting you a tutor to teach you to read and write."

"I'm a quick learner. What else would I do?"

He shrugged. "I don't know. I hadn't thought about it."

"You don't exactly see me as a lady of leisure, do you?"

"No, but . . ."

"Surely there will be *some* cases I can help you with." She grew excited just thinking about it. "I tracked Penelope all the way to Baton Rouge. I know New Orleans better than anyone, even you. I know how to protect myself—"

He sighed. "I'm beginning to think we'd be safer in Glory."

"We'd both be bored to death and you know it."

He kissed her again and she felt him smile against her lips. "I have a feeling life will never, ever be boring with you around."

"At least think about letting me work with you?"

He sighed. "I do have two cases already pending that will involve mostly research in the beginning. You'll have to put a lot of effort into learning to read."

"What kind of cases?" The quilt had slipped off her shoulders. She pulled it up higher. He reached out and tucked it around her neck.

"I'll be looking for two young women. Twenty-six and twenty-eight. Of Irish descent."

"My sisters," she whispered. "Laura's and mine. Oh, Tom. Do you think we'll ever find them?"

"I found you, didn't I?"

He pulled her into his arms, and in her heart Maddie knew that she was finally home.

**READ AN EXCERPT FROM BOOK THREE OF THE
IRISH ANGEL SERIES: *HEART OF GLASS*.
COMING SOON!**

## LOUISIANA 1876

Katherine Lane Keene leaned closer to the open window and studied the familiar landscape as the carriage rolled along the twists and turns of snakelike River Road. The legendary thoroughfare paralleled the Mississippi between New Orleans and Baton Rouge, where a century before, the swampy wilderness fronting the river had been sectioned into wedges of French land grants. Thriving plantations with steamboat landings and slave cabins flourished between occasional small settlements—Donaldsonville, Plaquemine, and White Castle—with their churches, cemeteries, and stores.

Despite the war, despite everything that had happened to the land over the past sixteen years since Kate had lived on River Road, the familiar scent of the rich, fertile earth was a constant. Countless shades of green expanded as far as the eye could see. Miles of long rectangular fields divided the land into holdings that stretched far and away from levees and the road. Acres of plantations once rich in sugar cane were overgrown, many formerly glorious mansions neglected. When the carriage passed Destrehan, one of the earliest Creole estates in the area, Kate's pulse jumped. They had nearly reached their destination.

She was in the midst of assuring herself that a lifelong dream might be about to come true, when Myra O'Hara spoke, startling her out of her reverie.

"I hear he's insane." Kate's traveling companion lowered her voice as if *he* could hear. She straightened her cocoa-colored traveling skirt and folded her plump hands across her ample waist. "Crazy as a loon, he is. Won't come out of the *garconniere*. Holed up in there like a madman."

Kate barely spared Myra a glance. "That's nothing but gossip and I'll take no stock in it until I've seen Colin Delany for myself."

She hoped she sounded more confident than she felt, for in reality, she had no idea what state Colin Delany might be in. She hadn't laid eyes on the handsome older brother of her best friend since she was thirteen years old.

If rumors were to be believed, the former Confederate soldier who had finally returned to *Belle Fleuve* plantation was not the same dashing, confident young man who enlisted with his father and rode off to war.

Kate turned to Myra. "This isn't just about *Belle Fleuve*. This is about how good the Delanys were to me. Besides, if Colin is as bad off as they say, then it's my Christian duty to help him."

Kate reached to the seat beside her for the long thick rolls of architectural plans tied with a black ribbon. She pulled them onto her lap and ran her gloved hand down the newsprint. She'd poured years of painstaking work into the plans for the reconstruction and refurbishing of the once grand house at *Belle Fleuve*, but it had been a labor of love.

Colin Delany would appreciate all the work she'd done. She was sure of it. After all, it was his father, Patrick, who had inspired her to study architecture.

"We're here." Myra raised her voice over the crunch and clatter of carriage wheels against the oyster shells lining the drive. "Wouldn't y'know it? It looks about to rain."

The carriage turned onto an *allee*, an arcade of ancient live oaks flanking a narrow lane leading to the wide front gallery of the main house at *Belle Fleuve*. Kate had instructed the driver to pull up near the *garconniere* next to the main house. These "boys' places" were staple outbuildings on most plantations. Separate from the main house, a *garconniere* provided privacy where young men could gather on their own, smoke cigars, gamble, and speak of things proper ladies should not hear. The two-story hexagonal structure at *Belle Fleuve* with its pointed finial on the ogee roof appeared to be wearing a jaunty cap.

As the carriage rolled by the main house, Kate slid a finger beneath her spectacles to wipe a telltale tear from the corner of her eye. It never failed to upset her—seeing the sad state of this once impeccable house. She would never forget the first time she had witnessed the toll the war had taken on *Belle Fleuve*.

Four years ago upon her return to New Orleans, she had settled into her mother's townhouse and then come directly here. Her Irish temper flared hot and furious when she saw a notice of auction due to failure to pay back taxes nailed to the front door.

Kate had torn down the offending poster and immediately returned to the city, marched into her accountant's office, and directed him to use funds from her inheritance to pay the back taxes on *Belle Fleuve*, with the stipulation that she remain anonymous.

Now she saw how the further passage of time had only added to the decay. More windows were broken. Woodwork was rotted. Gallery railings were splintered and missing. She knew inside there were shredded wall coverings and crumbling stucco that revealed the interior of original walls constructed of Spanish moss and sand, *bousillage entre poteaux*, as the French called them.

Restoration was needed now more than ever.

When the carriage suddenly stopped, her heartbeat accelerated and her plans were forgotten. All she could think of was seeing Colin again.

Myra put her hand on the full dolman sleeve of Kate's short-waisted violet cloak as they waited for the driver to open the door.

"You know there's no shame in turnin' back," Myra said softly.

"Everything is going to be fine. You'll see." Kate smiled at her longtime companion and friend and then added a wink. She wanted her confidence to be convincing. "Things will soon be right as rain."

The minute she mentioned the word rain, huge drops began to spatter against the roof of the carriage, and the air was suddenly filled with the scent of damp earth. Kate glanced up at low, dark, and angry clouds. The sky was about to open up at any second.

The driver hopped down, pulled his collar up around his neck and ears, and looked quite put out as he opened the door and stepped aside so that Kate could exit. She pressed the roll of drawings against her bodice, hunched her shoulders around them protectively, and ran for the door of the *garconniere*.

She was halfway there when she noticed hers wasn't the only hired vehicle on the drive. A scuffed, covered buggy was parked beneath a tree not far away. A Negro driver with his hat pulled low was perched on the high sprung seat. He watched Kate's progress in silence.

Hugging the plans, pressing close to the door of the *garconniere*, Kate reached for the weathered brass knocker. Before she could grab the ring, the door flew open and she found herself staring at a tall redheaded woman, who was apparently just as shocked to see her standing there. The woman stepped out and slammed the door behind her.

Standing toe to toe with the stranger, Kate smelled the overpowering scent of cheap perfume. The woman's hair was a garish shade of henna, her cheeks dusted with bright pink rouge, her lips carmine. Dark kohl outlined her small, close-set eyes. A slim painted brow slowly arched above her left eye as she studied Kate. Then a slow smirk curled her upper lip.

"Good luck with that one, honey." The frowzy redhead indicated the door behind her with a toss of her hennaed head. She looked Kate over from head to toe and barked a harsh laugh. "He'll chew you up and spit you out in no time."

With that, the fancy piece stepped around Kate and ran for the safety of the buggy. The woman scrambled aboard and the vehicle started down the drive. Kate wiped raindrops off the lenses of her spectacles with a gloved finger and raised her hand to knock again. When there was no answer, she twisted the knob and cracked the door open.

"Colin?" Kate held her breath in anticipation. She'd waited so long to see him again.

When there was still no answer, she pushed the door open a fraction of an inch farther.

"I said, get out!" A hoarse shout was followed by a deep growl, and something heavy slammed into the door. There followed a loud crash and the distinct sound of an object shattering against the floor.

Kate took a deep breath and quickly thrust the door open. Broken pieces of a ceramic vase crunched beneath her sturdy traveling boots. Across the room, a tall lean man, fully clothed but barefooted, was stretched out with one leg extended, lying on a narrow bed against the far wall. His thick, wavy black hair reached his shoulders; the lower half of his face was hidden beneath a thick dark beard and moustache. He bore little resemblance to the Colin Delany she remembered.

Stretching to reach as far as he could, his hand fell just shy of an oil lamp on his bedside table. She could tell by his furious expression that when his fingers came in contact with the lamp he had every intention of hurling it at her.

"Colin, stop!"

At the sound of his name, his head whipped around. He skewed her with a cold, hard stare. Dark shadows stained the skin beneath his deep-set black eyes. He winced in pain when he moved. As his dark eyes bored into hers, Kate saw that he'd finally realized she was not the woman who had just left. A sound escaped him, something between a rusty laugh and a snarl.

"You're not my type either," he rasped. "So go."

Shielding the architectural plans, she ignored the command and dared to take a step closer to the bed but remained out of reach. Her heart faltered when she noticed a cane propped against the bedside table littered with a tray of food and a half empty brown bottle of laudanum. This time when she spoke, she barely managed a whisper.

"Colin, it's me. Kate. Katie Keene."

Katie Keene.
Colin stared at the petite bespectacled mouse clutching a roll of paper as she hovered across the room. She was a far cry from the wench who had brazenly showed up earlier willing to do anything for a price. This one was no bigger than a minute and modestly turned out in an expensive traveling ensemble. She studied him from behind

her spectacles, her features shaded by the brim of a small hat jauntily poised atop thick brown hair.

His gaze swept downward from the lace around her high collar to the toes of her rain spattered boots before returning to her face. Behind small wire glasses, her intense blue-eyed gaze never wavered. Something about those eyes forced him to search through long forgotten memories. He knew this young woman but he had no idea how.

Katie Keene, she'd said. Suddenly he was assailed with painful flashes of recollection; memories of giggles and crinolines, hoop skirts with cascades of ruffles, and pleas for his time and attention. He pictured his sister Amelie and remembered.

*Katie Keene.* His little sister Amelie's best friend.

His eyes narrowed. Colin tried to intimidate the woman with a cold stare. She had nerves of steel, he'd grant her that. She hadn't budged an inch, nor was she frightened of him. If she was, her fear didn't show. Clutching that long roll of papers, she appeared to be dug in. Katie Keene wasn't going anywhere.

Or so *she* thought. He didn't care who she was. No, the truth was he cared too much because she had known him before. He needed no witness to what he had become. He wanted her out. She was too painful a reminder of a life that vanished long ago.

"Leave, Katie Keene, and don't come back."

She lifted her stubborn chin.

"It's Kate now, and I'll not go until I've had my say."

"Nothing you have to say interests me."

"Oh, I think it might." She dared take a step closer.

He made another attempt to grab the lamp until searing hot pain shot from his ruined ankle to his groin. He tried to turn a groan into a growl, hoping to frighten her away.

"Colin—" Concern stained her blue eyes. She took another step forward.

He held up his hand. "Stop right there. Don't you dare come any closer."

Thankfully, she halted.

"I want you *out*." He didn't need her help or her pity. He needed her gone.

For a second he thought she was going to comply until she glanced around uncertainly and walked over to a wooden chair drawn up to a drop-leaf table. She pulled the chair to the center of the room, stopping just out of reach again.

Fall rain spattered hard against the window pane behind him. This gray dismal day was proving to be even more tedious than all the other miserable days he suffered of late. Kate Keene was apparently determined to make this one memorably the worst.

As she perched on the edge of the hard bottomed chair, she carefully positioned the long rolled pages of newsprint on her knees. Then, acting as if he hadn't just bellowed at her to leave, she took a deep breath and started talking.

"I heard you were home and I have come to help."

"I don't need or want help. Yours or anyone else's."

"You may not want help but it appears you need it. Not only that, but *Belle Fleuve* needs to be restored before it's in total ruin, and I can assure you that I'm just the one to manage that. Thanks to your father's inspiration, I've spent the last few years educating myself as an architect. I don't pretend to be as talented as he was, but Patrick Delany would have wanted someone who truly cares about the house to do this, Colin. During the war and afterward I was in Boston and Ireland. I have studied—"

She quickly worked up a full head of steam, seemingly unaware that he was in excruciating pain. He couldn't care less about who or what inspired her or about restoring the house to its former glory. The place was still in as complete a shambles as the entire South even though the war was ten years ago. So was he for that matter.

He didn't want to listen to her, didn't care to see her plans. What he wanted was for her to leave him to his misery. He was in dire need of a hefty dose of laudanum while she blathered on about living in Ireland and studying architecture on her own. It was time to cut her off.

"Miss Keene, I have no intention of restoring this place." *Not even if I had the money. Not even then.*

His words shocked her into silence—but unfortunately only for a moment.

"Of course you are going to restore *Belle Fleuve*. You must."

"Why?" He closed his eyes, made an effort not to move his ankle.

Taken aback, she blinked her magnified owl eyes.

"Why? Because it's your home. Because it's … historic and magnificent, or it was. I have designs here that will make it so again. I'll admit I've made a few changes and additions, but I can assure you that they will not come anywhere near ruining the integrity of the original design. They are adjustments that take into account the needs of not only the occupants, but the staff."

*Staff?* He had barely enough money left to cover his own expenses and pay a pittance to the former slave who cooked for him in exchange for lodging for her and her husband.

Kate Keene began to untie the thin black ribbon wound around the drawings.

"Don't bother, Miss Keene," he said, willing her to listen. "I have no intention of living in that house ever again. I'd be rid of it in a heartbeat if I could find someone to take it off my hands, but plantation houses aren't even worth the inflated taxes the state demands. If I hadn't enlisted in the army after the war, if I hadn't donned a blue uniform, which seems to have gained me some leeway with the tax collector, I'd have lost possession of this land years ago."

She opened her mouth, and surprisingly, closed it again. Her cheeks were on fire.

He was elated to see her apparently struggling for words.

Finally she managed, "You can't be serious."

His unkempt appearance, his surly attitude, his rudeness, even the thread of flying missals had not stunned Kate Keene as deeply as the declaration that he couldn't care less and wanted to be rid of *Belle Fleuve*.

"This is your home, Colin, your heritage. Your ancestors are buried here."

"I look forward to the day it's no longer mine," he reiterated. "I have no use for this place anymore. It's not worth the paper the deed is written on."

As far as he was concerned, the grand pillared mansion was nothing but a tomb that housed memories of halcyon days that had faded to a cloudy dream. His father and mother had passed on years ago, victims of the war. He had no idea if he would ever lay eyes on his sister Amelie again. He had no notion of her whereabouts or even if she was still alive.

Nor had he any desire to move into the main house. He doubted he could travel the length of the narrow walk that connected the *garconniere* to the mansion even if he wanted to.

As if searching for a rebuttal, Kate Keene's sharp gaze was calculating behind her glasses. Yelling at her hadn't worked, so he attempted to reason again.

"I'm tired, Miss Keene. I'm feeling poorly, so please do me a favor and leave."

She formed her words slowly, as if choosing them very carefully.

"Even if I wanted to, Colin, I owe it to Amelie and your parents not to leave you in this state. Apparently you need more help than I imagined, so I have no recourse but to stay on."

Astounded, he forgot his injury and tried to sit up and was forced to clamp his jaw against a shout of pain. He closed his eyes and waited for the intense throb in his ankle and leg to recede. Finally he managed to take a shuddering breath.

"Stay on? There is no way in h —"

She cut him off with a quick wave of her gloved hand. "There is no need to be vulgar. I can see that you are in no mood to discuss this today. Perhaps in the morning you'll be more receptive."

"In the *morning*?" He couldn't believe her audacity.

Miss Keene rose very slowly, taking great care handling her plans. Then she made a show of shaking out her skirt and carefully returned the chair to its original location. Moving back to the center of the room, she paused and blinked rapidly behind her spectacles.

Then Miss Katherine Keene smiled a very irritating smile. Either he had gone completely mad or she was insane.

"There's no way I'm leaving you like this, Colin." Her words were laced with Southern syrup. "I'll send my companion back to town for our things and then find some way to make myself comfortable for the night. We'll have the house livable in no time, you'll see. You simply can't stay holed up out here like this." She looked around at the dingy paint and cracked plaster walls and shook her head. "It's depressing. No wonder you feel so terrible."

Colin shoved the fingers of both hands through his hair and gritted his teeth.

He pinned her with a hard, cold stare. "You are not wanted or needed here, so turn around, go back to New Orleans, and *don't come back.*"

She walked slowly to the door, crunched across the broken vase as if it wasn't there, and stopped. Before she reached for the knob, she slowly turned to face him again. Her tone was laced with softness, but there was no denying her determination.

"Your parents once assured me that I was always welcome at *Belle Fleuve.*"

"My parents are dead."

"Which is a blessing. If they were here, they would be appalled by your appearance and rude behavior. Since you are obviously not yourself, I'm going to forgive you for such odious conduct. I will see you again tomorrow. Perhaps then you'll be in the mood to go over the plans."

"You will leave *now*—" he bellowed.

When she smiled a most irritating smile, he noticed there was a dimple in her left cheek.

"I'm sorry, Colin, but I'm not going anywhere until you are capable of throwing me out yourself."

# Heart of Stone

## A Novel

*Jill Marie Landis*
*New York Times Bestselling Author*

She had the darkest of pasts. And he had everything to lose by loving her.

Laura Foster, free from the bondage of an unspeakable childhood, has struggled to make a new life for herself. Now the owner of an elegant boardinghouse in Glory, Texas, she is known as a wealthy, respectable widow. But Laura never forgets that she is always just one step ahead of her past.

When Reverend Brand McCormick comes calling, Laura does all she can to discourage him as a suitor. She knows that if her past were discovered, Brand's reputation would be ruined. But it's not only Laura's past that threatens to bring Brand down—it's also his own.

When a stranger in town threatens to reveal too many secrets, Laura is faced with a heartbreaking choice: Should she leave Glory forever and save Brand's future? Or is it worth risking his name—and her heart—by telling him the truth?

*Available in stores and online!*

## Share Your Thoughts

**With the Author:** Your comments will be forwarded to the author when you send them to *zauthor@zondervan.com*.

**With Zondervan:** Submit your review of this book by writing to *zreview@zondervan.com*.

## Free Online Resources at
## www.zondervan.com

**Zondervan AuthorTracker:** Be notified whenever your favorite authors publish new books, go on tour, or post an update about what's happening in their lives at www.zondervan.com/authortracker.

**Daily Bible Verses and Devotions:** Enrich your life with daily Bible verses or devotions that help you start every morning focused on God. Visit www.zondervan.com/newsletters.

**Free Email Publications:** Sign up for newsletters on Christian living, academic resources, church ministry, fiction, children's resources, and more. Visit www.zondervan.com/newsletters.

**Zondervan Bible Search:** Find and compare Bible passages in a variety of translations at www.zondervanbiblesearch.com.

**Other Benefits:** Register yourself to receive online benefits like coupons and special offers, or to participate in research.